"Are you looking for me?"

Startled by the man's remark, Anna turned abruptly. Her surprise increased when she saw the man himself. He did not look at all as she had expected an attorney to look. Well over six feet tall, the attractive young man seemed to be in his mid-to-late twenties. Curly black hair framed an oval face, drawing attention to the dark lashes fringing his clear blue eyes.

He moved toward her easily, crossing the room in but a few strides. His powerful form seemed unencumbered by the stylish dark gray vested suit he wore, with starched white shirt and black tie.

"If you're looking for William Sinclair, then you've found him. What can I do for you, Miss. . . ."

"Tyler. Anna Tyler."

"All right, Miss Tyler. How may I help you?"

Anna suddenly felt self-conscious. "I—I don't need any legal advice," she stammered.

His full mouth formed a winsome smile. "That's too bad. I thought I might be getting my first pretty client. If this isn't a business call, then to what do I owe the pleasure?"

Anna tightened her grip on the wallet. "I work at the Rosita Hotel. When I was sweeping the dining room, I found this."

D1488333

Dearest Anna

DEBORAH RAU

Serenade/SuperSaga
BOOKS
of the Zondervan Publishing House
Grand Rapids, Michigan

DEAREST ANNA

Copyright © 1986 by Deborah Rau
Serenade Super Saga is an imprint of
The Zondervan Corporation
Grand Rapids, Michigan

Library of Congress Cataloging in Publication Data

ISBN 0-310-47471-X

Edited by Ann McMath
Designed by Kim Koning

Printed in the United States of America

86 87 88 89 / 10 9 8 7 6 5 4 3 2 1

To John, Andy, and Becky

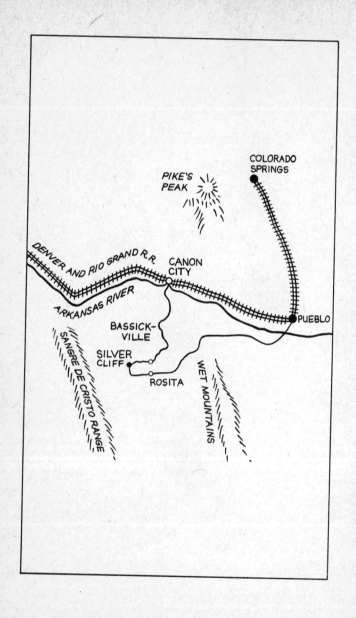

The central characters in *Dearest Anna* are fictional, but the historical information presented is accurate. The town of Rosita, Colorado, existed, as did its neighboring towns, Silver Cliff and Bassickville. The Grand Canyon of the Arkansas is known today as the Royal Gorge.

Although Rosita is now a ghost town, it had a colorful history. I have made every effort to authentically portray Rosita's story as I tell Anna's.

—Deborah Rau

Prologue
1862

Jacob hurried eagerly through the familiar woods, ignoring the path that lay hidden beneath the deep blanket of snow. His gray jacket, though tattered, hung impressively on his firm body, but his gray trousers fit more loosely now than they had ten months ago, thanks to army rations.

Despite the imperfect fit of his clothing and the shaggy condition of his light brown hair, he hoped Abby would think he looked quite handsome in his Confederate uniform. He chuckled, his blue eyes bright with anticipation at the thought of his young wife waiting just a short distance away. That she would be overjoyed to see him, he had no doubt. But he laughed as he fingered his bushy, blondish beard. He wasn't so sure she'd approve of that.

Although ten long months had passed since he had seen her, he could still picture her clearly. He had thought of little else during the months of fighting except her dark flashing eyes, long brown hair, and full rounded mouth. Abby had been his reason for going on, his motivation for enduring the horrors of war. Thoughts of her had kept him sane.

A sudden sound startled him, so he dashed instinctively behind a tree, ducking low while peering warily around the thick trunk, his hands firmly gripping his rifle. He relaxed when he spotted a deer scurrying through the thicket, but concealed himself a few moments longer just to be sure. He couldn't become careless now, not when he was so close. He had already experienced more close calls than he cared to think about. Now, traveling through neutral but Union-occupied Kentucky to spend his short leave with his wife, he was forced to call upon all his resources.

Jacob wanted to charge up to Abby's front door, joyfully announcing his return. Instead, he had hidden his horse near the creek, then walked the mile to the Logan's cabin. He still did not know how much—or how little—Abby had told her father. He would not allow his desires to endanger what little security she possessed.

From the very beginning, Caleb Logan had adamantly opposed Abby's relationship with Jacob, forbidding his daughter to even see the young farmhand-turned-soldier. Yet, regardless of Caleb's wishes, the two had continued their rendezvous and secretly married with the intention of heading directly for Texas to start a new life together. But their plans for departure were shattered by the outbreak of the Civil War.

Certainly by now, Jacob reasoned, Abby had informed Caleb of their marriage. But if for some reason she had not, any foolish actions on Jacob's part would only cause problems for his wife. Having no home or family where Abby could take refuge during his absence, he needed the assurance that she would be safe and well cared for in her father's house, especially since the war now appeared to be endless. So he stole steadily through the woods, his heart pounding faster with each step that brought him closer to his loving bride.

Halting at the edge of the woods just a hundred yards from the house, Jacob surveyed the clearing. He saw no one, but the smoke curling upward from the chimney indicated that someone was in the cabin. Abby was probably fixing supper. If so, Caleb might be tending the stock.

Jacob cautiously approached the back of the barn and pressed his ear to the cold, hard wood, straining to separate the assortment of noises inside. From the sounds, he detected only the presence of animals. He hesitated—perhaps Caleb had gone to Frankfort. His heart leaped at the prospect as he peered from behind the barn toward the warm, inviting cabin where he and Abby had spent one of their two nights as husband and wife. But he had to be sure. Gazing at the setting sun, he resolved to return to his hiding place to wait until he could get closer to the house without being seen.

As he turned in momentary retreat, a sight caught his eye. In a quiet corner behind the barn, next to his mother-in-law's grave, lay another mound, shrouded in snow, with a simple wooden cross erected at its head. Thoughts crowded and confused his mind as the grim meaning of the second grave pressed upon him. If Caleb were dead . . .

No longer feeling the need to conceal his presence, Jacob wandered toward the tomb. Another idea struck him, but he pushed the hideous thought away, refusing even to consider the possibility. The grave would be Caleb's. It had to be. And Abby would be in the house, alone. Alone but safe.

But when the name on the wooden marker came clearly into his view, he froze in disbelief. He could not read or write well, but he knew enough to recognize with horror the name inscribed there, ABIGAIL LOGAN. He stared, numb from the shock, his life suddenly as cold and dead as the frozen earth that covered his beloved wife.

He did not hear the footsteps that neared him, but, as if through a haze, he became aware of Caleb Logan standing next to him.

"How . . ." Jacob began, but the words stuck in his throat.

"She died of a fever," the stocky, gray-haired man barked. "She was weak from. . . ." He paused, then continued coldly, "From a sickness and she couldn't tolerate the fever. It was two weeks ago. February seventeenth."

Caleb reached into his pocket and removed a piece of paper. He shoved it into Jacob's hand. Jacob recognized the folded parchment as the marriage certificate he had left with Abby for safekeeping.

"I found this among Abigail's belongings. I have no need for it. Nor do you have any need to return to my home again."

Resentment vied with grief in Jacob's heart as he found his voice at last. "The marker should say Abigail Tyler. Not Logan. She was my wife."

"Not to me she wasn't. You ruined her life, Tyler. I'll not permit you to ruin anything else. Now get off my land. I never want to see you again."

Jacob felt suddenly exhausted, defeated. His gaze traveled to Abby's grave, then back again to Caleb. Of course he'd get off the land. There was nothing to keep him here.

Slowly, painfully, he grasped the folded marriage certificate in his palm and turned toward the woods, his feet like lead as he trudged forward through the trees. Somehow, in spite of his clouded vision and the settling darkness, he managed to find his way back to the creek. He mounted his horse sluggishly, aware only of the emptiness inside him.

Yes, he'd get off the land, and he'd go back to the war. Now he really didn't care if he lived through it or not.

Part One
1871

chapter

1

"WELL, ANNA, HERE WE ARE," Mr. Forrester exclaimed, pulling back on the reins to halt the horses in front of the white, two-story house. The wagon boards squeaked under his weight as the rugged man got off and lifted Anna down next to him.

She stood motionless beside the wagon while the dark-haired driver unloaded her trunk and satchel. His huge frame towered over her diminutive one. Although his kind face seemed to promise both protection and friendship, her heart once again flooded with panic.

The little girl glanced toward the house, her inner despair increasing as her eyes rested upon the black-and-white sign that hung from the porch awning—ST. MATTHEW'S HOME FOR CHILDREN. She hugged her rag doll tightly against her chest, half-hiding it beneath the long brown braids that hung over her folded arms.

A figure emerged from the front door, and Mr. Forrester nodded an acknowledgment. "Afternoon, Sarah."

"Good afternoon, Carl," Sarah called as she descended the three steps from the porch to the street. "I see you've brought along our newest family member."

The two adults exchanged quick, understanding glances,

then the woman approached Anna and placed a reassuring hand on her small shoulder.

"Welcome to St. Matthew's, Anna. I'm Sarah Johnson. Miss Sarah to all the children here. I'm so glad that you've chosen to live here with us. Let's go into the house. Mr. Forrester can put your things in your room, and I'll help you unpack later."

They entered the house, stepping into an attractively paneled entryway. "This building used to be an inn. But after they built the new road into Frankfort, it didn't get enough business and had to close down. So the church bought it, did some remodeling, and here we are."

Miss Sarah guided Anna through a doorway on the right into a large kitchen. She stopped when they reached a small table.

"Now, just have a seat and I'll find us something to eat. You must be hungry after that trip. Traveling fifteen miles on such a hot June day!"

As the tall woman rummaged through a cupboard, Anna watched her with great interest. She seemed nice. Her coal-black hair, pulled tightly into a bun at the nape of her neck, complemented her green eyes. Her fitted green dress drew attention to her slightly rounded waistline, but in Miss Sarah the plumpness just added to her attractiveness.

"Most of the children are in school now, in case you were wondering where they are," Miss Sarah explained. "The schoolhouse is the building next to this one. Have you been to school?"

"No, Ma'am. But my grandpa taught me to read and write."

"That's very good. And you've had a birthday recently?"

"No, Ma'am. I was nine, but that was in January."

Miss Sarah offered Anna two oatmeal cookies and a glass

of milk, which Anna eagerly accepted. After she ate, Miss Sarah took her upstairs to her room.

The pleasant square room housed two chests and five narrow beds, all neatly made and covered with colorful patchwork quilts. White curtains, rippling slightly in the breeze, hung at the two north windows. Anna noticed her baggage near a tall chest beside the corner bed.

"I see Carl's brought your things up," Miss Sarah noted. She suggested that Anna unpack, and showed her which drawer was for her.

Anna knelt to open her small trunk filled with the precious possessions she had brought from the farm. On the very top lay the Logan family Bible. As she pulled it from the trunk, a tintype slipped out from under the cover, dropping to the floor. Anna grabbed the enameled portrait anxiously and inspected it closely for damage.

"Is that your family?" Miss Sarah asked. Anna nodded. "Will you tell me who everyone is?"

Anna pointed to each person in the picture. "This is my mother, Abigail Logan. She died just after I was born. And this is my grandma. I never knew her, but I was named for her. And this. . . ." Her voice cracked. "This is my grandpa, Caleb Logan. He raised me until . . . until he got sick three weeks ago . . . and died."

"Do you have a picture of your father?"

"No. Grandpa would never talk about him. He just said that Papa never came back from the war, so I guess he must have gotten killed."

Miss Sarah touched Anna's shoulder again. "This picture is a real treasure, Anna, a beautiful reminder of the family that loved you very much. You are blessed to have it. Many of the children here don't have even that much to hang on to." She removed her hand. "When you finish unpacking, come back downstairs and I'll show you around. When school gets out, the children will all want to meet you." The headmistress then crossed the room, closing the door quietly behind her as she left.

Anna lovingly tucked the tintype back into her Bible, placing it in the bottom drawer with the rest of her personal belongings. She hung her three dresses in the closet, then pushed her empty trunk under the bed.

Anna glanced around the room again, taking in her new surroundings. This would be her home. She missed her old room in the loft of grandfather's cabin, and it hurt to realize that it was gone forever. Miss Sarah was kind, but she was a stranger. The other children would all be strangers. She wanted her grandpa. She wanted to go home. Sinking down onto her new bed and clutching her rag doll even tighter, she wept.

After a while, Anna made her way back downstairs to look for Miss Sarah. A colorful stitchery hanging in the entryway caught her eye. She examined the needlework closely, reading the words that had been sewn in an even, dark-blue cross-stitch.

> There is no man that hath left house, or brethren . . . for my sake . . . But he shall receive an hundredfold now in this time, houses, and brethren. . . .
>
> Mark 10:29, 30

Why would anyone choose those two verses for a sampler, she wondered. Especially when there were so many shorter verses in the Bible that made a lot more sense.

Anna left the entryway, found Miss Sarah, then accompanied her on a tour of the Home. The grounds at St. Matthew's Home for Children were the size of a small farm. Located four miles south of Frankfort, Kentucky, the ten-acre property included three buildings, pasture for the stock, a chicken coop, a goat pen, and a sizable garden. The Home seemed pleasant enough, yet Anna would have given anything to be back roaming her grandfather's tobacco fields or exploring his many acres of dense woodland.

For Anna, the remainder of the day's activities blurred together into a jumble of strange faces, chatter, and introductions as school let out and she met the seemingly innumerable mass of boys and girls who resided at St. Matthew's. She doubted that she would ever be able to keep all the names straight.

As she lay in bed that night, trying to fall asleep, she realized that she could not even remember the names of her roommates. She tossed and turned through the night, sleeping fitfully, her heart still clinging to the unlikely hope that she would waken in the morning to find that coming to the orphanage had just been a bad dream.

The next day dawned abruptly. Anna had been warned to expect the rising bell, but the sharp sound startled her so she sat straight up in her bed. She eyed the other girls in the room as they stirred in their beds. Two of them started to rise, but the third girl rolled over as if she were ignoring morning altogether. Anna glanced at the unoccupied bed next to her own, wondering where the fourth girl was. But her attention turned back to the other occupants when one of them spoke harshly to the still sleeping girl.

"Jessie, will you get up? Wake up now or you'll be late again!"

The girl speaking appeared to be several years older than Anna. Her brown hair hung just to her shoulders, its curly locks softly surrounding an attractive though disgruntled face. The girl began making her bed, stiffly pulling on the sheets and mechanically tucking them in at the foot of the bed.

Unruffled by the reprimand, the sleeping Jessie remained in bed but began stirring slightly. The second girl spoke encouragingly as she gently shook the sleeper's shoulders.

"Come on, Jessie. Rise and shine."

The second girl then began making her bed just as the first girl was doing, so Anna rose to make hers as well.

"I know you met us all last night, but in case you've forgotten, my name is Emily Summerfield," the second girl announced. She was younger than Anna by perhaps a year, slighter, and shorter by several inches. Her long red hair, badly tangled from the night's sleep, drooped around her freckled face and pugged nose.

Emily reintroduced the other girls, pointing to the first girl, who was in the process of getting dressed. "Thats Joanna Belden. And that," she went on, nodding toward the sleepy third girl, "that is Jessie Meyers. Your name is Anna Logan, right?" Anna nodded. "Clara isn't here right now, but you'll meet her before too long. That's her bed next to yours. Well, we'd better be getting dressed and get downstairs." Emily stepped to the farthest chest, removed some clothing, and started dressing.

Jessie stumbled out of bed and over to the chest, rubbing her partially opened brown eyes and yawning. As she threw back her head, her short dark hair bounced neatly into place about her round, impish face. She fumbled through a drawer for some clothing.

Following suit, Anna removed some underclothing from the chest, reached into the closet for her green dress, and began dressing, acutely aware of the absence of the privacy to which she was accustomed.

Joanna crossed the room, ignoring both her new roommate and her old ones as she scampered out the door.

"Don't pay any attention to Joanna," Emily advised after the older girl had closed the door. "She gets cross a lot. She doesn't like it here." The small redhead glanced at Jessie and breathed a sigh. "All right, Jessie. I'll make your bed for you or you'll be late again. Just hurry up and get dressed. Anna, could you help me?"

Anna hurriedly tied her hair back with some green yarn, then assisted Emily with the bed. When Jessie was ready, she and Emily headed out the door and down the steps. Anna followed hesitantly. At the foot of the stairs, Emily waved a hasty goodbye and scurried out the front door, leaving a worried Anna alone with her voiceless companion.

Finally Jessie spoke, her voice clear and musical, her face coming suddenly alive. "You're supposed to come with me. We're both on kitchen duty this session. Come on. I'll show you what to do."

Anna followed her transformed roommate through the door to the kitchen where Jessie greeted the girls already at work there, then through the kitchen to the dining room where she helped two other girls pull wooden boxes of forks, knives, and spoons from the large buffet.

"Just do what we do, Anna," Jessie instructed. "We have to set the table first. Twenty-five places."

Anna joined in with the three girls, confused by the sudden change in Jessie's personality. It was baffling that this now enthusiastic ten-year-old could be that same silent sleepyhead with whom she had just walked downstairs.

When the table was in order, Anna followed Jessie back to the kitchen. The room buzzed with motion as girls of all shapes and sizes performed the assorted tasks assigned to them.

By concentrating on her chores, Anna tried to ignore the

bothersome clamor of the other people around her. But despite her efforts, she felt smothered in the noise and traffic. How could she ever adjust to all this commotion? Thoughts of home tormented her again as she remembered the quiet breakfasts with her grandpa, the stillness of the mornings back on the farm. She swallowed hard and continued working.

When breakfast was ready, Miss Sarah sounded the clanging bell once again, and the house filled with even more people—eight boys, Mr. Forrester, and four small children from the nursery who were accompanied by Mrs. Forrester, a petite, light-haired woman. The meal seemed disturbingly noisy to Anna, the only quiet part being the prayer. And even that was interrupted by cries from one of the youngest toddlers.

After breakfast, Anna helped wash the dishes. She would have welcomed a nap after completing her chores. She could hardly believe her ears when Miss Sarah announced that only ten minutes were left before school would start.

Anna remembered little of her first day at school. She remembered almost nothing of the dinner and supper preparations in which she participated, or of the Home's evening activities. She remembered only that, despite the painful strangeness of St. Matthew's and her constant memories of home, she had no trouble falling asleep that night.

chapter

2

As THE DAYS PASSED, Anna grew more comfortable with the swift pace at St. Matthew's. The constant chatter at mealtimes still bothered her, as did the lack of privacy in her room. But she discovered pleasures that partially compensated for the negative factors.

She actually enjoyed attending school. She looked forward to the reading assignments, and took a keen interest in Mr. Forrester's history lectures.

She also relished the opportunity to form friendships with children her own age. Having spent her entire nine-and-a-half years in relative isolation at the farm, Anna had had little exposure to playmates. Even when those rare opportunities of seeing other children presented themselves, Anna had not fit in with them, for her attitude and personality reflected a sober, introspective nature uncommon in children her age. But the orphanage children were different. Having already endured the harshest of life's realities, they too exhibited a maturity beyond their years. Their shared losses gave them a special kinship.

At first Anna felt awkward in relating to her roommates. But after a short time she found herself enjoying their companionship, at least Jessie's and Emily's. Both girls were friendly, cheerful, and easy to talk to. But Joanna frightened her—the young girl always seemed to be in a foul mood. No matter what Anna said or did, Joanna managed to take offense. So Anna dealt with the problem the only way she knew how—by keeping her distance.

Avoiding a person who lived with her proved difficult. One evening, as Anna hurried into the bedroom to fetch her history book, she spied Joanna standing alone by the window, gazing out to the green lawn where Jessie, Emily, and a number of other children were playing a game of blind man's bluff. Ordinarily Anna would have greeted her roommate, picked up her book, and retreated. But tonight she decided to take a moment to try to talk to Joanna. After all, she reasoned, they were roommates. What possible harm could it do to try?

The conversation began pleasantly enough. Joanna started it herself by asking Anna for the correct chapter number on the history homework. Since Joanna seemed in a reasonably amiable mood, Anna ventured a question that she had been meaning to ask Jessie.

"Joanna, I've been wondering. If Mr. Forrester is the teacher here, how could he leave to go get me at the farm two weeks ago?"

The slim brunette stared out the window as she answered. "If he has to be gone, then one of the older children substitutes for him. Like Bobby Collins or Clara."

"Clara is our other roommate, right? Where is she, anyway?"

"In Frankfort, working."

"What kind of a job does she have?"

Joanna turned to face her, her expression cynical. "She doesn't have a regular job," she snapped. "She's just doing what we all have to do. Didn't they tell you?"

"Tell me what?"

Joanna seemed more than happy to disclose the information. "When people in town need work done, like cleaning, canning, or moving, they tell Miss Sarah and she picks different ones of us to go work for them."

Anna's brown eyes widened. "You mean I'll have to do that?"

"Yes, you will," Joanna affirmed. "Once you've learned the ropes, that is. Some of the people are really mean, too. They're only happy if you work like a dog, follow their instructions to the letter, and don't eat much." As Anna's inner fears were reflected in her face, Joanna added, "There is one way to get out of it, but I think it would be worse than being hired out."

"What's that?"

"If somebody adopts you."

Anna could not believe her ears. "Someone could adopt me?" she gasped.

"That's right. You're a little old for that, though. Most people want to adopt the little children in the nursery. But you never know. Just before you came here, some family adopted an older boy. He was eleven. How old are you?"

"Nine-and-a-half."

"Then you're probably pretty safe. But if it ever happens, watch out," she warned. "The people who adopt older children usually just want a free servant. If they adopt you, they save money because then they don't have to hire you out through Miss Sarah." She spotted a familiar figure on the lawn. "Oh, there's Millie. I have to talk to her."

Joanna departed, leaving Anna alone to cope with this new and frightening information. The very idea of being adopted or loaned out completely shook her. She didn't belong here. And she didn't want to belong to some strange family either, whether as an adopted child or as a hired worker. The insecurities that had just begun to settle down now resurfaced. She longed for the by-gone days of Grandpa's protection and the safety of the old Logan farm. Her future seemed no more certain now than when she had first arrived.

Try as she would, Anna could not erase Joanna's words from her mind. Although physically occupied with her chores and studies, she worried more and more through the following weeks. She was afraid to relax for fear that at any moment Miss Sarah would pull the rug out from under her. But during that time, the headmistress did not once bring up the topic of adoption or employment. So Anna kept her fingers crossed, hoping with all her heart that her luck would continue to hold out.

But one morning in mid-August, Anna feared that her good fortune had come to an end. As she stood at the kitchen table slicing cucumbers for pickling, Miss Sarah approached her.

"Anna, could you come to the office for a moment?" she asked. "There's someone here to see you."

Miss Sarah's voice sounded calm, yet Anna hesitated before following the woman into the small office. As she entered the square, pale blue room, a strange man rose from one of the chairs in front of the walnut desk. Remembering every word of Joanna's dreadful revelation, Anna's heart flooded with anxiety. She didn't want to go anywhere. She just wanted to be left alone. She swallowed hard before cautiously following Miss Sarah over to the desk.

"Anna, this is Mr. Crawford," Miss Sarah announced. "Please, Anna, have a seat."

Anna obliged but perched warily on her chair.

"Mr. Crawford is a lawyer. He is here to talk to you about your grandfather's estate." She turned toward the visitor. "Mr. Crawford, why don't you explain everything."

The attorney nodded, then turned to Anna. "Miss Logan, first let me say how sorry I am about your grandfather's death." He paused, but when Anna said nothing, he continued. "Your grandfather left instructions in his will leaving everything to you. I just wanted to bring you up to date on how things stand right now."

Anna relaxed, relieved that she wasn't being sent off somewhere.

"Because of your age, the court has chosen the Federal Bank of Frankfort as executor. That means that, until you are of age, they will handle your inheritance for you. They have just sold your grandfather's farm, and, if I do say so myself, they received an excellent price for it—five thousand dollars. Of course, the tobacco farm was a valuable piece of property. The stock was also included, along with the basic furnishings, except what you kept yourself."

His words hit her like a bolt of lightning. They had sold the farm. Grandpa's farm. Her home. She would never see it again, never again walk in their woods. The sale was inevitable, she knew, but somehow she had hoped it wouldn't happen. Her heart sank, yet still the attorney kept speaking, his voice even and unfeeling.

"Each year that you remain here, the bank will donate to St. Matthew's a contribution that should cover any expenses you might incur. The remaining monies will then be invested for you until you are eighteen or marry. In either event, all securities will then be transferred to you. Do you have any questions?"

A lump lodged in her throat, so she could only shake her

head. She had no questions. She would sort through all the other information later, but for now the only fact that concerned her was the sale of the farm. All that Grandpa had worked for now belonged to someone she didn't even know. And she really would have to stay here, because now she had nowhere else to go.

Still in a daze, she nodded a goodbye to Mr. Crawford as he left. After a moment, Miss Sarah crossed over to Anna's chair.

"I know how you must feel, Anna," she consoled. "It must all seem terribly final to you. I know how much you loved your home and your family. No one can replace the people you love. They're all different and they're all special. But you can learn to love other people and make a new family, no matter where you are. We want to be your family now, Anna, if you'll let us."

But Miss Sarah's words struck a raw nerve.

"How can you say you'll be my family?" Anna cried. "How can you say that, when Joanna told me that you'll make me go work for people, and that you might let someone adopt me?"

Miss Sarah's eyes lighted, as if she had just seen the full spectrum of Anna's thoughts. "I didn't realize that Joanna had mentioned so much to you," she began, her voice soothing and reassuring. "In the first place, adoption for a child your age is unusual. But if it comes up in your case, we will certainly consider your feelings. And as far as the employment program is concerned, the work system is good for all of us. You children receive practical work experience, and in the past some employers have been so pleased that they have offered permanent positions to the children when they were old enough. The system helps the Home earn some income, and the people who come to us for workers have their needs met. Granted, not all of the situations have been ideal. But despite whatever Joanna may have said, we keep a close watch on every one of our children. You will be no exception. So, please don't worry, Anna. It will be quite a while yet before you have to face any of that."

"It will?"

"You don't start in on the work program until you are twelve. So, you see? That's a long way off."

Anna drew a full measure of assurance from Miss Sarah's explanation. She felt a trust, a love, beginning to grow toward the headmistress. But her thoughts traveled back again to the sale of the farm.

"The graves. They're all back there. My mother's . . . my grandpa's. They'll take care of them, won't they?"

As Miss Sarah lovingly drew her to her breast, Anna wept freely. Somehow, as the tears flowed, Anna felt a lightness, as if Miss Sarah were sharing this burden with her. Strangely, in spite of the biting loss of the farm, for the first time in weeks she felt a ray of hope.

Anna always looked forward to the children's weekly excursion into town. Each Sunday, Mr. Forrester ferried the old wagon, laden with the well-scrubbed St. Matthew's residents, to the nine o'clock worship service at the Trinity Episcopal Church in Frankfort.

Anna had only been to church three times that she could remember, so the excitement of viewing the splendidly attired ladies and the beautiful stained-glass windows made concentrating on the long sermons quite difficult. Having grown accustomed to quiet Sunday mornings of reading the Scriptures with her grandfather, she was easily distracted in the crowded service.

After a particularly long, uncomfortable service in late August, Anna, Jessie, and Emily observed an excited cluster of children crowded around their wagon. In the center of the group stood a slender, pretty young woman who was eagerly hugging the boys and girls.

"Clara!" Jessie and Emily shouted at once. They raced down the church steps to greet their long-lost roommate.

Anna approached the wagon slowly, studying Clara carefully. She appeared to be about sixteen years old. Her oval face and bright blue eyes were framed by silky blond hair that curled on the ends and touched the middle of her back. Anna thought Clara was one of the prettiest girls she had ever seen.

Mr. Forrester loaded Clara's trunk and the boisterous group onto the wagon, then began the trip back to St. Matthew's. En route Anna learned that Clara's employer, who lived several miles west of the city, had agreed to meet Mr. Forrester at the church, thus avoiding the extra four-mile trip out to the orphanage. Jessie introduced Anna and Clara while they traveled down the bumpy road. But they did not have an opportunity to really talk together until that evening in the quiet of their room.

"How long have you been here, Anna?" Clara asked.

"Almost three months."

"Then you must have gotten here right after I left."

Jessie interrupted their conversation with a question that had been burning in Anna's mind all evening.

"What was your job like this time, Clara?"

"It was hard work, but it turned out well. Mrs. Campbell had just had their third child, the sweetest little boy named Jonathan. I just loved him, but he certainly created a lot of work. Between helping with him and watching the other children, plus doing garden work, I kept really busy." Her voice rang with exuberance. "Mr. Campbell is a teacher. He seems to think that he might be able to help me get a teaching position one of these days! Can you believe it, Jess!"

Jessie and Emily joined with her in her enthusiasm and fairly danced around the room. Clara then made an effort to restore order by changing the subject.

"By the way, how long .has Joanna been gone? And I didn't see Rose. Is she working too?"

Emily answered this time. "Rose and Jo both went to work for the same family. They're helping them move to a new house. Poor Rose! She's had to put up with Joanna now for two whole weeks!"

"Then Joanna's still the same," Clara remarked thoughtfully. "You'd think that she would have tried to adjust by now. That's really a shame."

The conversation diminished as the bedtime bell sounded and the girls retired. But as Anna lay in bed, her roommates finally asleep, a verse from the morning's sermon rang over and over in her mind—a verse she had repeated often with her grandfather. "And we know that all things work together for good to them that love God, to them who are called according to His purpose." For the first time in her life, Anna seriously questioned what the verse was saying.

All things, God? she pondered silently. *Even Grandpa's death? Even living at St. Matthew's?*

All things, the verse stated clearly.

But how could she really accept what had happened? She still missed her grandfather and was troubled over the sale of the farm. To accept her situation would mean telling God that she could trust Him in spite of what He had put her through. Could she? Could she really trust God?

She thought again of Joanna. She didn't want to be like

her. She wanted to be like Clara, like Jessie. She wanted to be happy, to be sure that she belonged somewhere. Had God put her here? If so, then He must want her to belong here, at least for now.

Purposefully, in the stillness of the night, she closed her eyes. She prayed, in thoughts more than in words. Yes, she would trust God. She didn't understand, but she would trust. And she would be happy, if He would help her.

Surprisingly, her acknowledgment flooded her with an inexplicable peace. She sensed a fullness of love and security that she had never known before. God was with her, and though she did not know what the future would bring, she felt confident that everything would work out. She slept peacefully.

chapter
3

As ANNA ADAPTED TO HER busy work and study schedule at St. Matthew's, one factor kept her often tiresome routine from growing monotonous—Jessie. The perky, dark-haired girl added a sparkle to life at the Home, brightening the days with her natural, free-spirited antics. Anna still marveled at the transformation she witnessed each morning when, somewhere between the rising bell's sounding and her breakfast duties, sleepy Jessie blossomed without warning into a bundle of energy.

How the two girls became such good friends Anna did not really understand, for their personalities differed tremendously. Anna enjoyed studying, Jessie did not. And while Anna preferred reading or taking part in quiet activities during free time, Jessie could hardly wait to get out-of-doors to run and play with the older children. Yet the two were drawn together despite their differences, or perhaps because of them.

Since Jessie did not excel in school work, Anna frequently helped her with assignments. But more often than not, those sessions proved frustrating for Anna since her ever active roommate seemed unable to concentrate on one subject for any length of time.

One evening, when Jessie asked Anna to quiz her on the next day's spelling words, Anna cringed inside. She wanted to refuse. Helping Jessie with spelling was absolutely the most useless exercise she could think of. To recite the letters, Jessie did not need to hold either a book or a paper and pencil. And with both her hands and eyes unoccupied, her mind wandered hopelessly.

But, as usual, Anna consented. After curling into a comfortable position on her bed, she patiently called out the familiar list of words to Jessie, who in turn pronounced her answers while roving nervously around the bedroom.

"Bandage."

"B-a-n-d-a-g-e."

"Kitchen."

"K-i-t-c-h-e-n."

"Handkerchief."

"H-a-n-k-e . . ." Jessie paused, then grimaced as she neared the window. "H-a-n-k-e. . . ."

"Think of it this way, Jessie," Anna coaxed. "It's a *kerchief* that you hold in your *hand*. HAND-kerchief."

But Jessie's attention was already fixed elsewhere.

"Hey, Anna, you haven't seen the new little goat yet, have you? Let's go over to the pen and see him."

"But Jessie, we need to go over these words," Anna sighed. "The test is tomorrow."

"I know." She shrugged her shoulders and moved toward the closet. "Don't worry. I'll go over them later tonight, after supper."

"But after supper you have to read the history assignment."

"Oh, I'll get it all done." Jessie reached for her jacket. "Let's go while we still can. It's almost time to serve supper."

Having learned the futility of debating with Jessie over such matters, Anna gave in. After she donned her heavy blue sweater, the two girls headed down the stairs and out the front door. But Anna halted on the front porch.

"Jessie, look at the sky. It's going to start pouring rain again any minute."

"Then we'd better hurry," Jessie insisted. She raced across the yard and toward the goat pen before Anna could venture another argument.

Anna followed reluctantly, stepping quickly but carefully to avoid slipping on the already soggy ground beneath her. Reaching the fenced area next to the barn, she stopped next to Jessie, who stood balancing on the bottom rail of the fence. Jessie pointed to the furthest corner of the enclosure.

"There he is," she exclaimed. "Isn't he adorable? Did I tell you that Danny helped birth him?"

"Yes, you did." Anna smiled as she caught a glimpse of the tiny brown kid half-hidden by the larger animals in the pen.

"Danny's really good with animals. And with tools too," Jessie boasted, elaborating on her brother's accomplishments. "He used to help Papa a lot, since he was the oldest and since he was the only boy. I helped Papa too, but mostly I worked inside with Ma, especially since Carrie and Margaret were so little."

Anna's attention turned abruptly from the animals to her friend. The cheery ten-year-old talked so easily of her family, even though everyone but she and Danny had been killed two years ago in the fire that had destroyed their farmhouse. Anna wondered if she would ever be able to do that—to talk freely about her losses without breaking into tears. But her thoughts traveled back to the immediate situation when her adventurous roommate made a suggestion.

"Let's go into the pen where we can see him better."

"Jessie, you know we can't do that! Only the boys and Mr. Forrester are allowed to go in there."

But Jessie would not be dissuaded. "I know that normally we're not supposed to go in with the animals, but this is different," she reasoned. "Since Danny helped with the birth, then that makes the little goat a kind of a relative, don't you see? So how can I get in trouble for visiting with him for just a minute?" With her position reinforced by her own rationalization, Jessie moved purposely toward the gate and pulled on the latch. "Are you coming?"

Anna shook her head, deciding to hold her ground. After all, rules were rules. Coming to look was one thing, but going in—knowingly disobeying—was another.

As Anna looked on, Jessie opened the gate and made her way across the enclosure, speaking all the while to her "distant cousin." "Hey there, little fella. Take it easy. I just want to see you, that's all."

With her eyes glued on Jessie and the kid, Anna did not notice a dark, quick movement at the gate. But when she heard a sound, she turned toward the noise and let out a cry of alarm.

"Jessie! That big goat! He's getting out!"

Both girls ran as quickly as they could toward the animal, but neither could reach the gate in time to prevent his escape. Frightened by the sudden commotion, the goat turned to run. Anna panicked when she realized that he was heading straight for the clothesline where three of Miss Sarah's aprons fluttered invitingly in the blustery wind.

Spurred by the knowledge of his destination, both girls raced forward, drawing upon all their energy to catch up with him. Once beside him, Anna lunged for his neck and

Jessie his middle, gripping him with all their might. But instead of stopping, the goat plunged stubbornly forward, dragging Anna and Jessie with him through the mud.

Despite their efforts, the powerful animal pulled them closer and closer to his target. Just as the girls were about to give up, they heard a boy's voice calling to them.

"Hold on! I'm coming!"

Just in time, a dark-haired boy ran to them with a rope, encircled the goat's neck, and relieved them of their lively burden. Exhausted, Anna and Jessie lay motionless on the ground as they looked up at Jessie's thirteen-year-old brother.

"Danny!" Jessie breathed, barely able to talk. "Oh, Danny . . . thank you . . . he almost . . ."

"I know. I was coming out of the barn and I saw the whole thing." He pulled on the rope to prod the animal back to the pen.

"I guess . . . I guess I forgot . . . to latch the gate," Jessie panted as she and Anna rose to their feet and followed Danny.

"Well, it's lucky for you that it was my turn to check the stock," Danny remarked as he pushed the goat back into the enclosure. After checking the latch, he turned to examine the two young girls beside him. He shook his head and let out a low whistle.

"You two are a real mess!"

Anna looked first at herself and then at Jessie, appalled to discover that they were both covered with mud. Miss Sarah would undoubtedly expect an explanation—and a good one, at that.

Just then, to her dismay, Miss Sarah stepped outside to gather her aprons. Spotting the filthy children at once, she hurried over to the barn to investigate.

"Anna, Jessie," she demanded, her tone stern. "What have you been doing?"

"Well, Miss Sarah . . . ," Anna stammered. "We . . ."

But Danny broke in. "I think I can explain, Miss Sarah. I was checking the animals and one of the big goats got out, and the girls helped me catch him. In fact, you can thank them for saving your clothes. The girls were dragged half-way over to the clothesline trying to hold the goat until I got a rope."

Taken aback by Danny's explanation, Anna's eyes widened. She gazed appreciatively at him, then studied Miss Sarah's face, wondering if she would find this story satisfactory. Apparently she did, for she plunged immediately into a tirade of instructions for the girls to follow.

"All right then, girls, you must get out of those clothes at once. And you'll need a bath. Head on inside now and let's get the water heating."

As they moved toward the main house, Anna glanced again at Danny, her heart warm with affection for him. He had been protecting his sister, she knew, and she had merely been caught in the overflow. But she liked the feeling. She hoped Jessie knew how blessed she was to have a brother.

Christmas at St. Matthew's bore little resemblance to the simple celebrations Anna and her grandfather had shared. Preparations started early as the children began secretly working on special gifts. Anna envied the older girls, enabled by their advanced skills to create a new shawl for Miss Sarah and a baby quilt for the Forresters' expected child. But she worked hard at knitting a pair of slippers for Millie, whose name she had drawn in the girl's Christmas gift exchange. She and Emily, both newcomers to the art of knitting and purling, struggled together under Clara's able supervision, while Jessie busied herself with a mysterious weaving project on the loom in the parlor.

But the real excitement began the week before Christmas. School was cancelled, and after giving the Home a thorough cleaning, the children tackled the joyous job of decorating St. Matthew's. Anna viewed her home with pride as she toured it anew, happily noting the holiday changes they had made. A homemade pine cone wreath hung in almost every room. Large red candles circled with pine boughs brightened the dining room table. And sprigs of holly and mistletoe, tied with red bows, adorned the doorways. Holiday baking began too. As the welcome aroma of sugar cookies, gingerbread, and caramel-covered popcorn permeated the house, the level of excitement in Anna's heart heightened to a point near bursting.

With only two days left before Christmas, Anna finished her table-setting tasks, then scurried to find Miss Sarah. The headmistress had promised her a piece of cloth and a string with which to wrap Millie's recently completed gift. The items secured, Anna hurried upstairs and removed the hidden present from the trunk beneath her bed. She tied the blue slippers in the green fabric, then patted the parcel proudly. She only hoped that Millie wouldn't notice the slight unevenness on the toes.

As she hid Millie's gift in her bottom drawer, her eyes fastened upon her family Bible. She carried it to her bed and opened it, looking at the familiar tintype still tucked safely under the front flap. Her thoughts raced backwards to the farm, to Grandpa's quiet ways, to the happy times they had shared. She missed him terribly, even now.

She leafed through the large Bible to find the middle section where the family history had been recorded. Though the names and dates were all indelibly inscribed on her mind, still she read them again.

Caleb Logan, born September 6, 1820
    died June 1, 1871

Married, Caleb Logan to Anna Simons
    March 24, 1844

Anna Simons Logan, born January 13, 1821
    died July 30, 1860

Abigail Christine Logan, born April 10, 1845
    died February 17, 1862

Anna Kathleen Logan, born January 22, 1862

As her eyes scanned the memorized page, her many questions resurfaced. Where was her father? Why had her grandfather avoided talking about him? Why had he refused to acknowlege him in the family tree?

She thought back on the little information her grandfather had given her—that her parents had married just as the war began and that her father had never returned, so was presumed dead. With the actual date of her father's death unknown, she could understand her grandfather not listing it. But where were the other dates? Where was his birth date, the marriage date? Why had they been omitted? What was his name?

Above all else, Anna longed to possess the answer to her last question, to be allowed the privilege of knowing her own father's name. For, no matter who her father had been or what he had done, she certainly owned the right to know his name—*her name*. Her heart pulsed with a tinge of anger over her grandfather's purposeful silence. For the first time that she could remember, she felt a conscious resentment toward him.

Her thoughts were interrupted as Joanna entered the room. Anna watched her uncertainly. For some reason, Joanna's temper flared even more easily this holiday season, so Anna said nothing.

Joanna spoke first. Attracted by the flash of Anna's tintype, she stepped closer to the bed to get a better look.

"Who's that?"

Anna turned the picture to give her a clearer view of it. "My family. My grandparents and my mother."

Joanna studied the likenesses thoughtfully. "You look like your mother."

Surprised by the kind remark, Anna did not know how to respond. Her eyes met Joanna's briefly, and in that instant, Anna glimpsed a spark of sadness, of deep pain unmasked.

"Where's your father?" Joanna questioned further.

Anna glanced at the empty lines in her Bible. "He died in the war."

Joanna walked to her bed, picked up a book, then stepped over to the door. But before leaving, she turned to face Anna. This time as her eyes glared into Anna's, they reflected not sadness and pain, but bitterness and anger.

"You know, maybe you can stand living here, but it's only because you know everybody is dead and you can't go anywhere else. But how would you feel if you were me, and you knew that your father was alive?" Her sharp voice rose. "Surprised? Well, it's true. Two years ago my father put me here. He said he just couldn't handle everything with my mother being dead. Well, how did he think *I* felt?

How did he think I'd handle losing him too? But I'll show him, believe me. Someday, when I get out of here, I'll show him!"

She stomped out the door, leaving Anna in a state of confusion. She understood now Joanna's attitude, Joanna's bitterness. Anna had experienced that same bitterness just moments ago toward her grandfather. She shuddered. God help her, she didn't want her bitterness to grow, as Joanna's had. They both had cause, that was true. *God help her,* she prayed. *God help them both.*

Her encounter with Joanna spoiled the remainder of the evening for her, but by morning she had shaken her muddled thoughts. The church service, through joyous carols and Scripture passages, drew her thoughts back to the birth of Christ, God's gift to man. Her heart was filled again with love and with the spirit of the Christmas season.

That evening, Christmas Eve, Anna thrilled at the viewing of her first Christmas tree. The eight-foot pine stood proudly in the parlor, spreading a wondrous scent through the room. Everyone helped trim the tree, then they exchanged gifts. To Anna's delight, Millie seemed sincerely pleased with her new slippers. Anna beamed, too, at the cream-colored sweater she received from Clara.

But to Anna, the most wonderful gift of all was the one Miss Sarah gave to each child—a small, brown, hand-stitched tree ornament, shaped like a gingerbread man, with each child's name stitched across the stomach. Each of the children tied his own ornament to the tree. As Anna stood back to view the sight, she was filled with love and thankfulness. Her name hung there, along with Clara's, Jessie's, and the rest. Her name belonged there, as she belonged at St. Matthew's. This was her family. This was her home.

Part Two
1876

chapter
4

THE COLD FEBRUARY WIND nipped at Anna's cheeks and nose as she tied her green woolen muffler tighter around her neck. She wished that Mr. Patterson would drive his carriage faster, but he continued guiding the horses cautiously down the frozen roadway.

She glanced toward Mr. Patterson, a short, balding man about forty years old. In spite of the difficulties she had had while working for his family, she had grown quite fond of him during her four-week stay in his home.

"I want to thank you again, Anna, for all your help," he remarked. "I know my family isn't the easiest to get along with."

Anna agreed entirely with his evaluation, but she found herself replying sincerely, "Oh, that's all right, Mr. Patterson."

Her work experience at the Patterson home had been quite trying. Naomi Patterson, a fretful hypochondriac, had demanded considerable attention. Pamela, the eldest daughter, proved to be a spoiled fifteen-year-old who constantly put on airs. The three younger children—Jimmy, eleven; Kelly, nine; and Christy, six—were less irritating, but Anna feared that their personalities would conform to Pamela's unless Mr. Patterson recognized and dealt with their unruly behavior.

"I hope things work out well for you in Colorado," Anna commented. "What was the name of the town you'll be moving to?"

"Rosita. It's a little mining town. Well, now, it's not *too* little. Jeff says there are about a thousand people there."

"Jeff is a relative?"

"My youngest brother." Mr. Patterson's tone sparkled as he spoke of his venture. "Jeff says that Colorado is the place to be. Pretty country, nice people, and a good future with all the strikes they're making. Rosita is booming, and Jeff and his wife Kate are expanding their boardinghouse to add a hotel and dining room. He wants me to be a partner. You know, ever since the war ended, I've dreamed of going west. Now, come spring, we'll be heading out. That is, if Naomi's health improves."

Anna winced inwardly at the mention of Mrs. Patterson's physical condition. She felt certain that Mr. Patterson's dream would never come true if it depended upon his root-bound wife. Her heart went out to the kind, timid man. She prayed that he would find the strength to pursue his goal in spite of his wife's indifference.

When they reached St. Matthew's, Anna jumped from the carriage. While she waited for Mr. Patterson to climb down and unload her satchel, her dark eyes flashed with impatience. She removed her muffler, then shook her head to push her long, light brown hair away from her face. Her fine facial features and maturing figure made her appear older than fourteen.

With Mr. Patterson ready at last, they made their way up the steps. Despite Anna's average height, she felt tall as she stood next to her very short employer. When they reached the porch, they were greeted by Miss Sarah.

"Welcome home, Anna," she cried as she and Anna embraced happily. Miss Sarah then turned to speak to Mr. Patterson. "I trust that Anna was able to be of help to you. She is one of our most reliable workers."

"Indeed. Indeed she was. She's a very capable young lady."

The headmistress smiled proudly at her attractive ward. "Well, Anna, there are some people in the dining room who will be very happy to know you're back. Mr. Patterson, would you care to join us for supper?"

Not waiting to hear his response, Anna scurried to find her friends. Her one disappointment was not finding Jessie, and learning that she had been sent out to work just the week before. But her happiness at being home countered her momentary sadness.

That evening, Anna caught up on all the news while she and her roommates dressed for bed.

"We got a letter yesterday from Clara," Emily mentioned. "She just got three new students, so now she has sixteen altogether. She sounds so happy."

Anna smiled, pleased that her friend had reached her goal of becoming a teacher. She thought again of poor Mr. Patterson and hoped that he would experience the same fulfillment.

Anna suddenly realized that Joanna's bed was vacant.

"Where's Jo?"

Emily hesitated before answering. "We don't know."

"What?" Anna gasped. "What do you mean, you don't know?"

"She ran away. Two weeks ago we got word from the people she was working for. They said that she ran off with some boy from town. Joanna left a note saying that she was getting married and moving away, and so not to bother looking for her. That's all we know."

Greatly distressed by the news, Anna thought of nothing else for the rest of the night. Poor Joanna. Never content. All Anna could do now was pray that, somehow, Joanna would finally find what she was looking for.

In no time at all, Anna slipped back into her comfortable routine of schoolwork and chores. She also took on several sewing projects. She made two sorely needed shirts for a new St. Matthew's resident, then cut and hemmed new sheets and pillowcases for the nursery.

But her routine changed abruptly in mid-April when Miss Sarah called her into the office. After Anna took a seat in the chair next to the desk, Miss Sarah asked her a curious question.

"Anna, what did you think of the Pattersons when you were at their home?"

Anna thought for a moment, then replied politely but honestly. She related her negative evaluations of the family members, but included her sympathy and affection for Mr. Patterson.

"Then you think that, if Mrs. Patterson has her way, they won't go to Colorado?" Miss Sarah asked.

"That's right."

"Well, you may be right. Mr. Patterson was here to see me this morning. He seems determined to make this move, but he is facing a number of obstacles. He has left his furniture-building business and has sold his home, but now Mrs. Patterson's condition has him quite concerned."

"What condition?" Anna argued. "That woman is no sicker than I am. If she ruins everything for her husband when he's been dreaming of this for so long. . . ."

"She's expecting a baby, Anna."

The words took Anna completely by surprise.

Miss Sarah continued. "Mr. Patterson was wondering if you would consider helping him."

"But how?"

"He will need help packing and getting the house in order for the new owners. He asked for you since you did such good work for him the last time. But he was also wondering if you would consider going west with them, to help Mrs. Patterson on the journey, and to help them get settled—just until the baby arrives and they adjust to everything. I know it's a lot to ask, Anna. You would have to leave in two weeks and you would be gone for a year."

Shocked by the unexpected proposition, Anna stared at Miss Sarah blankly. Going west with the Pattersons? For a year? She had barely endured Naomi Patterson's demands and Pamela's rudeness for the month she was with them. The prospect left her speechless.

"You don't have to answer right now, dear," Miss Sarah assured her. "Just think about it—and pray. You'll know the right thing to do."

Anna spent the rest of the day and most of that night struggling with her thoughts. Her immediate reaction was a definite no. Yet a small voice kept nagging at her, reminding her of the sparkle in Mr. Patterson's voice when he spoke of the little Colorado town. She had prayed for God to give him the strength to pursue his dream, and he was at last pursuing it. Now he was in danger of losing what ground he had gained if she refused to help.

But she didn't want to be a part of his decision. She cringed at the thought of a year with Pamela. Yet she remembered again the familiar verse that had helped her so many times before. "And we know that all things work together for good to them that love God. . . ." All things. Had it come to that again?

She grappled with the problem through the night, sleeping but a few hours as she thought about the difficult decision facing her. But when she woke the following morning, the answer seemed surprisingly simple. Mr. Patterson needed her help. She could not in all good conscience refuse him.

She would go to Colorado.

chapter
5

THE TREK WESTWARD began in early May, 1876. After a week of packing and repacking, Anna watched the Pattersons' four tightly packed crates being loaded onto the railroad car at the Lexington station. She clutched her satchel tightly, then boarded the train with the family.

Since Mrs. Patterson expected to experience frequent fits of nausea, they selected seats at the far end of the car near the toilet. Though occasionally annoyed by Naomi's constant complaints, Anna felt a touch of sympathy toward the stout, dark-haired woman who was leaving her home for a different life in a strange place.

Pamela spoke little during the trip, save to whine about the annoying crowds, the smoke that irritated her eyes, and the inadequate dining facilities. But, undaunted by Pamela's negative remarks and Naomi's illness, Mr. Patterson, Anna, and the three younger children enjoyed the long ride. They stared out the windows, observing with delight the scenic countryside that seemed to change constantly during the three-day journey to Denver.

Once in Denver, the group boarded the smaller narrow gauge Denver & Rio Grande Railroad that carried them, first, the 115 miles south to Pueblo, then the remaining 45 miles west to Cañon City. The beauty of the Colorado countryside struck Anna with awe as she viewed the endless eastern plains broken sharply by the vast, towering peaks of the Rocky Mountains. Still solidly covered with snow, the mountain slopes were dotted with huge green pines and bare aspen. She marveled at the solid permanence of the lofty peaks, and the quiet stillness of the clear, invigorating air. Thinking back on her decision to come, Anna wondered at her hesitancy. To live in such beauty even for a year would be a wonderful privilege.

Lord, thank You for creating so much beauty, and for letting me experience it, Anna played silently.

Late Friday afternoon, when the party reached Cañon City, they found Jeff Patterson waiting for them. He embraced his brother heartily and welcomed the other family members with a sincere warmth. But when he greeted Anna with some reserve, it occurred to her that her presence must have been totally unexpected.

She liked the young man at once. He bore little resemblance to his older brother. Roughly thirty-five years old, Jeff Patterson moved confidently, his compact, muscular frame handling with ease the Pattersons' heavy crates.

As he began loading the cargo onto his wagon, he let out a low whistle. "What'd you do, Rich? Bring half of Kentucky with you? I think we'd better freight most of this over to Rosita. There's no way the team can pull both a load like this and passengers up the grade we've got tomorrow." Jeff's intense brown eyes twinkled under an abundant growth of thick brown hair. His full beard was neatly trimmed. "By the way, did you bring the things I wrote to you about?"

"Yes, indeed," Richard affirmed. "Woolen blankets, carpentry tools, mason jars, and yellow gingham."

After loading the boxes, Jeff and Richard assisted the ladies and children onto the wagon. Jeff then drove them down the main street of the small city to the hotel where he had reserved rooms for the night.

Insisting that they were totally exhausted, Naomi and Pamela chose to have dinner in their rooms. The rest of the party consumed a hearty meal in the hotel dining room, all the while questioning Jeff concerning what would await them in Rosita.

"Is our hotel like this one?" Jimmy asked. Unlike the other family members in appearance, Jimmy was taller and lighter, his auburn hair touched with red and his oval face sparsely splashed with pale brown freckles.

"No, not exactly," Jeff responded. "Our place is smaller, and it still needs a lot of work. The basic framing on the hotel is done, but only half of the rooms are actually finished inside. There's a lot to do, and I hope you young folks are willing to work hard."

The children responded enthusiastically. The peaceful surroundings and the promise of a simpler lifestyle seemed already to be asserting a positive influence on them. Anna's heart glowed with that knowledge as she noted the look of contentment on Richard Patterson's face. How thankful she was that she had come—that they all had come.

"Actually, Rich, there *is* a lot to do," Jeff continued. "We've been swamped since we opened the hotel last week. Kate is so desperate for help in the kitchen that she's even put *me* to work out there. But we've purposely neglected hiring anyone permanently until you and your family arrived. We thought we could divide up the duties and see if we couldn't just handle everything ourselves—make a real family business out of it." He glanced awkwardly toward Anna. "By the way, is Naomi all right? She and Pamela both looked a little green around the gills. Rough trip?"

Richard then described his wife's weak physical condition and the expected baby, including the explanation for Anna's presence. However, Anna still sensed a reservation in Jeff's expression, as if he inwardly doubted any real need for her services. Defensively, she glanced away from him to speak to her employer.

"Mr. Patterson, if we have a thirty-mile trip ahead of us in the morning, I should put the children to bed. It's getting late."

At that, Anna accompanied the children upstairs where she saw Jimmy to his room and guided Kelly and Christy to the room they were sharing with her and Pamela. She helped the young girls into their nightgowns and tucked them into bed, then changed to her nightclothes as well. She would have loved to stay up a little longer to write a letter to Jessie. But Pamela was a light sleeper, and the light would undoubtedly bother her. Since Anna was unsure of her standing with Jeff, she didn't want to add to her problems by disturbing Pamela. So she blew out the lantern, climbed into her bed, and fell asleep.

Early the following morning, the group piled into the crowded, rickety wagon. Spring had technically arrived weeks ago, but the higher altitude hindered the arrival of the season's warmth. Anna and the Pattersons bundled up in sweaters and scarves to protect themselves from the surprisingly cold weather.

The hard winter and the spring thaw had both taken a toll on the rugged roadway, so the wagon jerked and bounced along the weather-beaten thoroughfare. Its uneven movements caused considerable complaining from Naomi and Pamela.

Just a few miles south of town, the wagon left the rolling valley road and began climbing an incredibly steep, winding grade. Anna's heart pounded as the wagon creaked slowly forward, traveling just a few feet away from the mountain's edge. Behind them, Cañon City disappeared from view as it hid itself in the narrow, scenic valley. All other foothills and landmarks to the east blended subtly with the great plains, their seemingly endless expanse broken abruptly by the awesome presence of Pike's Peak.

Once up the incline, when Jeff guided the wagon through Oak Creek Canyon and away from the precipitous heights, Anna relaxed and enjoyed the intriguing scenery. Huge pink and white granite formations lined the roadway, their stark appearances softened by the surrounding pines and blooming wildflowers. She listened attentively as Jeff pointed to the various local greenery—the bushy green piñon pines, the lovely wildflowers, and the now familiar aspen.

As the day passed, the road led away from the winding gorge, crossing through rich, green meadows. Occasionally Anna glimpsed snowy peaks in the far distance, but the half-timbered mountains around her blocked any clear view of them.

Darkness had settled on the Wet Mountain Valley as the wagon at last bumped slowly into Rosita. Nestled in the rolling hills, the town lay quiet, its dimly lit cabins twinkling a welcome to the weary travelers.

"Welcome to Rosita," Jeff announced proudly. He stopped the wagon in front of a large, two-story building bearing the sign ROSITA HOTEL, ROOMS AND MEALS.

The Pattersons alighted from the wagon and headed for

the front door, leaving Anna to care for Kelly and Christy, who lay sleeping in the corner of the wagon. Noting Anna's dilemma, Jeff offered his help, and the two promptly scooped up the slumbering children and moved toward the hotel.

Inside the shadowy entryway, the straggling group met a pleasant young woman with honey-colored hair, who guided the Patterson family into the dining room to the right of the entry. As she did, Anna followed Jeff through the parlor on the left, down a corridor, and into a small room that housed two bunks and a chest. They tucked the children into the lower bunks, then moved back down the hallway to the kitchen.

The room lacked the brightness and spaciousness of the kitchen at St. Matthew's, Anna thought, but housed adequate work area and equipment. A stout, black cookstove and small icebox were against the west wall. Underneath a tiny window to her left stood a large wooden table with two long benches running the length of the table and a wooden chair at each end. The counters and pantry along the far wall were interrupted by two solid doors, and swinging doors to her right led into the dining room.

Even as Anna stared at the swinging doors, they parted, and the blond woman entered the kitchen. Her blue eyes twinkled and she grinned as she crossed the room toward Jeff.

"Well, do you think you can spare the time to say hello?" she chided.

"Oh, I think so," Jeff smiled. He pulled her to himself and embraced her warmly. "I've missed you, Katie."

"I've missed you, too."

As their lips met, Anna cast her eyes to the floor, touched but embarrassed by their open display of affection.

The couple seemed not to notice her discomfort as they turned to face her.

Jeff's eyes focused on Anna. "Now, lest this young lady get the wrong impression, allow me to introduce my wife. Anna, this is Kate Patterson. And Kate, this is Anna . . . I'm sorry. I don't know your last name."

"Logan. Anna Logan. I'm pleased to meet you, Mrs. Patterson."

"Kate," she insisted. "Richard just told me that you've come along to help Naomi."

Anna nodded, sensing Jeff's silent skepticism once again.

"And please call me Jeff," he added. "If you keep calling me Mr. Patterson, we'll never know if you're talking to me or to Rich. Anyway, 'Mr. Patterson' sounds so formal. It makes me feel as old as the hills."

"I don't suppose you want me to comment on that last statement, do you?" Kate teased.

Anna grinned, feeling slightly more at ease with her new acquaintances. She then volunteered her help in preparing a late dinner for the hungry troop that waited in the dining room. After a tasty meal of roast beef sandwiches and applesauce, Anna and the others retired to their rooms.

Despite the fact that she was dead tired, Anna did not fall asleep immediately. Jeff's attitude troubled her greatly. She was sure that he saw her as an extra burden, as an intruder into their family venture. But, she decided with firm resolve, she would do her best to prove him wrong.

chapter

6

ANNA ROSE EARLY THE NEXT MORNING. Since the three
Patterson sisters shared the room with her, she dressed
quietly so as not to disturb them. She then made her way
down the dark hallway to the kitchen, where she spotted
Kate at the far counter, vigorously stirring a large bowl of
batter.

"Good morning," Anna announced.

Kate turned. "You're up bright and early." She wiped her
hands on her white apron and brushed a streak of flour
from the long sleeve of her pale green dress. "Everyone else
is still in bed. Did you sleep well?"

"Very well. I'm just used to getting up about now to get
breakfast started. Can I help?"

"Certainly." Kate directed Anna to a cupboard containing
tableware, and Anna busied herself setting the table.

"How many men are boarding here now?" Anna asked.

"Twelve. That's our limit. The boarders eat here in the
kitchen. The dining room is for hotel guests and local customers."

"What time do you serve breakfast?"

"At about six-thirty, or a little earlier if I can manage it.
The hotel dining room is open from seven o'clock to eight-

thirty, so I can usually get our boarders taken care of before the rush comes from out front. We serve dinner from eleven-thirty to one-thirty, and supper from six to eight."

While Kate poured heaping ladles of pancake batter onto two long, hot griddles, Anna brewed coffee. The kitchen then began filling with hungry men. First to arrive was Jeff, who emerged from one of the bedrooms directly off the kitchen. Anna heard no sounds coming from the second bedroom, so she assumed that Richard and Naomi were still sleeping.

The boarders soon filed through the hall door and took their accustomed places at the table. Anna gazed at them in surprise. She had expected to see old, bearded prospectors in simple, even shabby attire. Instead, she viewed a tidy, well-mannered group, some young and clean-shaven, and several dressed in stylish vested suits.

Anna watched in amazement as the huge stacks of pancakes disappeared from the platters as quickly as she set them on the table. Though the boys at St. Matthew's had had good appetites, she had never seen such hearty eaters as this group. Most of the men ate quickly and quietly, departing for parts unknown when they had finished. But several lingered over their coffee to chat with Jeff and to meet Richard, who had recently joined the gathering.

As Kate had predicted, they barely finished serving the boarders before the dining room began filling with the hotel guests and local patrons. The time passed quickly as Kate made more pancakes and Anna prepared bacon and eggs for the guests who requested them. Anna then fed the children and delivered a breakfast tray to Naomi while Kate closed the dining room. When at last they were able to sit down, they were more than ready to eat their own breakfast.

But just as Anna sat down at the kitchen table, she spotted Pamela standing in front of the swinging doors. Pamela's pink Sunday dress hugged her thick waist snugly. The delicate lacework at the collar and cuffs drew attention to her pale, wide throat and chubby hands. Her black hair, which barely touched the pink collar of her dress, was secured behind her ears with two gold barrettes, giving her round face an even fuller appearance.

"Good morning, Pamela," Anna ventured. "Did you sleep well?"

"No, I did not," she replied coldly. "If I'm to be forced to share a room with the three of you, I shall expect you all to be more quiet in the future." She then spoke to Kate. "By the way, I have been sitting in the dining room for several minutes now, waiting to be served. Perhaps Jeff should install some type of service bell out there."

"We eat in the kitchen, Pamela," Kate remarked firmly. "The dining room is for hotel guests *only*. Your table service is in the cabinet to your left. Help yourself."

Anna tried hard to conceal a grin as she watched Pamela's reaction. Obviously disgusted with Kate's order, she hesitated for a moment, then noisily retrieved the necessary utensils from the cupboard and carried them to the table. Her green eyes squinted warily as she noticed Anna scooping a heaping spoonful of the fluffy scrambled eggs onto a plate.

"I do hope those eggs are well done. I detest runny eggs."

They consumed the meal in relative silence. Pamela found the eggs too hard and the griddlecakes too dry, yet she managed to consume generous portions of each. Finishing first, she rose from the table and entered her mother's room. She returned as Anna and Kate were sharing the last three pancakes and dividing the small amount of remaining eggs between them. Pamela crossed the kitchen, stopped when she reached the hallway, then turned to address Anna.

"Anna, Mother finished her breakfast some time ago and would like you to remove her tray. Also, I understand that church starts in thirty minutes. I suggest you stop dawdling over breakfast and get the children dressed. We wouldn't want to be late on our first Sunday here. You'll be staying here with Mother this morning while we're gone, in case Father forgot to mention it to you."

As the young girl marched down the hallway, Kate breathed a heavy sigh and glanced toward Anna. Neither spoke as they finished eating, then Kate completed the kitchen chores while Anna located Jimmy and told him to get dressed for church. She then prodded the youngest Patterson girls into their room and helped them into their Sunday apparel. After accompanying the neatly dressed girls to the parlor, Anna left them in Richard's charge, then retreated back down the corridor to the kitchen.

The room stood empty and strangely silent. Noting the half-filled teapot still perched on the warm stove, Anna poured another cup for herself, then leaned wearily against the counter. She surveyed the room thoughtfully, grateful for a few moments of privacy. The work here would be harder than back home. But Kate was easy to work with, and the year would pass quickly enough. A year. At the moment, it sounded like an eternity.

The distant sound of organ music filtered in through the open window. Anna recognized the faint but familiar tune of "A Mighty Fortress." The song drew her mind back to the pleasant Sundays at St. Matthew's—the enjoyable trips to and from church, the relaxing afternoons of reading alone or playing games with Jessie. Jessie. How she longed to see her. The endless preparations for the trip and her hectic schedule with the Pattersons had left Anna little time to grow homesick. Now, in the quiet stillness of her strange new surroundings, she thought of her family fondly. She longed to share the excitement of her journey with them, to describe the beauty of the countryside, to confide her frustrations to the people who would understand. Feelings of loneliness pressed upon her and she wished for the comfort and security of a familiar face.

A sudden noise at the back door interrupted her thoughts. As she glanced toward the sound, the door opened and an older, gray-bearded man entered the room. Anna recognized him as one of the boarders. Billy, she thought they had called him. He wiped his dusty boots on the doormat and removed his shapeless felt hat as he stepped into the house. His faded shirt was partly covered by a brown leather vest with the initials "BF" burned onto the left pocket. He moved slowly and naturally, as if he had all the time in the world but none of its cares.

"Good morning," Anna ventured.

"Mornin'. You got any more of that?" He nodded toward the cup she held in her hands.

"Yes, but it's not very hot. And it's tea, not coffee."

"Don't matter to me, so long as it's wet." Billy walked to the table and sat at the back bench. "So, what do you think of Rosita?"

Anna carried his tea cup over and joined him at the table. "Well, so far it seems fine. I haven't seen much of it, since we arrived so late last night, but I think I'll like it here. The mountains are beautiful. I've never seen anything like them."

"And you won't, either. They're a sight to behold."

"Have you lived here long, Mr. . . ."

"Billy. The name's William Friedrich, but folks all call me Billy. Yep, I've been here as long as anybody. I came in with the first load of bricks, back in April of '73 when the camp first started."

"You're a miner, then?"

"Couldn't you tell?" he laughed. He gulped his drink, then pushed the empty cup to the middle of the table. "Yep, I'm a miner—prospector's a better word. I'm on my own. Most of the folks here work for the big mines. The Senator, the Humboldt, the Pocahontas—there's a mess of 'em."

"Where is your mine? Is it near town?"

Billy gave her a quizzical glance, then shook his head. "You sure are green, ain't you?" When Anna appeared puzzled, he explained further. "You just don't ask a prospector where his mine is, 'cause he won't tell you the location. Too many claim jumpers. I wouldn't tell my own grandmother where my mine is."

"Oh, I'm sorry. I didn't mean . . ."

"That's all right. You'll learn."

Afraid to ask any more questions, Anna said nothing for a few minutes. But at length her apprehension gave way to her curiosity.

"Do you know why they named the town Rosita?"

Billy seemed pleased with her interest in the subject. "There's two stories on that. The first one is that it's because of all the wild roses that grow around here. Second—and all the womenfolk like this one—is that some Frenchman named it after his Spanish sweetheart. After she died, he got to wandering around and found this spot so pretty that he named it after her." Noting a soft gleam in Anna's eyes, Billy let out a short burst of laughter. "See, I told you ladies like that last one!" As Anna grinned, he asked her a question. "How come you ain't at church with the rest of your family?"

"Oh, they're not my family," she explained. "I just work for the Pattersons. Mrs. Patterson is expecting a baby in October, and they wanted me to come out with them to help them until the baby comes and until they get all settled. Mrs. Patterson isn't feeling well, so I'm staying here this morning in case she needs anything. I would be at church too, otherwise."

"How old are you?"

"Fourteen."

"And your folks let you come all the way out here by yourself?" the old prospector inquired, his raspy voice reflecting a touch of disapproval.

"My parents are dead. My grandpa raised me until I was nine, and I've been living in an orphanage since then."

Billy seemed momentarily lost for words, and their conversation ended as Kate emerged from Naomi's room.

"Is there anything I should be doing now?" Anna asked.

"Yes, there is," Kate replied. "On Sundays we don't start serving dinner until twelve-thirty. So we have a while yet before we have to start frying the chicken. You go take a walk, rest, or whatever."

"But what if Mrs. Patterson . . ."

"I'll be here to check on Naomi. Now get going," Kate demanded pleasantly.

Anna needed no further prodding. After stopping by her room for her sweater, she headed out the front door, anxious to see Rosita in the daylight.

She noted immediately that the Rosita Hotel was situated in the heart of Rosita's business district. The stores and shops had been built in a square to form a wide plaza. Directly across from her, in the center of the plaza, flowed a spring that she suspected was the town's water supply.

She glanced to her left, studying the buildings that lined the eastern end of Tyndal Street. Her eyes darted to the brightly painted signs that signalled the various businesses. Webb and Tomkins Hardware. Post Office. Grand View Hotel. F. L. Miller & Company.

As she turned her gaze to the west, she gasped in surprise at the sight that awaited her. The distant peaks that she had glimpsed only in part yesterday now spread in full view. Before her, framed by the partly timbered mountains and the deep blue sky, loomed the most magnificent mountain range she had ever seen. The Sangre de Cristos. Their beauty astounded her.

She moved toward them, walking the entire length of Rosita's business district. She then continued on until she reached the top of a slight incline where the road began winding away from the settlement. She stopped there, overwhelmed by the indescribable natural beauty around her.

But as she turned to retrace her steps, another vista confronted her, shocked her, with an impact almost as staggering. For there, mingled with the immense beauty of nature, was terrible ugliness. Scores of mines pushed outward on the sides of the hills, blackening the landscape with their crudely built frames and their growing piles of waste. Hundreds of cabins, roughly hewn and unpainted, crowded the sloping hills, as if their construction had been a necessary afterthought. Even the town itself, with its rough, dark buildings, some with false fronts and gawdy signs, appeared out of place in such a serene setting. Nowhere had she ever witnessed such a disturbing contrast.

Unsettled by these conflicting pictures, her heart rushed with a flurry of differing responses. She felt awed by God's power, evidenced in the beauty of the mountains, but angered at man for his destructive presence. So this was Colorado, a land of contradictions. What a strange new country she had found.

But the contemplating ended when Anna arrived back at the boardinghouse. As she busied herself with the tasks at hand, the day passed quickly. It seemed that she had no sooner completed dinner cleanup than the hour had arrived to start supper. She spoke little with anyone, her conversations limited to a few passing remarks with Billy and instructions from Kate and Jeff.

With the dining room at last closed for the evening and the kitchen work finished, Anna retired to her room. The hour was still fairly early, but she felt extremely tired. Tomorrow would be washday, Kate had mentioned. The thought of facing an unknown but undoubtedly enormous amount of dirty laundry depressed her. She pushed the thought from her mind, blew out the lantern, and climbed into her upper bunk.

She tried not to think about it, yet she wondered what the Pattersons were discussing—if she were one of the topics—as they held their family conference around the kitchen table. She rolled onto her side and pulled her blanket around her shoulders, dismissing the subject as best she could. For all she really cared about right now was getting a good night's sleep. She had the feeling that she was going to need it.

chapter
7

ANNA WAS RIGHT. Monday was exhausting. When she stepped outside to begin doing the laundry, she could not believe her eyes. Never had she seen such a monstrous pile of dirty clothes and bed linens. Even though the boarding house employed two Mexican women to help with the task, the job was still enormous.

On Tuesday, Anna and the two Mexican workers had to iron the stacks of Monday's freshly laundered garments and sheets. Pamela and Naomi were no help at all. Naomi spent her days resting, complaining all the while of nausea and fatigue. When Richard at last convinced Pamela to help with the kitchen duties, she was in the way more than she helped. Kelly, Christy, and Jimmy, though willing to work, were now enrolled in school.

All day Wednesday, Anna helped Kate bake half a week's worth of bread and rolls for their hungry customers. She also helped cook and serve the meals and looked after the children when school let out. Though accustomed to long hours, Anna found herself totally exhausted as the day finally drew to a close. She had performed these same weekly chores at St. Matthew's, but there she had had help from all the other children. With Richard and Jeff occupied with the necessary carpentry projects, she and Kate were left to care for everything else. She could understand why Kate and Jeff had asked Richard to help them. She wondered, though, just how long she could handle her boardinghouse responsibilities in addition to her duties with Naomi and the children.

That night, after tucking Kelly and Christy into their bunks, Anna headed back to the kitchen to prepare the pot of tea that Mrs. Patterson had requested. She delivered it to Naomi who lay reading in bed, then stepped back out into the kitchen. She paused to rest against the bedroom door as she closed it behind her, shutting her eyes for a moment. When she opened them, she spotted Billy emerging from the hallway. He nodded a greeting, so she smiled weakly.

"Kate said I could sneak a few rolls," he announced. "Mind if I help m'self?" Shen Anna shook her head, Billy pulled an empty cup and a platter of cinnamon rolls from the cupboard. He removed a pitcher of milk from the icebox and crossed over to sit at the table. "Can you sit a spell, little lady?"

Anna made her way over to the table, grateful for the chance to rest a minute. Billy scooped a roll from the platter and took a hefty bite.

"I don't know what Kate did to these rolls," he mumbled, "but they sure do taste extra good."

Anna perked at his remark, since she had made that particular batch. He slid the platter toward her, so she reached for a roll too.

"Looks to me like you're burnin' the candle at both ends," he commented, his gravelly voice sounding more stern than usual.

Knowing that at this point she could start crying with little provocation, Anna sampled her roll instead of answering. She took comfort in his reprimand, though. At least someone cared enough to notice that she was tired.

"For being new out here, you're doin' a mighty fine job," he added, giving her a quick wink. "You must be used to workin'."

Anna kept eating and remained silent.

"Jeff's brother seems to know his business," Billy continued. "Him bein' out here should be a considerable help to Jeff. Yep—they've got themselves a fine little place here. I like Rosita. But one of these days, I plan to move on back to Californy."

"You've been all the way to California?"

"Yep."

"Have you seen the ocean?" she questioned, momentarily feeling a surge of new energy.

"Sure have."

Billy needed little encouragement to get him started on a detailed account of his travels and adventures. Anna listened attentively. She didn't mind at all that their conversation was keeping her up late, so pleased was she to have someone to talk to. But, at length, Billy insisted she go to bed. He did promise, though, that they would pick up where they had left off at another time.

The next morning, however, Anna regretted her decision to stay up so late, for Thursday was cleaning day. After spending the day scrubbing every inch of the boarding-house and hotel with Kate, Anna could barely find the strength that evening to help Kelly and Christy into their nightgowns. Finally, she changed into her own nightclothes and climbed into her bunk. Her muscles ached from the staggering workload, and her mind struggled with the negative thoughts that pressed upon her. She couldn't do it. Not any longer. Not at this pace.

Tears trickled down her cheeks, so she buried her face in her pillow to muffle the sobs. Loneliness crept upon her as her mind traveled back to her family in Kentucky, so far away.

Lord, she prayed in the silence of her mind. *Lord, I can't do it. I'm all by myself, and there's too much to do. I just can't do it. And I'm tired . . . I'm so tired.*

She slept.

Early the next morning, Anna stood in front of the squat cookstove browning sausage in two large, cast-iron skillets. As the pleasant aroma drifted upward to her nostrils, she could almost taste the robust flavor of her favorite breakfast—sausage, eggs, and biscuits.

"Good morning, Anna," called a voice from behind her.

She turned to see Richard Patterson standing a few feet away. "Good morning," she responded. She turned again to the stove and peeked into the oven. She didn't want the biscuits to burn.

Richard stepped closer to the stove. His green eyes darted nervously from the skillet to the worn wooden floor.

"With all the traffic in this kitchen, these floorboards sure do get a workout. I suppose they'll need to be replaced one of these days. But not for a while, I'd say, with all the other jobs that need to be done first." He paused, then added with a cheery note, "Jeff and I will be going over to the sawmill this morning to order some more timber. I hope to get a good start on some furniture for out in the dining room."

Sensing that his jovial tone did not match his mood, Anna prodded him on with a question.

"How do the children like school here?"

"Fine. Well, the girls seem to enjoy it, but Jimmy is not

one for studies. Once he gets to know some of the other boys, though, I'm sure he'll do fine. I think he just feels a little strange having Mr. Baldwin living under the same roof."

Mr. Baldwin. Anna thought back on the various boarders as she tried to place the schoolteacher's name with the proper face. Hiram Baldwin. Appropriately named, she decided, as she remembered the tall, lean gentleman with the rapidly receding hairline.

As an uncomfortable silence settled on the room, Anna grew concerned by Mr. Patterson's odd behavior.

"Mr. Patterson, is there something you'd like to talk to me about? Have I done something wrong?"

"Oh, no . . . no . . . you haven't done anything wrong. Not at all," he stammered. "It's just that, well, there is something we should discuss, and, well, it concerns last night. After you retired, we had another family meeting to discuss the business here and to assess the situation. And I was wondering, we were all wondering if . . ."

"If what?"

"I know that when I originally asked you to come, it was under the assumption that you would help Naomi and take care of her duties with the children and the household until we got more organized. I just didn't realize how much work we were getting into. I thought *I'd* be the one helping Jeff and Kate. I didn't really understand that the whole family would be expected to participate in the actual day-to-day workings of the business. Neither did they." His voice dropped, reflecting as it did a tinge of disappointment.

"I appreciate all you've done so far, Anna. You've jumped right in and helped with everything, you've looked after the children and Naomi, but there's just too much to do, and I refuse to make you do all of it." He spoke with conviction, his tone more forceful than Anna had ever heard it. "Would you be willing to alter our original agreement?"

He hastened to explain. "Pamela has agreed to help her mother and to watch over the children, which I should have insisted upon originally. If she does this, and I intend to see that she does, you would be free of those responsibilities. Under those circumstances, would you be willing to stay on for the year, working strictly as a paid boarding-house employee? I know this is not why you came out here. Heaven knows, you could have gotten similar work back in Kentucky. So, if you would like to, you can go back home. I don't want to be unfair to you. But, well, we do need help. And you are so . . . you are so . . . adaptable." Mr. Patterson waited, anxious for a reply but hesitant to demand one.

Surprised by the proposition, Anna searched her heart for the right response. She could go home. That alternative had not even entered her mind, at least not realistically. Her heart raced at the prospect. If Pamela were really to assume the task of caring for Naomi and the children, then her presence would no longer be required. The business needed more workers, that was true. But she didn't have to be one of them. Jeff had hired two women to help with the laundry, so he could hire someone else to take her place. As Mr. Patterson had said not a moment ago, she could have taken a comparable job in Kentucky, nearer home. Her thoughts ran to Jessie and Emily, and she pictured them clearly. But as she did, she saw also the harried face of Richard Patterson as he asked for her continued help.

She then considered an aspect that she had not thought of before. If she were to return to St. Matthew's, she would undoubtedly face new employment situations. Not all of her past work experiences had been pleasant ones. Maybe staying in Rosita for the full year wouldn't be so bad after all. Mr. Patterson had always been fair in the past, and his generous offer now indicated that he intended to remain so. Since Jeff must have consented to his brother's proposition, she could assume that he approved of her work and no longer considered her a millstone.

She faced her employer confidently. "I agreed to stay for a year, Mr. Patterson, and I will. But you will have to notify St. Matthew's of the change in my duties, and they'll have the final say."

Richard's lips formed a pleasant smile, emitting as they did a noticeable sigh of relief. "I'll write to them right away. Thank you, Anna. I . . . we really appreciate it."

The alarming smell of overbaked biscuits alerted Anna to her immediate duties. She hurriedly yanked the oven door open to remove the golden rolls. Kate entered from the back door, carrying the extra wood she had gone to collect, and the familiar breakfast bustle began.

After breakfast, when Kate left to take care of some shopping, Anna found herself with nothing to do. Deciding to write a letter to Jessie, she gathered her writing materials, stepped into the parlor, and selected a comfortable chair near the fireplace. She placed her ink bottle on the low stone hearth, then picked up her pen and began.

Dear Jessie,

Greetings from Colorado. I miss you and hope you are well. I am fine. The journey out was really interesting. I can hardly describe what a beautiful place Colorado is. The scenery is wonderful. There are huge mountains covered with snow right near Rosita. I can see them clearly whenever I'm outside. They're called the Sangre de Cristo Mountains. Billy, a boarder here, says that's Spanish for the "Blood of Christ."

I've gotten to know Billy pretty well, and I really like him. He's about sixty years old, and he has a gold mine that's hidden somewhere high up in the mountains. He has traveled all through the West, and even lived in California for a while. So he knows quite a bit about history. He has been answering a lot of my questions about Colorado and Rosita.

There are a lot of Mexican people out here, so a lot of the places have Mexican names (like Rosita). Even Colorado is a Spanish word that means "colored red."

There is a lot of work to do here. At first I didn't think I could handle it. But Mr. Patterson has come up with an idea that should work out better. He will be writing to Miss Sarah about it very soon, so I'll let him explain it all. Please tell Miss Sarah that I won't mind Mr. Patterson's new arrangement if it's all right with her.

Give my regards to everyone. I will try to write again soon.

Your Friend,
Anna

"Good morning," boomed a deep voice from behind her. When Anna turned with a start, the man added, "I'm sorry. I didn't mean to startle you."

Recognizing the man as a boarder, Anna studied him as he walked to the sofa and seated himself. Attractive and in his mid-twenties, he wore a spotless white shirt and a dark blue vested suit. Thick black hair, impeccably trimmed and parted on the left, accented his clear gray eyes. His name, she thought, her mind going blank. What was his name?

"Jason Ryker," he stated as if he understood her dilemma. "I see you're busy. If I'm disturbing you, I could talk to you some other time."

"Oh, no, it's all right," she responded, glad for some company. "I've just finished. I'm sorry that I didn't re-

76

member your name right away. I still don't know very many of the people here."

"That's perfectly understandable. Your name is Anna Logan, is that correct?"

She nodded. "What is it that you do, Mr. Ryker?"

"Jason, please. I'm a journalist. I write for the *Rosita Index*. Have you read a copy yet?" Anna shook her head. "It's a fine newspaper, published weekly. We're very proud of it." He spoke distinctly, with a spark of pride. "Rosita is a nice little town. All in all, it's pretty quiet and peaceful. Not like most of the mining towns you've probably heard about."

Hesitant to mention that she had heard very little about *any* mining town, Anna remained silent while Jason continued.

"I'm sure you're aware that most mining towns have, shall we say, undesirable histories, to say the least. Many camps have an overabundance of saloons and gambling halls, an extreme shortage of respectable ladies, and constant instances of fighting, claim jumping, and killing. But, as I said earlier, Rosita is a quiet town. There have been occasional problems, of course. Why, just last fall we had some full-scale fighting. The 'Pocahontas War,' we called it. An organized party of scoundrels took over the Pocahontas mine, and their leader, Walter Stuart, cleaned out the bank. There was an entire day of gunfighting right outside on Tyndal Street! But, since then, life here has been calm, with only a few outbursts, like the shooting last Saturday night."

"The shooting?"

"Yes. Didn't you hear about it?"

Anna resented the implication of ignorance that his tone inferred. "Mr. Ryker, I mean Jason, we had just arrived, and I have been very busy."

Oblivious to her injured feelings, Jason flashed a charming smile. "I suppose you have been. The incident took place on Sunday morning, actually, at 2 A.M. Some men tried to break into Townsend and Son, a saloon a few blocks down the street—the one connected with the Rosita Brewing Company. Mr. Townsend owns them both. He was inside the saloon at the time of the break-in. He fired a shot and hit one of the men, Jake Webber."

"Was Mr. Webber hurt?" she inquired, suddenly conscious of the fact that listening to Jason talk was very much like reading a newspaper article.

"He died later during the day. There will be a coroner's inquest, but I'm sure that Mr. Townsend will be acquitted. After all, he *was* protecting his property."

The revelation of mining camp violence unsettled her, as did the news of an actual shooting so close to her lodgings. She wanted to inquire about the possibility of an Indian attack, but, giving the matter more thought, decided not to. Mr. Ryker would probably laugh. She'd wait and ask Billy.

"Who's the letter to, or am I not allowed to ask?"

"It's to a friend back home. In Kentucky."

"Let me see," Jason pondered. "You're from Lexington, if I remember correctly."

"Frankfort. The Pattersons are from Lexington."

"Well, Kentucky's loss is our gain. By the way, have any of the boarders started teasing you yet?"

"Teasing me? Why would they do that?"

"Oh, they're big on joking, and you'd be a likely target, with that southern accent."

"Accent? I don't have . . ."

"Oh, yes, you do. But if they give you a hard time about it, don't worry. It's very slight, and I'll venture to assume that most of the young men around here will find it quite charming. I know I do."

She flushed at the compliment and was on the verge of forgiving his earlier insult when he transgressed even further.

"Speaking of young men, do you have one waiting back in Kentucky? Because if you don't, I'll give you about four months out here—six at the most."

"What do you mean?"

"Before you get married." He made the statement matter-of-factly, as if his prediction left no possibility of error.

"Oh, I don't think so," Anna replied coldly, irritated by his overly confident manner and his poor choice of subject matter. "I'm only fourteen."

Either not sensing her displeasure or ignoring it, her forward companion continued to talk. "Well, fourteen is marriageable age out here. And there are plenty of eligible bachelors in Rosita—quite a few in the boardinghouse. Adam Burdick, for one. He's the young blond boy who rooms here with his father, Sam. But he's got a lot on his mind at the moment. They've been mining for a month now, trying to earn enough money to bring the rest of their family out from Ohio. After two weeks underground, Sam made Adam quit the mines and take safer work as a clerk at F. L. Miller & Company. Adam's not too happy about it, but I don't blame Sam at all. The mines are dangerous. A lot of men go in and never come out. I wouldn't want a son of mine in that business."

Uncomfortable with the direction their conversation had taken, Anna ended their talk by politely mentioning her need to post her letter and get back to work. Jason accompanied her as far as the post office, then headed west down

Tyndal Street toward the newspaper office.

After delivering the letter, Anna walked back to the boardinghouse, thinking about Jason's recent comment.

"Four to six months," she repeated defiantly, still angered by his clear vision of her future. "Well, we'll just have to see about that!"

chapter

8

WHETHER OR NOT ALL of Jason Ryker's predictions would come to pass, one of them did. The joking began during Anna's second week in Rosita. The target was not Anna, but Pamela.

On Monday morning, as Anna leaned over her washtub to scrub a grass stain from Jimmy's Sunday britches, Pamela emerged from the back door with a yellow frock dangling over her arm.

Oh, good, Anna thought sarcastically as Pamela began her approach. *Just what I need. Another dress to wash.*

But as Anna started to resume her task, Pamela's movements caught her eye. The plump girl was walking slowly, all the while clanging a spoon in an old tin can. The two Mexican workers, Teresa and Elena, glanced toward Pamela as well. But they immediately returned to their scrubbing, muttering something in Spanish.

Reaching her destination, Pamela tossed the cotton dress onto Anna's enormous stack of laundry. "Here. I forgot to give this to you this morning." She was turning to leave when Anna, overcome by curiosity, blurted her inquiry.

"Pamela, what in the world are you doing with that can?"

"Oh, didn't they tell you?"

"Who are 'they,' and what didn't they tell me?"

"The men. The boarders. Especially Mr. Goddard and Mr. Campbell. They've been concerned for my safety and were kind enough to inform me of the danger of mine varmints."

"Mine varmints?" Anna's eyes narrowed as she stared at Pamela.

"Yes, mine varmints. They live underground, but with all the activity here, many of them have been forced to seek refuge elsewhere. They prefer woodpiles and holes. Sharp noises scare them off."

"Pamela, I don't think. . . ." She stopped short, suddenly aware of a repugnant odor. Sniffing the air, Anna found to her surprise that the aroma emanated from her stocky companion. "Uh, Pamela . . . what is that . . . smell?"

"Oh that? That's snake repellent. Billy gave it to me." With that, Pamela turned to retrace her steps, clanging steadily as she retreated.

Anna shook her head and chuckled, wondering both at Pamela's gullibility and at the grown men who were pulling such childish pranks. Yet, the more she thought about Pamela's behavior, the more humorous the entire situation seemed. Soon she found herself laughing until she was near tears. Even Teresa and Elena joined in with her until she finally forced herself to stop and concentrate on the business at hand.

But Anna was not the only one laughing. At suppertime, as she served the beef stew and oatmeal bread, Anna sensed an undercurrent of amusement rippling around the table as news of the occurrence spread. With their stifled giggles and whispers, the men reminded Anna of a bunch of schoolboys.

Halfway through dessert, Hank Goddard, the brown-haired culprit largely responsible for the prank, rose from the table. He was about to step out the kitchen door when Anna, acting on impulse, surprised herself with her own forwardness.

"Oh Mr. Goddard," she called. "Don't leave yet. You forgot something." She crossed the room and handed him a tin can and a spoon. "You wouldn't want a mine varmint to bite you, now, would you? Do be careful!"

Her action sparked a howl of laughter. As she joined in the merriment, she felt for the first time an affinity for the varied group of men. The heavy weight of loneliness lightened ever so slightly as she glanced around the table at the happy faces. No, they were not her family. But maybe, just maybe, they could be her friends.

Aside from pulling pranks, Anna discovered another habit the boarders practiced—eating in the late evening. Several of the roomers seemed never to get enough to eat. Understanding their needs, Kate always made sure to have extra dessert or leftover sandwich fixings available. Though many of the men took advantage of the late night snacking opportunity, three partook with extreme regularity: Billy, Adam Burdick, and Adam's father, Sam.

On Wednesday evening, the three men took their customary places at the long kitchen table. They eagerly sliced pieces from the applesauce spice cake that Anna had placed before them. Though Anna had been ready to call it a day, she changed her mind when the men asked her to join them. She enjoyed the few opportunities she had had to visit with them, and she didn't want to pass up a chance.

"This cake sure hits the spot," Billy stated. "Anna, did you make this?" She nodded. "I'll tell you, whoever marries you will have found himself a real gold mine."

Adam interrupted. "Speaking of gold mines, isn't it about time for you to 'head for the hills'?"

Billy flashed an easy grin. "Well, now, it just might be. Then again, it might not." A sly gleam glinted in his brown eyes. "Sam, you ever see a bunch of young folks as nosey as the ones nowadays?"

"No, I haven't. I don't know what the world is coming to."

Anna took several bites of her cake, all the while listening as the men exchanged their comical remarks. She could think of nothing to add to the conversation, at least nothing that would be of any interest to them. But she felt grateful that they had wanted to include her in their evening get-together. It was nice to feel like she was a part of things.

"I hear the East Leviathan is producing some good ore now. That true, Sam?" Billy inquired.

Sam nodded. "We're working a good solid vein, and it looks like we'll be busy for a while."

"Sounds good." Billy's expression then grew serious. "That's too bad, though, about Ted Zimmerman."

"What happened?" Anna asked.

"He died this morning in a fall," Sam explained. As he spoke, Anna noticed that his eyes darted directly to his son, as if to reinforce his reason for making Adam quit the mines. So, she thought, Jason's information had been correct.

"You know, Sam," Billy announced. "I'm surprised that you're as good a miner as you are, you being from back east. Most easterners can't tell the ore from the tailings. I remember one fellow I ran into out on the trail. He was from Tennessee. He had his mule loaded down 'til that poor ol' critter could hardly move. I never could convince him that what he'd found was leaverite, not gold."

"Leaverite?" Adam asked. "What's leaverite?"

"Oh, that's the fancy name for 'fool's gold,'" Billy explained.

"I didn't know that," Sam admitted. "Leaverite, eh?"

"Yep. Leaverite," Billy repeated. "Because if you find it, you should just leaverite there in the ground, since it ain't worth a plugged nickel."

Billy's humorous quip caught Anna off guard, and she nearly choked on the bite of food she was swallowing. But after recovering, she found herself giggling. Her overt reaction to his joke seemed to please him, for Billy's face fairly beamed with a broad, mischievous grin.

At that moment, the stocky, bearded prospector reminded Anna of her grandfather. Not because of his humor, for her grandfather had never displayed much of that. But because of her warmth, his good nature. Grandfather had been such a kind, loving parent. Although Billy bore no physical resemblance to Caleb Logan, he definitely made her think of him.

As the evening grew late, the friendly gathering broke up. Billy and Sam bid Anna goodnight, but Adam lingered to finish drinking his third glass of milk. Anna began to gather up the dirty dishes.

Alone in the kitchen with the eighteen-year-old boy, Anna felt strangely self-conscious. Her mind flew back to Jason's inference of a possible romantic involvement between them. But, despite the awkwardness, she continued with her chores. Adam remained quiet until she reached into the cupboard to pull out silverware.

"What are you doing?"

"I'm setting the table. I thought I'd get a head start on tomorrow morning."

Adam reached for some tableware.

"Adam, you don't have to help, really."

"I know. But I'd like to," he insisted. He worked on one side of the table while Anna moved down the other. "Doing this reminds me of home."

"That's Ohio?" Anna's uneasiness began to fade. For Adam was acting no differently toward her than the boys at St. Matthew's had.

"Cincinnati. I guess we were neighbors, then, since you're from Kentucky."

"Will your family be joining you soon?"

"I'm not sure," he sighed. "It will probably be a few more months before we'll all be together again."

"How many brothers and sisters do you have?"

"Three. Helen is your age, then I have two brothers who are much younger. You know, I knew I'd miss them all, but I had no idea how much. It's really been rough just suddenly not being able to see them anymore." His face reddened as he added, "I'm sorry, Anna. Billy mentioned that you lost your family. I didn't mean to . . ."

"That's all right," she assured him. "All that happened a long time ago. I'm doing fine now. You don't need to apologize."

With the table in order, Anna and Adam parted company. As Anna dressed for bed, she recalled her conversation with the young boarder. She should never have allowed Jason's inference to color her opinion of Adam. He was really very nice and not the least bit pushy. It had been very thoughtful of him to apologize to her. His concern for her feelings touched her, for people seldom seemed to give much thought to her difficult station in life.

Yes, she decided, Adam seemed like a special person. She hoped that she would be able to get to know him better.

She had no trouble getting to know Billy, though. Since he didn't have a regular job in town like the other boarders, he spent a good part of each day in or around the boardinghouse. Never one to hurry away from the table after meals, he frequently lingered to chat with Anna while she cleaned up the kitchen.

Whenever she could, Anna would join Billy and the group of boarders who visited each evening in the parlor. Billy made it a point to include her in their conversations. He gladly answered any questions she had about the state, the town, or the West. He seemed almost grateful for such a willing audience. The old prospector soon found a special place in Anna's heart.

One Thursday morning, Billy was still sitting at the table when Kate and Anna finished serving in the dining room. Ready for her own breakfast, Anna cleared some of the dirty dishes off the table so Kate would have room to set down the platters of fried cornmeal mush and sausage that she was bringing from the stove.

"Now it's our turn to eat!" Kate exclaimed as she and Anna sat down. "Would you have a little more breakfast with us, Billy?"

"I don't see how I can turn you down—not when it's mush, anyway. That's my weakness, you know."

"I know," Kate chuckled.

Anna got up to get Billy a clean plate and silverware. Then she took her seat and enjoyed the good, hot breakfast. When Billy helped himself to seconds, Anna couldn't help but wonder. Had she only imagined feeding him just an hour earlier?

"I wish I could pack some of this mush in with my gear," he lamented.

"It's still a little early to leave, isn't it?" Kate asked.

"Yep. It won't be thawed out enough in the high country. I'm gettin' itchy to move though. I want to get back out in the open spaces again."

"I think I understand what you mean," Anna nodded. "When I was a little girl, I used to hike in the woods with my grandfather. But when I went to the orphanage, I really missed having the freedom to just walk around in the trees or sit by the creek whenever I wanted to. It was always so peaceful and relaxing in the woods—and so pretty. I'll bet it's beautiful up in these mountains."

" 'Specially this time of year," Billy confirmed. "Tell you what, Anna. Sounds to me like you're about as ready as I am to see a little bit of old Mother Nature. There's some real pretty spots not far from town, too. When you get a bit of spare time here, just let me know. We can take off and clear some of this city life out of our systems."

Billy's invitation did more than please Anna. It met an emotional need. For now she had a friend. Someone in Rosita cared about her. She didn't feel so lonely anymore.

The very next afternoon, Anna found herself with some unexpected free time. She could hardly wait to take Billy up on the promised outing. But though she looked all through the hotel, she couldn't find him anywhere.

"Just my luck," she muttered to herself. "The one day I have the time, Billy's not here."

Not wishing her free time to go to waste, Anna considered what to do. She had so wanted to go hiking with Billy. Well, she would just do a bit of exploring on her own.

She took one step outside the hotel, then stopped. Dark clouds hung in the sky. But the sight encouraged her. With the threat of rain, she and Billy wouldn't have been able to go hiking anyway. She thought for a moment, then decided to take a short walk and see what she could before it started raining.

Anna strolled west down the street until she reached the edge of town. She was about to turn south to explore the pine-covered hills, but a gate, stretched between two stone pillars and bearing a wooden sign, caught her attention. Curious, she walked down the road until she could read the sign clearly. ROSITA CEMETERY.

Anna paused, then, seeing no one about who would object to her intrusion, lifted the metal latch to open the gate. She walked slowly among the graves, reading with interest the names, dates, and inscriptions etched on the markers. Several freshly dug mounds, one a tiny one, were interspersed with the others. Anna's heart went out in pity to the people who had been left behind to bear such losses.

So many people, she thought as she surveyed the surprising number of graves. Each one loved, each one missed by someone. Her mind pictured again the three graves she had left in Kentucky. She realized that, even after all the years that had passed, after all the changes in her life, the pain was still there. Lessened by time, true, but still present.

A clap of thunder and the light splash of raindrops drew Anna's thoughts back to her immediate situation. She returned to the gate and hurried back down the road toward town. But as she retreated, the reality of three words struck her with incredible force. She had seen the words engraved on many of the tombstones. *In Loving Memory*. She realized again that she had no memory at all of her father. She had long since resolved her bitterness toward her grandfather's silence, trusting God that, for whatever Grandpa's reasons, he had done what he had thought best. Still, she longed for the impossible—to have some knowledge of her father.

Yet, she remembered, as a flicker of hope touched her heart, she *did* have knowledge of her father—her heavenly

Father. And He loved her and had promised to meet her needs. She would just have to allow Him to take the place of her earthly one. She felt a sudden warmth as peace gently filled her heart. Anna knew without a doubt that she was loved and that not even death could separate her from this love.

chapter
9

As TOUCHES OF SPRING reached even the highest elevations, Billy began preparing for his departure. The bearded
prospector talked incessantly of his plans to further excavate
his gold mine, but remained closed-mouthed concerning his
departure date. Then, to Anna's surprise, he chose an early
hour before dawn one chilly Tuesday morning to slip away
unannounced.

Though Anna attributed Billy's sly action to his mistrust
of human nature and his fear of being followed, she still
felt hurt. After all, she was his friend. He certainly could
have trusted her enough to say goodbye.

With Billy gone, the days seemed longer. His friendly
presence and bountiful compliments on her cooking had
made her tasks at the boardinghouse seem easier. She
thought about him as she kneaded a batch of bread dough
the next morning. She wondered just what kind of diet he
would be having now that he had to cook his own meals.

Her shoulders ached from kneading, so she stopped for a
moment and walked over to the window. She could see Jeff
and Richard Patterson in the back yard, cultivating a garden patch. A part of her wanted to help with the digging
and planting as she had done at St. Matthew's and at her

grandfather's farm. But her practical side appreciated being excluded from the gardening chores. She had enough to do as it was.

She finished kneading the dough and set it aside to rise. She then checked the progress of her first batch which was rising in three baking pans on the table. Noting that the volume had doubled, she placed the pans in the hot oven and began mixing yet another batch of dough. She looked up to see Kate pushing open the swinging dining room doors.

"Did you think I was never coming back?" Kate called cheerfully as she marched directly to the table to deposit the bulky package she was carrying.

"Oh, I knew you'd come back eventually."

"Like when I got hungry?"

"Yes, or when you started missing Jeff, whichever came first."

Kate removed her cream-colored shawl, tucked her white blouse more securely under her full blue skirt, and reached for an apron. "Goodness, you've gotten a lot done already."

"Oh, I managed to keep busy." Anna stirred four eggs into her sticky batter. "Did you get everything you'll need for Jeff's shirt?"

Kate nodded. "I found some blue fabric that should make up nicely. My two problems now will be finding the time to sew on it and keeping it a secret until Jeff's birthday. It's almost impossible to surprise anyone around here. There are too many people who can let the cat out of the bag."

"We had the same problem back home," Anna remarked, reflecting on the many birthday and Christmas projects she had tried to make in secret, not always successfully. "If you need a place to hide the material, I have room for it in my drawer."

"Thank you, Anna. That would be a help."

"Maybe you should put it in my room now, before we forget and leave it out on the table where Jeff will see it."

"That's a good idea." Kate disappeared with the package momentarily, then rejoined her co-worker in the kitchen.

"Kate, all this talk of sewing reminds me that I'd like to start working on a gift for the Pattersons' baby," Anna mentioned. "I'm not sure what to make, though. Do you have any ideas?"

Kate rummaged through the cupboard for another mixing bowl and began measuring flour into it. "Well, let me think. The Ladies' Auxiliary at church is working on a quilt. That's a surprise, by the way. I thought I'd knit a sweater and hat. I did hear Naomi mention that she'll be needing dressing gowns."

Anna's face brightened at the suggestion. "That would be fine. I've never made one, but they look simple enough. Maybe I could even do some embroidery on it. I love to sew."

"Never say things like that around here, Anna," her slender employer warned. "We just might put you to work on the new tablecloths and curtains for the dining room."

"I wouldn't mind at all," Anna answered. "But it does seem a shame to cover up that new table. Mr. Patterson did a beautiful job making it."

"Yes, he did, but there's still so much to be done." As Kate spoke, Anna noted a touch of discouragement in her naturally soft tone. "I guess that's the way life is, though, especially out here."

"Have you always lived in Colorado?" Anna asked, suddenly aware that, after spending nearly a month with Kate, she knew almost nothing about her background.

"In Colorado? No. I'm from Kentucky—Lexington—just

like Jeff. Jeff traveled a lot before we met. He has always loved the West. In fact, we met while he was home visiting his family after his first trip to Colorado. Before he proposed, he gave me fair warning. He always told me he intended to settle out here somewhere. So, after we were married three years ago, I wasn't surprised when he decided to move here. Rosita was new then, but looked promising. My parents owned a small hotel and restaurant in south Lexington, so, with my experience there and the need here for housing, well, everything just fell into place."

"Do you ever wish you could go back?"

Kate thought carefully before replying. "At first I did. Life is harder out here. The work is constant, but I don't think I have to tell you that! And the winters!" She laughed brightly. "You haven't spent a winter here yet, so you don't know how cold it can get. But going back isn't an option, Anna." Her voice grew serious as she added simply, "Jeff's here." She spoke with such quiet conviction that, for a moment, Anna almost envied Kate the close relationship she shared with her husband.

The women worked silently for a while before Kate made a surprising remark.

"In case you were wondering, Anna, I had a good reason for getting back so late this morning. I am happy to report that I've just signed up a new boarder."

"A new one? Where will we put him? I thought we only had room for twelve."

"That's right. But with Billy gone, we have room now."

Anna's heart sank. "You mean—Billy's not coming back?" She asked the question as calmly as she could, trying to mask her concern.

"Oh, he'll probably come back," Kate replied matter-of-factly. "He has for the last few years, anyway. We can't leave his place vacant, since he's gone for months at a time. But if his diggings give out, he may just head in another direction altogether. You never know with Billy."

That revelation completely dampened Anna's spirits. She continued through the day preparing the assorted baked goods, but she did so with a heavy heart. Billy had never once told her that he might be gone for months, possibly forever. He knew that he might never come back at all, yet he had left without even saying goodbye.

She had thought that Billy was her friend. Didn't he care about her feelings at all? Perhaps she was just expecting too much from their relationship. But then, she wasn't exactly sure what she was expecting. She wasn't sure of anything at all, except of how she felt. Deserted.

By mid-June, Anna had not yet received official word from St. Matthew's concerning her change in duties. She felt confident, however, that Miss Sarah would agree to the new arrangement. Upon occasion, Anna questioned the wisdom of her choice. But on the whole, she felt that Richard Patterson's revised job assignments were working out well.

Pamela managed to carry out her responsibilities with a minimum of prodding from her father. Naomi, who both felt and looked much better, no longer passed the days in bed, but spent a great deal of time in her room sewing maternity clothes. Both Naomi and Pamela purposely avoided being in the kitchen any longer than necessary. In fact, they seemed to avoid the entire boardinghouse whenever possible, leaving for hours at a time to visit with their new acquaintances in town.

Anna's favorite day of the week was Friday. The day usually proved to be more of a day of rest than Sunday, and she generally found some time in mid-morning or mid-afternoon to spend on herself. The third Friday in June proved no exception, so, after lunch, Anna headed toward F. L. Miller & Company to look for the fabric she needed to make her baby gift.

As she strolled happily down the street, the full skirt of her blue gingham dress could not disguise the extra bounce in her step. For today, two things gave her extra confidence. First, she would be making her purchase with money that the Pattersons had just paid her. She could hardly believe it—her own money! And she had earned every penny.

Secondly, she had just styled her hair in a different way. The high, braided bun, an imitation of one of Kate's frequent hairdos, drew attention to Anna's deep brown eyes and clear complexion. She felt the becoming new style combined well with her maturing figure to lend her an air of adulthood.

As Anna entered the general store, a flood of scents greeted her—the pungent aroma of tobacco, spicy cinnamon, musky leather. Several customers, none familiar to her, browsed through the stacks of merchandise that were displayed on shelves or in open barrels. Anna joined them eagerly. After perusing the bolts of fabric, she could find nothing that satisfied her. She wondered if Adam had any more material stored in back.

An easy smile formed on her lips as she thought of the attractive young boarder. During the last few weeks, their relationship had budded into a relaxed, mutual friendship. Adam had been the only one at the boardinghouse to suspect how much she missed Billy. Once he understood her feelings, he never lost an opportunity to encourage her. She wondered if perhaps his continued homesickness for the rest of his family had made him more sensitive to her lone-liness. She glanced around the room in search of the young blond clerk.

But as she surveyed the room, she realized with displeasure that she was being watched. An unkempt, middle-aged man just down the aisle kept eyeing her. Her gaze met his for a split second, so she darted her eyes downward to ignore his lurid stare. But from the corner of her eye she could see him approaching. As the distance between them narrowed, she detected the strong odor of alcohol.

"Afternoon, honey," the tall stranger wheezed through yellow teeth. "You new around here?"

Anna wanted to run, but she froze in her tracks. "Well . . . yes . . . ," she stammered uneasily. She searched the store desperately for Adam, spying him at last atop a ladder in the back of the store. But his back was to her as he reached for a barrel perched on the highest shelf.

She started to walk past the man. "If you'll excuse me, please. . . ."

But he gripped her arm firmly in his thick, rough hand. "What's your hurry?" he asked, his voice menacing and his grasp tightening painfully.

Frightened by his action, Anna jerked loose from his hold and backed out of his reach. Then she all but ran across the room to the counter where Adam was working. She wanted to turn around to see if the stranger was still in the store. But instead she leaned against the counter, feeling both angry and embarrassed.

Adam stepped down off the ladder and turned to slide his heavy load onto the counter. His eyes lit up as he peered over the wooden barrel. "Anna! What can I do for you today? Say, I like your hair that way. You look. . . ." After taking a second look at his shaken customer, his voice took on a tone of concern. "What's wrong?"

She breathed deeply. "Is he gone?"

Adam glanced quickly around the room. "Who?"

"That man."

"Which one?"

Feeling braver with a friend nearby, Anna turned to point out the culprit. "Oh, good. He's gone."

"Anna, was the man bothering you?" Adam demanded. When she nodded, he raised his voice. "Then why didn't you say something? For heaven's sake, I would have helped you if you'd have let me know!"

She appreciated his assurances, but as they came in the form of a rebuke, she found herself fighting a sizable lump in her throat.

Sensing her reaction to his sharpness, Adam lowered his voice. "I'm sorry. I didn't mean to shout at you. It's just that—well—I don't want anything to happen to you. Are you all right?"

When Anna nodded, Adam continued. "You know, even though Rosita is a reasonably safe place to live, it's still a mining town. So it will always attract its share of troublemakers. I hate to say it, but this type of situation may very well come up again sometime. So let me give you some advice. If it happens when you're around other people, just scream or make some commotion. That should bring help right away. But if it happens when you're alone, well, you just run like the dickens. Understand?"

She nodded again and attempted a smile.

"Now, what say we get things back to normal," he stated decisively. "Can I help you find something, or are you just browsing today?"

"I'd almost forgotten why I came," Anna admitted. "Do you have any more flannel out back? I was hoping to find some pale yellow or green, but I didn't see any."

Adam shook his head. "No, I'm sorry. Everything we have is out front already." He lowered his voice to a whisper. "I'll tell you what, though." He leaned across the counter, motioning for her to lean closer to him as well. "I happen to know for a fact that Jackson's Emporium on Quartz Street just got a new shipment of fabric in yesterday. If I were you, I'd check over there first before settling for any of our stuff."

Chuckling over the suggestion, Anna replied cheerfully, "Thanks. I'll do that. But not today. I think I'll just go back to the boardinghouse now."

Adam gave her a quick, understanding wink. "I'd like to see you safely home, but since I'm the only employee here right now, I'd best not leave the premises." He accompanied Anna to the front door, then added, "However, there's no rule that says I can't watch from the door until you get there."

Comforted by his kindness and concern, Anna thanked him for his help before leaving the store. She walked the short distance from Miller's to the boardinghouse, then waved to Adam as she reached the front door. Adam returned her signal and disappeared back inside to resume his duties.

But instead of going directly into the hotel, Anna glanced again toward Miller's. Somehow, the afternoon's episode had cast Adam in a slightly different light. She couldn't really put it into words, but when she finally stepped inside the hotel, she felt strangely secure and protected.

chapter
10

IN ROSITA, AS IN ALL OF COLORADO, the approach of the Fourth of July generated much speculation. A territory since 1861, Colorado had applied for statehood in 1867, only to have the bill vetoed by President Johnson. So the bid in 1876 became a principal topic of conversation during the final weeks of June. Even Anna found herself caught up in the excitement as she listened to the boarders debating the issue at mealtimes.

"Jason, do you think Colorado will achieve statehood this time?" she asked one evening as she sat by the fire in the parlor.

"Probably," he replied. "But I'm not so sure that it will matter much to anyone—except, of course, to the people of Colorado."

"Why do you say that?"

"Because there's too much going on elsewhere. Don't forget. This is not just a regular Fourth of July. It's America's Centennial. And, as if all eyes weren't going to be on Philadelphia as it is, there is also the fact that the city is hosting the Centennial World's Fair. *That's* what's going to make all the headlines, my girl. *Not* whether or not Colorado becomes the thirty-eighth state."

As if Colorado's bid for statehood did not already have enough competition in the newspapers, an event in the Dakota Territory drew the nation's eyes to that section of the country. For on June 25, 1876, George Armstrong Custer suffered disastrous defeat at the Little Big Horn.

Yet despite the nation's seeming lack of interest, Colorado's request was approved in a vote on July first. Although President Grant would not be publicly announcing Colorado's admission until some weeks later, the newest state immediately began a joyous celebration. Not to be outdone by her sister cities, Rosita gladly began celebrating on Sunday, July second.

In church that morning, Anna learned of the scheduled festivities. The opening event was to be a session of music and speeches that very afternoon in the spacious field just east of town.

"Anna, are you joining the celebration today?" Jason asked as Anna deposited a platter of fried chicken onto the crowded kitchen table.

"Oh, I don't know. If I have time, I may go see what's going on. Do you know who's going to be speaking?"

"Who cares!" laughed Hank Goddard. "Anyway, you should be more concerned with getting your box supper ready."

His remark reminded her of her confusion on that subject. "What *is* a box supper? When Pastor Warren announced it this morning, I didn't know . . ."

The response to her question made her wish she had never asked it.

"What's a box supper?" chided Hank. "My goodness, Anna, where in the world are you from? *Everybody* knows what a box supper is!"

"Now, Hank, don't go getting personal," interjected Sam.

"You know how those people from Kentucky are."

Even Adam was unable to resist teasing her. "Yes, everybody knows that a box supper is a supper that's in a box."

Anna shook her head and proceeded with her serving duties. As the boarders chuckled over their comments, Jeff explained.

"A box supper is a social for single men and women, Anna. Each girl fixes a nice meal and wraps it in a decorated box. Then the boxes are auctioned off to the men. The men don't know whose box they're getting, so you end up having a picnic supper with whoever bids the highest amount for your box."

"That's how I met my wife," added Hank. "So you never know what's going to happen. You may just find yourself a husband in the bargain."

"No, thank you!" Anna declared. But the chiding continued.

"Now, don't be a wet blanket. It's fun," Jeff remarked. "Besides, if you don't go, there are going to be some mighty sorry young men out there. Like the two Lowry boys. After church they both asked me to tell them what your box looks like so they can bid on it. So you've already got two fellows interested in having you for a supper partner."

"Make that four," Adam corrected. "Jim Walker and Matt Buchanan asked me the same thing."

That revelation sparked even more jesting. Anna was thankful when it was time to start serving in the dining room. But the topic was far from finished. As she and Kate began their cleanup duties, Kate brought up the subject once again.

"You really should reconsider going to the box supper," Kate mentioned in her quiet, unassuming tone. When Anna said nothing, Kate continued. "Everyone has a good time. And the socials aren't to be taken seriously. Oh, sure, you have to eat with the person who buys your box. But everyone stays in the same area, so it's really just a big picnic. And all the couples mingle because they're self-conscious and don't necessarily want to be alone with their partner. So you could meet a lot of nice young people." Still receiving no response, Kate added, "A lot of the girls there would be your age. You might make some new friends."

Kate's last remark hit home. For though Anna felt a kinship with Kate, Jeff, and the boarders, she knew that she needed friends her own age, friends like Jessie and Emily.

"But Kate, the box supper will be right at supper time. I can't leave you with so much to do."

"Yes, you can. Jeff and Kelly can help me. Please, Anna, go."

With Anna's qualms resolved, the two women found a box and decorated it with fabric, yarn, and wildflowers. They then filled it with chicken, biscuits, and spice cake. Knowing that their cleanup chores would make them late, Anna entrusted her box to Jeff. He promised to deliver it to the church and then save a place for her and Kate at the meeting.

The speeches had already begun when Anna and Kate made their way to the crowded field. The citizens of Rosita listened attentively to the current orator, a man Anna had never seen before. His address appeared to be centered on the founding of Rosita, a subject that Anna usually found interesting. But another matter had captured her attention. The ladies had not changed from their Sunday clothes. She should have worn her good suit, not her simple blue work dress.

She would have turned in retreat, but just then Kate spotted the Pattersons sitting on their blanket some twenty yards away. She prodded Anna forward with a touch to her arm.

As they neared the blanket, the Pattersons tried to make room for them. Jeff had managed to save a seat for Kate, but there was no room for Anna. She was about to sit on the grass when a voice called to her from a nearby group.

"Miss, over here."

She turned to see a good-looking young man about eighteen, with black hair, green eyes, and a pleasant smile. He motioned to a vacant spot on the quilt that he shared with what looked like his parents and two sisters.

"We have room for you. Come over here."

He motioned again. Since Anna felt conspicuous standing, she accepted his offer.

"Thank you," she whispered. She sat down and directed her attention to the platform. But, as she did, the speaker finished and the crowd broke into loud cheers and hearty applause. She glanced back to the young stranger seated next to her.

"Who was the man who just finished speaking?"

"Carl Wulsten. He was one of the first settlers in Fremont County. In 1870, he founded the German colony of Colfax. But their settlement didn't work out. He stayed on, though, and has become one of Rosita's leading citizens."

As the next speaker reached the podium, Anna realized that she had not introduced herself. "Thanks again for the seat. By the way, my name is Anna Logan."

"I know," he responded with a grin. "I'm Matt Buchanan. And these are my sisters, Sarah and Maggie, and my parents."

Anna nodded an acknowledgment, then turned her eyes

back to the speaker. But through the four speeches that followed, she had difficulty concentrating. She kept trying to recall where she had heard Matt's name before. The Buchanans were friends of the Pattersons, she knew. But she had heard his name in connection with something else, and recently, she thought. Then she remembered—he was one of the men that Adam had mentioned, one of the men who wanted to know which box belonged to her. Her face reddened, and she was thankful that she wasn't looking at Matt. Instead her eyes wandered to the Pattersons where, for a moment, Anna thought she saw Pamela glaring at her. For the life of her, she couldn't imagine why.

When the meeting ended, Pamela wasted no time in joining the Buchanans.

"Oh, Matt," she cooed. "How terribly thoughtful of you to make room for poor Anna. I do hope you've thanked him, Anna."

"She has," Matt answered, darting a pleasant glance to Anna as they rose from the quilt.

"Well, we had better be on our way," Pamela blurted. "Sarah, Maggie, don't you think we should be going? We wouldn't want to be late for the box supper." She directed her remarks to Anna. "Sarah and I worked all afternoon getting our boxes ready, and, if I do say so myself, they are beautiful. Mrs. Buchanan has prepared some of her excellent barbecued roast beef especially for our boxes. Wasn't that kind of her? Such a thoughtful family." As Pamela flashed a smile at Matt, Anna detected in his eyes a look of exasperation. Politely controlled, but present nonetheless.

"I suppose we should go," Matt concurred. "Anna, would you care to join us?"

"Yes, Anna," Pamela added. "We'll be walking right

past the Rosita Hotel on our way. We'd be happy to drop you off."

Pamela's behavior awakened Anna's sense of defiance. "I'd be happy to join you," she replied decisively, unshaken by Pamela's icy glare. "I don't have to work tonight, so I'm planning on attending the box supper too."

"Splendid!" Matt exclaimed.

The group commenced the lengthy walk from the field to the Methodist church. Under normal circumstances, the walk would have been a pleasant one. But en route to the church, Pamela babbled until Anna thought she would scream.

Once at the church and away from Pamela, Anna found herself enjoying the social event. As she mingled with the friendly group of young people, she grew less self-conscious. She even attempted to set two nervous young girls at ease. One of them, a petite redhead named Claire McMahon, joked anxiously as the Reverend Warren walked to the front of the room to begin the auction.

"If anyone saw me carrying mine in, the pastor won't even get a nickel for it," she maintained. "I threw it together so fast, I'm not even sure what I put in it!"

"I know what you mean," Anna laughed. "I didn't decide to come until the last minute either."

The boxes were displayed on two long benches in the front of the room. As each package was purchased, the buyer went to stand behind his chosen parcel. Several beautifully wrapped boxes sold for 65 cents, one for 75 cents. Anna felt certain that no one would bid on hers.

But her fears were unwarranted. When three bidders pushed the price of her box up to 80 cents, Anna thought she was dreaming. Two other men joined the bargaining, raising the price even higher, until even the Reverend Warren seemed surprised. At last the bidding closed at $1.60, with Matt Buchanan claiming final possession of the small package.

"I guess you know I cheated," Matt admitted as they walked together to the churchyard where picnic blankets had been spread for the occasion. "Adam Burdick told me which box was yours. I had to bribe him, though."

"You mean you had to pay him?" Anna's dark eyes widened at the idea of Adam behaving so unscrupulously.

"Oh, no. Not with money. With information."

"Information?"

"Yes. He wanted to know which boxes belonged to Pamela and Sarah."

"But he didn't . . ."

"I know. He wanted to know which boxes *not* to bid on."

As Anna stifled a laugh, Matt presented a surprising proposal. "Anna, would you come with me to the town dance on Tuesday night? I thought I'd better ask you now before someone else does."

"The dance?"

"Yes, at the City Hall. It's the final event in Rosita's Fourth of July celebration. Everyone comes. Families, even the old folks."

"Well, I don't know. I have to work."

"It doesn't start until eight o'clock."

"Well, Matt, I. . . ." She paused, her face flushed from embarrassment.

"Oh, I see," Matt remarked quietly. "If you'd rather not go with me, I understand."

"Oh, it's not that," she cried. "It's . . . well . . . I've never been to a dance. I don't know how."

His face lightened at her confession. "That's no problem, really. I can teach you. It's easy. And you'll have to learn sometime if you're going to be living around here."

"I'd have to check with the Pattersons first."

"And if they say it's all right, will you come with me?"

Anna smiled up at him and nodded.

After a pleasant dinner and a lengthy walk through town, Matt escorted Anna back to the boardinghouse. She stepped into the entryway, and hearing low voices in the parlor, moved into the dark, empty dining room. She didn't want to see anyone, not yet.

She sat in a chair and mentally reviewed the events of the day. She had enjoyed getting to know some girls of her own age. Claire McMahon had suggested that they get together soon. The perky redhead bore a definite resemblance to Emily, but her outgoing personality reminded her of Jessie.

What surprised her was the attention she had received from the boys. Five young men had purposely vied for her box. And two others, in addition to Matt, had invited her to Tuesday's town dance. They wanted to spend their time with her. They were interested in *her*. The idea overwhelmed her, confused her, delighted her. She felt special. They liked her for herself. Not for her clothes, not for her family, just for herself. She, Anna Logan, was special.

She rose from her chair and walked toward her room. By accepting Matt's invitation, she would undoubtedly incur Pamela's wrath. And she would be teased unmercifully in the morning when Adam related her box supper success to his fellow boarders. But she didn't care. Tonight nothing mattered. Because she was special, and no insults, no worries, no jesting could spoil the joy she felt in her heart.

chapter

11

THE BOX SUPPER MARKED THE beginning of Anna's friendship with Claire McMahon. The tiny redhead stopped by the boardinghouse to visit with Anna that next Friday. Since Anna still had dinner dishes to wash, Claire offered her assistance.

"So, are you going to tell me or not?" Claire asked.

"Tell you what?"

"About the Fourth of July dance on Tuesday night. What else?"

"The dance? It was fine."

"Fine. Is that all you can say?" Claire sighed. "I was hoping for a few more details."

"Like what?"

"Like, since you danced with just about every available boy in town, which ones did you like best? And did any of them ask to call on you? And did Matt Buchanan ask to call on you when he brought you home?"

"Claire!" Anna cried, taken aback by her bluntness. "Don't you think those questions are just a little bit personal?"

"Oh, then he *did* ask you!"

"He did not! And of course I danced with a lot of boys.

But it was a square dance, so you just naturally dance with everyone else. You did too, you know!"

"All right, just calm down," Claire laughed. "I was just curious, that's all." She waited a moment before adding, "I've always thought Matt was good-looking. But then, who wouldn't? He's positively beautiful! Personally, though, I prefer the ranch-hand type. You know, like Jim Lowry. Yes indeed, there's just something about a cowboy!"

Anna grinned. "Claire, are you always so . . ."

"So straightforward?"

"No, so silly!"

"I'm afraid so," Claire affirmed solemnly before unleashing a burst of laughter.

The two girls finished the dishes and spread their wet dishcloths on the counter to dry.

"Thank you for helping me, Claire. I'm glad you came by this afternoon. My days are pretty full, but on Fridays I can usually take some time off. Is there anything you'd like to do? I have about two hours before Kate and I have to start supper."

Claire thought for a second. "Let's go shopping. I don't have any money, but I like to look."

They headed out the front door into the warm sunshine. As they traveled down the street, Anna ventured a question that she had been wanting to ask since Tuesday night.

"Claire, I really liked the dress you wore to the dance. Did you make it?"

"No, my mother did. Why?"

"I was wondering if you could give me some ideas on a party dress. I don't have one, and I was thinking about making one in case I would end up going to another party or something."

"In case? You'd better plan on it! I'd love to help you. In fact, I have an idea. Let's go over to Miller's. They have some catalogs of ladies' fashions, and we could probably get some good ideas there."

Delighted with their new plans, the two marched enthusiastically into F. L. Miller & Company where Adam happily gave them access to the store's brochures. Though Anna made no definite decision, she returned to the boardinghouse two hours later full of ideas.

But once back in the kitchen, all thoughts of fashion flew from her mind as she spotted an envelope on the table. A letter from St. Matthew's. She grabbed the envelope and tore it eagerly, pulling out two pieces of paper dated June 14, 1876.

Dear Anna,

We were happy to hear from you, and although we miss you, we were pleased to know that your position in Rosita is satisfactory.

Mr. Patterson has written to inform us of your change in duties. He has asked that you be allowed to stay the full year as an employee of the Rosita Hotel. Normally, we would not agree to an employment situation that is so far from our supervision. But in this instance, we feel that we can make an exception.

I have written separately to Mr. Patterson and will continue to correspond with him throughout your stay. We trust that you will inform us if at any time you become dissatisfied with the conditions there.

We miss you, Anna, but, knowing you, I'm sure that you have made many new friends by now. Jessie is enclosing a letter also, so I will let her give you all the news from here.

Affectionately,
Sarah Johnson

The handwriting on the second page of the letter was

indeed that of her close friend, Jessie.

Dear Anna,

I was so happy to hear from you. I was working in Frank-fort when your letter arrived, so it sat here unopened for a week. Emily could hardly stand not knowing what was in it until I got back.

I worked for three weeks for a dressmaker, helping her while one of her workers was ill. You would have loved it, but I was glad when it was over. You know how I hate sewing. I think that's why Miss Sarah assigned the job to me. You know how she's always making you do things that are "good for you."

Anna couldn't help but grin at her friend's comical re-minder of Miss Sarah's training technique. How well she remembered her own encounters with that principle. She read on.

I have some good news for you. Danny was offered a per-manent position with that smithy he's been working for in Lexington. He is so happy. Also, he has become quite serious about a girl named Karen. So, I may have a sister-in-law one of these days.

We're busy with garden work now. Is it warm enough in Rosita to garden, or are you up too high in the mountains? From your description, it sounds beautiful there.

Miss Sarah is ready to post this, so I will close for now. Emily sends her regards and promises to write soon.

Love, your friend,
Jessie

How good it felt to hold the messages in her hand. The distance between her family and herself lessened for a brief moment as she reread the letters. She had anticipated the reaction to Mr. Patterson's proposal, so its final acceptance came as no surprise. She felt a flutter of warmth at each reference to being missed. But the news of Jessie's brother pleased her most. She knew how much he had wanted that position. She thanked God that his future now seemed more settled.

Thoughts of Danny's situation brought to her mind something that Kate had mentioned not long ago, something about when she and Jeff first decided to open the boardinghouse. How had she phrased it? *Everything just fell into place.* That was it. Well, things were falling into place for Danny now, and Anna took pleasure in his good fortune.

But as she considered his happiness, she grew anxious. Her own future concerned her deeply. St. Matthew's held legal guardianship on each child until he or she either turned eighteen years of age or married. But they generally placed their wards in permanent employment by the time they turned sixteen. So, before long, she would face the task of deciding which career to pursue. Miss Sarah had once mentioned a dressmaking apprenticeship program in Lexington. But, though Anna enjoyed sewing as a hobby, she was not too happy with the prospect of sewing every day to make a living.

She purposely pushed all thoughts of her insecure future from her mind, deciding not to worry about the subject yet. She would just be happy for Danny, and hope that, in time, things would fall into place for her as they had for him.

By mid-July, after another careful study of the catalogs at Miller's and a painstaking evaluation of available materials, Anna finally reached a decision on her party dress. After selecting the fabric and notions at Jackson's Emporium, she approached the project with both excitement and trepidation.

Claire stopped by regularly on Friday afternoons to check Anna's progress and to offer suggestions. Anna hinted that perhaps Claire's mother might be able to offer some helpful advice, but Claire seemed to avoid inviting Anna to her home. Deciding that she might be imagining her friend's evasiveness, Anna began questioning her about her family. But each time she did so, Claire grew uneasy and unresponsive. Although puzzled by Claire's behavior, Anna acknowledged her need for privacy and avoided the subject of family as best she could.

Anna was unable to finish her new dress in time for the town's official statehood celebration on August first, so she donned her blue Sunday suit for the occasion. Accompanied by the ruggedly handsome Buck Lowry, she enjoyed the potluck supper immensely. Both Matt Buchanan and Adam had invited her too, but only after she had already accepted the offer from the older of the two Lowry brothers.

Anna did manage to have her dress done for the Saturday night church social two weeks later. Adam had made her promise to reserve the next social event for him, so he escorted her to the church that evening. When he and several acquaintances complimented her on her lovely dress, Anna's heart surged with pride at her handiwork. The lace-trimmed lavender cotton gown had turned out beautifully. She could hardly wait for Claire to see it.

But the sparkly redhead was not there. Anna's first thought, that Claire might not have been invited, seemed ridiculous when she viewed the abundance of available men mingling with the relatively few single women in the mining town. Besides, escorts were not necessary. Knowing Claire's penchant for socializing, Anna thought she would have come with or without an escort—unless she were ill. The more she considered the possibilities, the more sure she became of the conclusion. Claire must be ill. Nothing else she knew of would have kept her friend away. Though the activities and several admirers diverted Anna's attention periodically, her concern deepened as the festivities drew to a close with no sign of Claire.

After bidding goodnight to the people at the church, Anna and Adam began walking back to the boardinghouse. Anna's concern for Claire left her disquieted, so she said nothing. Adam seemed preoccupied with thoughts of his own, so he did not speak either. If she had been with anyone else, Anna would have found the silence awkward. But with Adam, there was no need for words.

The crispness of the night air caused her to shiver, so she pulled her shawl more tightly around her shoulders. "If the nights are this cold in August, what are we going to be in for come winter?" she ventured boldly, deciding that a conversation with Adam might help to shake her fretful mood.

"Don't ask me. I haven't spent a winter here yet, either," he reminded her pleasantly. "From what I hear, the snow can start as early as September. I just hope it doesn't snow heavily until after Mother and the children have been here for a few weeks. I don't want them getting discouraged right away."

"I imagine they'll be so happy to see you and your father that they won't care what the weather is like. Do you know yet when they'll be arriving?"

"In two weeks, on September ninth." Anna could hear the excitement in his voice. "Father and I just finished making the final arrangements this afternoon. They'll be taking the train into Pueblo, and then they'll catch the stage into Rosita. You'll like Mother. She's quite a lady. And I would be surprised if you and Helen didn't hit it off well. Frank and Jonathan, well, they manage to get into mischief most anywhere they go, but they're fine boys. I think you'll like them."

"I'm sure I will. Are you going to have the house ready in time?"

"I think so. The outside is almost done now. And with some lamps, we can work as late at night as we need to to finish the inside. We really appreciated your bringing supper over to us the other night, Anna. I confess I'm going to miss your cooking when we move out of the boardinghouse." He chuckled as he added, "Mother is a wonderful cook, but I can't say the same about Helen. Maybe you could give her some lessons."

Anna wished he hadn't brought up the subject of his moving. She would miss having him at the boardinghouse. She would still see him, of course, but she suspected that his family would take up all of his spare time for quite a while. She wouldn't think of mentioning her feelings, though. Adam was so looking forward to this reunion. She didn't want to put a damper on his excitement.

By the time they arrived at the boardinghouse, Anna's spirits were low. She retired to her room, where Pamela had just arrived from the same social event. Normally she would have been forced to endure Pamela's idle chatter about her escort and whether or not he was socially and financially acceptable as a potential beau. But tonight the plump young lady made relatively few remarks, for which Anna was grateful.

As she lay in bed trying to sleep, Anna was plagued with negative thoughts. Why hadn't Claire come to the social? Was something wrong? And why did she exclude Anna, her best friend, from her home life? She also thought of Billy. Couldn't he at least have trusted *her* with his plans? He had been gone so long. Did that mean that he had been hurt?

Or could it be that he wasn't even coming back? And Adam. How would his family's presence affect their relationship? When his family was far away, he had needed her friendship as much as she needed his. But they would be in Rosita soon. As happy as she was for him, she was selfish enough to resent his family's intrusion.

Silent tears stung her cheeks as she thought about her three friends. Her relationships with Adam, Billy, and Claire were the closest she had come to experiencing a feeling of family in Rosita. But Adam wouldn't need her anymore. And neither Billy nor Claire trusted her enough to share their private thoughts with her. And wasn't that what a family was all about? Sharing the good, the bad, the secrets?

But as she inwardly accused them, she felt pangs of guilt. How could she blame Billy and Claire for not confiding in her when she herself still withheld certain facts from them. She had never told them of her anxieties for her future, nor of her inner distress concerning her father's identity.

She wondered if she would ever find someone she could trust completely, someone with whom she could share her deepest, darkest secret. Where her father was concerned, she had not even confided completely in Jessie.

When she was small, she had always believed that her grandfather's silence had to have been caused by something that her father had done—something terrible or unmentionable. But as she grew to know many of the children at St. Matthew's and learned of their backgrounds, another possibility entered her mind, cutting her soul to the very quick. She had never dared breathe this idea to anyone, for she feared that her grandfather's reason for never mentioning her father was that her father and mother had never married. If so, then she was illegitimate.

Why else would she bear her mother's maiden name? No crime that her father might have committed could have been so horrible as to necessitate such complete silence. If her fears were true, if her father had not loved her mother enough to marry her, then he most certainly would not have wanted a child. Perhaps her mother had not wanted her either. Tears streamed down her cheeks as she considered that painful possibility.

The squeak of Pamela's bed startled Anna back to reality. She stifled an urge to sob, in case her roommate would hear her and ask unwanted questions. Rolling over onto her side, she lay awake for a long while before finally falling into a fitful sleep.

The following morning Anna arrived at church early, hoping to talk to Claire before the service began. But when she could find neither Claire nor her mother anywhere, she decided that something must indeed be wrong. Late that afternoon, she marched resolutely down Tyndal Street, determined to investigate the situation. Turning right onto Euclid Avenue she traveled a considerable distance until she reached an attractive stone dwelling with a split-rail fence, the landmark Adam had described when he gave her directions to Claire's house. The third house on the left past the fence. She spotted the small wooden cabin and moved purposefully toward it.

The house bore a definite resemblance to the neighboring homes with its dark, rough hewn timbers, small window, and wide front porch. As she reached the front yard, she stopped to pet a small gray goat that was tied to the fence post. Leaving the friendly animal, Anna stepped onto the porch. Then she halted abruptly as she suddenly realized that something was very wrong.

chapter
12

ANNA HEARD A DEEP, loud voice booming from inside. Through the window she could see an unfamiliar figure shouting angrily. From the man's thick reddish hair and beard, she felt certain that he was Claire's father.

He caught a glimpse of Anna and moved away from the window. His voice dropped suddenly, then Anna heard a sharp, crashing sound, as if a door were being slammed from somewhere inside.

Hesitant to knock but afraid not to since she had been seen, Anna tapped lightly on the door. After a moment of dead silence, the door opened just a crack.

"Anna!" Claire exclaimed. "What are you doing here?"

Anna felt terribly awkward. "I was . . . well . . . I missed you last night. I . . . I thought you might be ill. I guess I came at a bad time. I'm sorry."

Claire opened the door a little further. "It was nice of you to check on me. Did you get your dress finished?" Anna nodded. "I can't wait to see it. And I'm anxious to hear about your evening. Who did you go with?"

"Adam Burdick."

Anna squinted in an attempt to see her friend more clearly through the shadows. But as she did so, she let out a gasp. Claire's normally attractive face looked blotched and distorted. Her eyes were swollen from crying and her right cheek bore an unsightly bruise.

"Claire, what happened?" But even as she worded the question, she feared that she already knew the answer.

"It's all right, Anna, really," Claire answered, her voice calm and consoling. "I'll be fine. It's just that my father gets upset sometimes, and then he drinks, and . . . it's his work right now. Things have slowed down at the stamping mill and he's been terribly worried." She glanced behind her for a moment. "I have to go now. Pa left, but Mama's pretty upset. I'll come by the boardinghouse once things have settled down again. Thanks for thinking of me, Anna."

Anna reached for Claire's hand and clasped it firmly. "If I can ever help you . . ."

"I know," she replied. "Thanks." At that, Claire disappeared back into the dimness of the cabin, closing the door softly behind her.

In a daze, Anna turned and retraced her steps, ignoring the playful goat that wanted more of her attention. She could now understand Claire's quiet moods and her reluctance to invite her to her home. But what baffled her was how the young girl could maintain a cheery, non-complaining attitude in the light of the abuse she and her mother had to endure. Claire's love and strength of character impressed Anna deeply.

As Anna walked back down the road, she paused for a moment to sort through her muddled thoughts. Her mind struggled to grasp all the discoveries she had just made. Aside from learning of Claire's difficult situation and being drawn closer to her, the afternoon visit had revealed yet another startling insight. Having a family could be just as painful as not having one at all.

The slowdown in business did not affect only the stamping mill. Through the month of September, the entire community felt the sting of a recession. Both the Pocahontas Mine and the Pennsylvania Reduction Works shut down completely, and the Humboldt Company discharged many of its workmen. Many smaller diggings ceased being productive, so their owners chose to clear out before winter's icy descent would make departures impossible.

Adam's mother, sister, and two brothers managed to arrive right on schedule and, as Adam had hoped, several weeks before the heavy snows began. As Anna suspected, she saw very little of her friend during the first weeks after his family's reunion.

Other families moved in to join their working husbands and relatives. But the influx of new citizens ceased dramatically. At the boardinghouse, as the Burdicks, Hank Goddard, and Otis Campbell moved out, only one boarder, a quiet newcomer named Tim Randall, arrived to take their places. The young, brown-haired Texan had been fortunate to find employment at the sawmill at a time when few companies were taking on new workers.

Though aware of the economic slump, Anna did not physically experience its effects. September brought with it more canning of the harvest. So, in addition to their regular workload, Anna and Kate put up quantities of applesauce, cider, and carrots to join the jars of canned corn, beans, and beets.

As the women finished their canning chore, Richard and Jeff completed their latest project—the construction of an enclosed back porch off the kitchen. The spacious room filled quickly with piles of firewood and bushels of raw apples, carrots, potatoes, and onions. The addition also provided Anna, Teresa, and Elena with adequate workspace for washing the laundry, a task Anna was grateful to tackle indoors instead of outside as the days grew noticeably colder.

Adam's involvement with his family proved to be only temporary. Once they became more settled, he began frequenting the boardinghouse once more. Anna berated herself for the selfish thoughts she had had about his family earlier. The pleasant ex-boarder spent a good many evenings in the parlor, chatting with his former roommates and befriending Tim Randall, who was roughly the same age. Sam often accompanied him. The two never came for meals, but seldom turned down an invitation to share an evening snack.

In October, the frequent snow flurries turned into heavy snowfall. Rosita's few operating mines continued what production they could manage despite the weather. But outside travel ceased, and when it did, so did business at the hotel.

With fewer overnight guests, Anna had less work to do. The dining room continued to attract a reasonable number of local patrons, but in general, Anna was able to finish her chores earlier than usual. She spent much of her free time visiting with Claire, but she also enjoyed stopping by Miller's to see Adam or working on sewing projects.

Aside from easing Anna's workload, the heavy snows brought her another pleasant surprise—Billy's return.

Anna wanted to drop everything to visit with him as soon as he walked through the door. But he had timed his arrival right during supper, so she had to wait until after her cleanup chores were completed. She then joined Billy and a gathering of boarders in the parlor.

"Welcome back," she ventured quietly. "How did your trip go?"

"Fair enough," Billy replied. "I can't complain."

A sly smile lighted Jason's face. "Not even about the food?"

"Well, now that you mention it, there were some times when I'd have done most anything for a taste of Anna's cooking. Yes siree, that meal tonight was worth its weight in gold."

"So, Billy, you've managed to miss two major political events," Jason remarked. "You've heard about Colorado's admission to the United States?"

"Yep. But that's only one thing. What's the other one?"

"Elections. Last week we voted for our state officials."

"Who's governor?"

"John Routt."

Billy seemed pleased with Jason's answer. "At least we're getting off to a decent start with a Republican in office. But I don't figure that newspaper of yours was much help in putting him there."

Certain that the two men were on the brink of one of their famous oral battles, Anna intervened.

"Billy, did you notice that the Burdicks are gone? They moved into their own house with their family. Otis and Hank left too." Afraid that she had not yet succeeded, she added, "Business seems to have slowed down considerably since you left. Jason, do you think the mines are really in trouble or could the slump be due to the bad weather we've been having?"

"Bad weather?" Jason retorted. "Anna, bad weather hasn't even started yet!"

Her ploy worked, for the group immediately veered their conversation away from politics to less explosive topics such as Colorado winters and Rosita's economic condition. When the evening drew to a close, Anna retired to her room in high spirits. For Billy was back, and she felt as close to him now as she had before he left.

"You mean that woman hasn't had her baby yet?" Billy exclaimed after Naomi Patterson tottered past them. The expectant mother was clinging desperately to Pamela's arm as she and her daughter inched their way down the snow-covered sidewalk.

"No, not yet," Anna answered, amused by Billy's comment. "But she's due any day now, so it shouldn't be much longer."

The sun shone brightly against the snow. Anna tried to block its blinding glare by squinting as she and Billy walked down Tyndal Street. Anna was enjoying both the chance to get some fresh air and the opportunity of spending part of her Sunday afternoon with her friend. She was about to ask Billy more about his trip, but she said nothing, for her thoughts were distracted by the breathtaking view of the Sangre de Cristos as they stood clothed in solid white against the darkening sky.

"Looks like a storm's on the way," Billy announced.

They continued their walk, plodding through sizable snow drifts to make their way to the edge of town. There, they turned to study the familiar scene of houses, businesses, and mines nestled among the foothills. Once again, Anna reflected upon the strange mixture of beauty and ugliness that always struck her whenever she visited this particular location.

"At least the snow covers up some of the mines," Billy sighed. So, Anna mused, the contrast troubled Billy too. Yet as she pondered his reaction, she realized that the ugliness must appear even more pronounced to a man who had spent his life living and traveling through the mountains.

"Billy, I really don't understand why mining has to mess everything up so much," she complained. "In all the pictures I've ever seen, the miners just work alongside creeks with those little pans. Why can't they do that here?"

Billy smiled at her remark but did not laugh. "That's placer minin'. It's the easiest kind. But there's not much of it goin' on now. With placer minin', the gold is loose, mixed with either gravel, sand, or dirt. To separate it out, you just need water, patience, and a pan, rocker, or sluice box. But placer minin' only works on gold that's not in ore form. You can never pan for silver. It's always found as an ore."

"And the mines here all produce silver?"

"Yep. There's some traces of gold, but it's mostly silver."

"How do you know where to start looking for it?"

Billy grinned again. "Aah!—that's the question! You don't know. In placer minin' when the loose gold flows in the creek, you just try followin' it to find where it's comin' from. Once you're away from the water, you look for hills or ground that contain a lot of quartz. Gold is found in quartz. But then, I'd be happy enough just to find it in pints, or even half-pints." He paused just long enough for them to chuckle at his joke.

"With silver, well, it goes pretty much the way it happened here. A couple of prospectors start diggin' around a bit and find some ore, not real rich but rich enough to get them curious. They go a little deeper, and they hit a big vein.

"Now, when you have to start diggin' shafts and tunnels really deep to follow the veins, that's lode minin'. The problem is that around here you're diggin' into rock. Solid rock. Gettin' the silver out of the rock is the trick.

"First, since you can't just dig with a shovel and pick anymore, you have to drill holes in the rock and blast it with dynamite. Then you have to haul all the rocks to the surface and separate the waste from the ore. The waste goes in the piles you see outside a mine. The ore is the rock that has a reasonable amount of metal in it. The ore then has to go through stamp mills, concentration mills, and smelters. Colorado rock is stubborn. Even smeltin' doesn't get as much pure silver out as we'd like." His face tensed and his eyes reflected a touch of sadness. "Yep. It's a messy business."

"Jason told me that a lot of men die while working in the mines. Is that true?"

Billy shrugged. "Either minin' accidents or saloon brawls. If you die in a mine, they name the shaft after you." His expression relaxed once again. "I figger I'd rather have a saloon named after me than a mine shaft."

His humor lightened the seriousness of their conversation. They commenced walking again, this time turning back toward town. They slipped, skidded, and laughed all the way back to the boardinghouse.

But upon their return, both immediately sensed an uneasiness in the atmosphere. The parlor was unusually empty, hosting only two boarders who greeted them with an awkward reserve. As Anna made her way down the hallway, Kelly and Christy slipped past her to enter their room, their behavior strangely quiet and their expressions grave. Once in the kitchen, Anna discovered the reason for the heavy silence. Naomi Patterson had gone into labor.

chapter
13

RICHARD PATTERSON SAT AT THE TABLE, nervously watching the bedroom door as his wife's low moans filtered through the thin walls. When a sudden loud cry reached his ears, he rose from the bench and walked to the parlor. Jeff followed him after pausing long enough to say, "If you need any help with supper, Anna, let me know."

Since Dr. Sperry, Pamela, and Kate were all tending to Naomi, Anna felt certain that she would be of more help by simply taking care of the mealtime responsibilities. In fact, she felt relieved that circumstances had permitted her an escape from assisting with the birth. She proceeded with supper, grateful that Kate's absence had given her plenty to do. But the increased work did not occupy her mind entirely, for she could not block out the painful cries that echoed from the bedroom.

The strained atmosphere lifted six hours later. At ten P.M., Michael Thomas Patterson entered the world safe and sound, his mother exhausted but well. Though worn out from the ordeal herself, Anna gladly prepared a late-night celebration by pulling Monday evening's cake from the pantry and brewing some coffee.

But the merrymaking did not last long. The newest Patterson's schedule included frequent fits of screaming and bouts with colic. His bellows penetrated the boardinghouse walls with an annoying regularity and irritated many of the boarders. After three weeks, Richard concluded that his family needed a house of their own. So he and Jeff launched an immediate search for suitable lodgings.

Because of the economic slump, a number of houses were available for immediate occupancy. The men located a small rental home on Quartz Street that, with a little work, would adequately house the family until they could build a larger dwelling come spring.

Eager to make the move as soon as possible, Richard and Jeff worked steadily through the week making the necessary repairs. Finally, on Saturday, November 11, the momentous event began. Richard and Jeff packed the crates of belongings onto their wagon and transported them to their new home.

To Anna's delight, Kate insisted that she move her belongings into the bedroom off the kitchen that Richard and Naomi had been using. The room was small, but it sparked her sense of pride and allowed her once again to experience the warm welcome world of privacy.

Anna put her newfound privacy to good use by starting right away on her Christmas projects. She could crochet Claire's shawl in the parlor while chatting with Billy, Jason, and the others, but she could not very well work on Billy's muffler or Kate's embroidered apron in their presence. So, as Christmas approached, she spent more and more evenings in her room.

Expecting to feel a little lonely through the holidays, Anna was pleasantly surprised. Kate practiced traditions similar to those at St. Matthew's—baking gingerbread and shaped sugar cookies. She was more than happy to let Anna prepare the Home's delicious caramel popcorn. Together the two women decorated the boardinghouse with pine cones and pine boughs tied with red ribbon, topping their endeavors by hanging Kate's beautiful pine cone wreath over the fireplace. The rooms radiated a special holiday warmth.

Caught up in the excitement of gift preparations, Christmas caroling, and assorted social functions, Anna whirled happily through the season with little opportunity to miss her friends in Kentucky. In fact, she did not even have time to send a letter to Jessie until three weeks into the new year. She felt a twinge of guilt as she reread the note that she had finally gotten around to writing.

January 23, 1877

Dear Jessie,

Your letter dated November 12 arrived just last week. I was happy to hear that you are well. Mail service has been extremely slow since the heavy snows hit, so I am not sure how long it will take for this letter to reach you. I hope you have received my other letters by now.

Even though the Pattersons have moved, I still see Mr. Patterson almost every day. I see the rest of the family at church each Sunday. The baby is almost three months old now.

I wish you could see our dining room now. Mr. Patterson and Jeff have gotten all the tables and chairs made, and I'm almost finished with the tablecloths and curtains. The room looks really pretty.

I had a nice Christmas. Kate, Jeff, and the boarders surprised me by going together to buy me a new winter coat. Do you remember my old blue one? It just wasn't warm enough for out here.

The whole town got a wonderful Christmas present, too, though it came a little late. A man named Edmund Bassick discovered a rich vein just one and one-half miles from Rosita that contains both silver and gold. It promises to be one of our biggest strikes ever. They've named it the Bassick Mine, and it has brought new life to the town.

Greet everyone there for me. And please give Mr. and Mrs. Forrester my best wishes concerning their new positions at the orphanage in Knoxville. It will seem odd not having them there when I get back.

Love,
Anna

Anna sat at the kitchen table, staring at the paper in front of her. She had thought that writing to Jessie might help her settle down and go to sleep. But now she felt more awake than ever. Her eyes wandered around the dark, quiet kitchen, coming to rest on the clock that ticked softly on the small ledge above the icebox. One-thirty.

She could hear the freezing wind whistling through the cracks in the walls, so she knew without looking that the blizzard outside was still raging. With the current snowstorm bringing postal service to a standstill, she didn't know why she had even bothered writing at all. Jessie might never get the note.

She glanced again at the words she had written, noting the two sections that troubled her. Her eyes stopped first on the date. January 23, 1877. Yesterday had been her fifteenth birthday, and no one had acknowledged it. Her friends here could not be blamed for the oversight, since she had never told anyone the date. But then, no one had ever asked her. At St. Matthew's she would have had a cake, along with a present or two from her friends. Miss Sarah would have exempted her from chores and given her the day to do as she pleased. Here she had spent the entire day scrubbing dirty laundry on the cold back porch.

She thoughtfully reread the last sentence. "It will seem odd not having them there when I get back." When I get back. She did want to go home. She wanted to see everyone, to be around her friends again. But how strange her old life would seem. She had grown so accustomed to her life in Rosita.

Of course, living in Rosita had its drawbacks. The work was hard, and the winter had been bitterly cold. But there were also advantages. Here she had her own room, and she had made a good many friends. Also, though she would never admit it to anyone, she took pleasure in her popularity with the young men. When she returned to Kentucky, she would miss the social occasions that were not a part of her St. Matthew's life. Then, too, she would miss her wages. She had been able to save money and make purchases, and she rather enjoyed the feeling of independence that her earnings inspired.

She shook her head and stared at the letter, wondering at her dilemma. She wanted to go back. But, for the first time, she realized that she also wanted to stay. And she couldn't do both.

But did she have a choice? Her agreement with the Pattersons had stated clearly that the arrangement was for one year. She knew that, as did they. She doubted that the Home would let her stay in Rosita permanently. But would the Pattersons want her to? Did *she* really want to?

She closed her eyes. "Lord, I'm not sure which way to go, or even if I have a choice. I just don't know why I feel so unsettled inside when it comes to going back. I want to go back, but I also want to stay here. So please help me to know what I should do, and show me where You want me to be."

She opened her eyes, sensing as she did a calm, peaceful feeling rising to replace her confusion. She rose from the bench and walked to her room, ready at last to go to sleep.

Anna posted her letter the following morning, but, as she had suspected, the envelope sat in the post office for two weeks until the weather moderated enough to permit riders access to Rosita. When that happened, the dining room filled to overflowing with ranchers who were taking advantage of the lull in the weather to pick up supplies in town. Although Anna's feet ached as the busy Wednesday evening progressed, she was delighted with the unexpected increase in business.

Halfway through the supper hour, as Anna was busy serving in the dining room, Tim Randall motioned her from the doorway. Certain that the quiet young boarder would not interrupt her at such a hectic time without good reason, she stepped out into the entry where he stood waiting for her.

"I know you're busy, so I'll only keep you a minute," he assured her in his soft, steady drawl. "But I just came from the back porch, and I thought you should know that your friend is out there waiting to see you. She looks upset, and my guess is she's been out there for some time. She won't come inside because she knows you're busy."

"My friend?"

"You know, that little redhead."

"Claire? But what . . ."

Tim's dark eyes grew serious. "I just thought you should know, because she'll probably freeze if she has to stay out there much longer."

"Thank you for telling me, Tim. I'll go see her right away."

Anna hurried through the dining room and kitchen and out the back door onto the cold porch. She surveyed the dark enclosure, spotting Claire at last in the far corner next to the storage shelves. She crossed over to her friend. Even in the darkness Anna could see Claire's eyes glistening with tears.

"Claire! What are you doing out here? Why didn't you come inside?"

"I didn't want to bother you," she murmured, her teeth chattering and her voice strained. "I know this is a bad time to be coming, what with supper . . ."

"Don't you worry about supper. Let's take care of you first. Now, how long have you been out here?"

"Oh, I don't know. A while, I guess."

"You must be freezing!" She nudged Claire toward the door. "Come on inside, and you can tell me all about it."

But Claire stood firm, ignoring Anna's prodding. "It's my father," she blurted. "But I'm sure you figured that out already." Tears trickled down her cheeks and she wiped at them awkwardly with her gloved hand. "I've been so scared for the last few days, Anna. He's been in a terrible mood. But when he reads the letter we got today. . . ." Her voice broke, so she paused for a moment. "It was from my Uncle Ed in Cheyenne. My brother Tommy passed through there two months ago, and he . . . he's in trouble with the law again. It's really serious this time. Pa . . . Pa will be so angry. Mama thought I shouldn't be there because . . . well . . . whenever Pa's mad at Tommy or Russ, he takes it out on me, since I'm the only one left."

She looked up at Anna, her voice pleading. "Anna, I need . . . I was wondering if you could let me stay here tonight. I'll pay you. But I need to . . . to be away from the house until Pa calms down."

"Of course you can stay tonight. You can stay as long as you need to. And don't you even mention paying. You're my best friend, and you can stay in my room with me."

"I don't want to get you into any trouble."

"You won't, I promise," Anna insisted as they walked to the door. "Now, you just go into my room and warm up while I fix you some hot cider. We can talk more about all of this as soon as I'm finished working."

"Anna, I . . . I don't know how to thank you," Claire whispered. "I don't know what I'd do if you weren't here."

Anna gave Claire's shoulder a gentle squeeze as she guided her to her bedroom. She then resumed her duties, and by the time the dining room closed, Claire felt enough revived to join her and Kate in their own late but well-deserved supper.

Claire stayed for two days. During that time Anna felt their friendship growing even stronger. As Claire opened her heart, relating her experiences and her fears, Anna in turn found herself confiding her own secrets, including her most private thoughts about her father. By the time Claire's mother stopped by on Saturday morning to assure Claire that all was safe at home, Anna found herself once again struggling with her thoughts about leaving Colorado.

After Claire left, Anna and Kate stood at the kitchen counter, occupied with their various baking projects. Kate mixed up yet another batch of oatmeal cookies while Anna shaped cinnamon rolls from her second batch of sweet dough.

"You know, Anna, it won't be long until your year here is over," Kate mentioned as if reading Anna's thoughts. "I've been wondering just what you'll be doing once you get back to Kentucky. Do you have any plans?"

"No, not really."

"I know that you met Richard when you were working

at his home. Will you be taking on jobs like that again?"

"Yes. Until I'm sixteen. Then St. Matthew's will want me to take a permanent position somewhere."

"Oh, so that won't be for a while then, will it? You've still got what . . . ? A year and a half before you're sixteen?"

"No. I'm fifteen now."

Kate looked up in surprise. "Fifteen? When were you fifteen?"

"On January twenty-second."

"Anna Logan! Do you mean to tell me that you had a birthday and you didn't tell me?"

Anna stared back at the flattened dough on the counter to avoid Kate's flashing eyes.

"Anna, I don't know what I'm going to do with you!"

Neither spoke for several moments, then Kate made evident the fact that their original conversation was not yet over.

"Do you have any idea what kind of permanent job you'll end up with?"

Anna breathed a heavy sigh. "Well, Miss Sarah has mentioned to me that she thinks I'd do well as a seamstress."

"Do you think you'd be happy with that, though? I know you enjoy sewing, but I also remember how glad you were to finally get those tablecloths and curtains finished. It's none of my business, but I'm just not sure that being a seamstress would be such a good idea."

"I'm not so sure that I'll have much choice!" Anna blurted.

"I'm sorry. I didn't mean to upset you," Kate remarked. "I was just trying to see how you felt about going back to Kentucky. You have been such a good worker, and we have really enjoyed having you out here. We were just hoping that you might want to stay on with us permanently."

Surprised by Kate's proposal, Anna did not know what to say.

"You don't have to answer me now," Kate continued. "I know it's a lot to think about. We'll certainly understand if you want to go back home. But we did want you to know how we feel, just in case. Colorado can kind of get into your blood after a while."

"I'll think about it," Anna answered softly.

The two commenced their tasks again, with Anna deep in thought concerning their conversation. In fact, so intent was her concentration on Kate's offer that she did not notice the unusual flurry of activity in the parlor that night. But as she headed for her bedroom when her work was done, she heard a commotion in the hallway. She turned to see Adam, Sam, and all the boarders filing into the kitchen and over to the table. As she watched them, Kate turned from the counter holding a cake in her hands. At her nod, the room echoed with loud, cheerful shouting.

"Happy Birthday, Anna!"

"We may be late, but we're sincere," Kate called. "Now, get over here and cut this! I still have to make the coffee!"

Taken aback by their action, Anna felt like running into her room to cry. But instead, she crossed over to the table and began cutting large slices of cake for the jovial group of men around her. When she retired at last, she realized how very much she had grown to love the little cluster of people God had given her in Rosita. But she felt more confused than ever as to what she should do.

chapter
14

As much as Anna wanted to stay in Colorado, she could not bear the thought of cutting her ties completely with her St. Matthew's family. She tried to sort through her feelings as she dressed for bed that night. When she had first accepted Richard Patterson's job offer nine months ago, she never dreamed that she might never see any of her Kentucky family again. That's what staying in Colorado would mean.

If she stayed, how could she afford the time or the money to go back even for a visit? Jessie, Emily, or Miss Sarah weren't likely ever to travel to Colorado either. Never to see them again seemed almost as severe a parting as death. What was the difference, really? For all practical purposes, they would cease to exist for her—departing from her life just as completely as her grandfather had.

Grandfather. She still missed him. Almost without knowing it, Anna stepped over to her bureau to pull out the old family Bible. She stared at his likeness on the tintype, then at her grandmother's and her mother's. She couldn't help wondering again about her father.

Grandfather would have told her about him eventually, she concluded. He was probably just waiting until she got older. She remembered how much he had disliked discussing personal topics with her. So, most likely, he just never felt comfortable with the subject of her parents' marriage. She felt certain, though, that when she really needed to know about her father, her grandfather would have told her. After all, he had loved her. He couldn't have known that he would just suddenly die, that he would not be there to answer her questions. It wasn't his fault.

She thought back to her life on the farm, to the time of her grandfather's illness. She could still see herself as a child, frantically trying to help him when he collapsed in the barn. She would never forget that frightening night when she ran through the woods to the nearest neighbors to ask them to bring the doctor. She had been so afraid that she would find her grandfather already dead by the time she got back with help. But he had lived for three more weeks. Three weeks of being unable to talk or respond to her, of living in a dark haze.

Her mind returned to St. Matthew's, to her adjustment there. The people certainly hadn't replaced Grandfather, but they had made their own place in her heart when she finally let them in. She hated the thought of permanently leaving either Miss Sarah or Emily. But Jessie meant more to her than anyone. She was like a sister. How could she possibly part with her?

The next morning, not even the church service could distract Anna from her troubled thoughts. She visited with others only briefly in the churchyard before making her way back to the boardinghouse. There, she went about her work and spent most of the day in an unusually quiet manner as she contemplated the decision before her.

Thanks to several late-coming customers and an accident with her coffeepot, Anna's chores in the dining room took her longer than usual that evening. When she finally closed up the front room, she found that Kate had already put the kitchen in order and was in the process of laying out an evening snack for the boarders. At the table, Anna spotted the familiar trio once again. Adam and Sam had come by the boardinghouse. They now sat at attention with Billy, awaiting Kate's signal before demolishing the pan of cinnamon rolls she was placing before them.

"Will you have a bite with us tonight, Anna?" Adam asked.

"Not tonight. I'm just not hungry. But thank you anyway."

As she headed across the kitchen toward her room, Adam left the table and intercepted her just as she reached for the doorknob. "Could I talk to you for a minute?" Her tall young friend glanced back at the table, where Jason had just joined the party. "But not out here. In the dining room."

Puzzled by his request, Anna let him guide her through the swinging doors and over to a table in the corner. The light from the kitchen illuminated the dining room enough for her to see his face.

"Adam, is something wrong?" she asked as he sat down on the chair across from her.

"That's what I'd like to know," he replied. "You're not yourself, Anna. The minute I got here, I could tell something was bothering you. Do you want to talk about it?"

She dropped her eyes. "Oh, Adam, I don't know if talking about it will do any good."

"Why not give it a try? Even if it doesn't solve anything, it can't hurt, can it?"

"No," she answered, touched by his concern. "It's the Pattersons. They want me to stay here permanently."

He didn't act the least bit surprised. "They know a good thing when they see it," he quipped. His expression grew serious. He started to say something, but checked himself. Then, after looking at her for a long, silent moment, he made one simple, sincere statement. "I understand."

As Anna studied his face, she felt that he really did. She wouldn't need to give him all the details of her inner struggle. Those difficult months apart from his family had taught him a great deal.

"It isn't that I don't want to stay," she admitted. "I love my job here. I can't quite imagine going back and leaving Kate and Jeff, Claire, Billy, and . . . and you." She paused, not knowing just what to say next.

"It's Jessie, isn't it?"

She nodded slowly, blinking in amazement at his insight. "I just . . . Jessie means so much to me, I just can't say goodbye."

"This is a difficult decision, Anna. I wish I could make it easier for you." After speaking, Adam relaxed back into his chair, contemplating her problem. Then suddenly he bolted upright. "Anna, you're fifteen, aren't you?"

"Yes."

"And St. Matthew's will place you in a job when you're sixteen?"

"Yes."

"Is Jessie older or younger than you?"

"She's a year older. She's . . ." Anna stopped short.

Adam finished the sentence for her. "She's sixteen already." His tone softened as he drew his conclusion. "Then the Home may already have placed her in a job somewhere."

Anna sat frozen in her chair. She hadn't even thought about Jessie's age until now.

Adam reached across the table to rest his hand atop hers. "Anna, by the time you get back to St. Matthew's, Jessie will be the one who will be saying goodbye to *you*."

She glanced back down at the table. Adam was right. She hated to admit it, but he was right. Even if the Home placed Jessie in a neighboring town, Jessie's job would probably keep her as busy as Anna's kept her. And if she went back, Anna had no guarantee that St. Matthew's would situate her anywhere near Frankfort. Realistically, how often would she and Jessie see each other? She remembered many of the older children who had left St. Matthew's when she was there. She had never seen most of them again. And now the time had come for her to leave. She wanted to cry.

So she did. Adam moved next to her and wrapped his arm around her shoulder, comforting her. But even as she wept for her past, she felt a surge of hope for her future. For she had made her decision. If the Home would permit, she would stay in Rosita.

The next morning she informed Kate, Jeff, and Richard of her desire to stay. They were delighted and promised to contact St. Matthew's about the matter. After writing to Miss Sarah herself, Anna debated writing to Jessie as well. She decided against it, at least for the time being. For if the Home said no, she wouldn't have to tell Jessie at all.

In late March, as Anna awaited word from St. Matthew's, she received a letter from Jessie. The very sight of her friend's handwriting on the envelope stirred Anna's desire to see her. As she held the letter in her hands, she began having second thoughts about her decision to stay.

Wishing to read the note in private, Anna slipped into her room before opening it. Dated five weeks earlier, the letter had obviously been delayed by the weather.

February 22, 1877

Dear Anna,

I enjoyed your last letter so much. Thank you for writing. I hope that by the time you read this your weather will be warmer. Even with your descriptions of the winters there, it is hard for me to imagine what they must be like.

I am writing this letter with mixed emotions. I have some good news for you, but there is also some bad news to go with it. The good news is that, as of March 26, I will begin a permanent job as a bank clerk for Commerce Bank. You know how I enjoy being around people. And, though my spelling and history often left much to be desired, I was always rather good at arithmetic. So this job is perfect for me. The bad part, however, is that the bank is located in Knoxville, Tennessee.

I have always known that we would be separated eventually by the various occupations we followed, but I had hoped to lessen the pain by finding a position close to you and Danny. I know that Knoxville is where God wants me, at least for now, so I must simply trust His leading. Knoxville is not too terribly far from Frankfort, so I am hopeful that we can see each other once in a while.

I hope this letter will not upset you too much. I just wanted you to know about my plans. I had hoped to be able to stay at St. Matthew's until you arrived here, but now that will not be possible. I will, and do, miss you, Anna. I will let you know my new address as soon as I know what it is myself. I am anxious to hear from you.

Love,
Jessie

Though momentarily stunned by Jessie's announcement, Anna sensed a new peace and serenity. The letter merely reinforced her own decision. Jessie felt certain that God wanted her in Knoxville. And Anna knew now, beyond a shadow of a doubt, that He wanted her in Rosita.

Anna trusted that God would work in Miss Sarah's heart too. So she settled back into her regular routine without worrying about the Home's reaction to her request. When word arrived in early May granting her permission to stay, Anna was not surprised. Their approval was conditional, however. Legally Anna would be their ward until she turned eighteen. So she and the Pattersons would have to correspond with the Home on a regular basis. As her guardian, the Home could and would call her back to Kentucky if they ever felt such a move would be in her best interest.

The conditions did not bother Anna. In fact, they gave her added security. She liked knowing that the Home would still keep an eye on her, that Miss Sarah would still care about her even though she couldn't be with her in person. She wouldn't be losing her St. Matthew's family after all. She could keep in touch with each one of them, sharing in their lives through letters, thoughts, and prayers.

She thought again of her new friends in Rosita. Claire wasn't Jessie, and Billy wasn't her grandfather. Her Rosita family would never be able to replace her St. Matthew's family, just as St. Matthew's had never taken her grandfather's place. For each family, each person, was special to her in their own way. Even her father owned a little corner of her life, a place that would forever remain empty now because of her grandfather's death.

But as Anna looked back, her heart filled with peace. Yes, she had left many loved ones, and she still struggled with the unknown secret of her past. But God was bringing her a whole houseful of new people to love and care for. And there was room in her heart for all of them.

Part Three
1878

chapter
15

THE COLD OCTOBER AIR cut through Anna's lightweight shawl as she hurried down the wooden sidewalk toward F. L. Miller & Company. As she neared the storefront, a sudden gust of wind whipped at the full skirt of her blue cotton dress and drove light flurries of snow in her face. She paused and glanced upward, scanning the darkening sky. The billowing gray clouds did not pose any immediate threat, but she recognized again the clear signs of winter. Having already spent two long, cold winters in Colorado, she wasn't sure that she was ready for the third one to start yet.

Once inside Miller's, Anna stood by the door, her slim frame shivering as the wintry chill gave way to the building's welcome warmth. Instinctively she lifted her hand to her light brown hair, checking for any hairpins that might have slipped loose from the high, braided bun.

"Could I interest you in a new winter coat today, ma'am?" called a familiar voice.

Anna flashed a grin in Adam's direction. He always made shopping at Miller's a pleasant experience.

"I have a coat already, thank you," Anna answered. "I was just too lazy to get all bundled up for such a short walk down the street." She surveyed the store. "It certainly is quiet in here today."

"That it is." He frowned momentarily. "But it's good to know that we do still have *some* customers. Can I help you find something?"

"No, I'm just looking."

Anna stepped over to examine the shop's collection of yard goods. She was not expecting to find anything new, so she was surprised when she spotted a bolt of peach-colored cotton.

"Adam, where did you get this beautiful material? I thought you said you wouldn't be getting any more yard goods in for a while."

He crossed the room to investigate. "Oh, that was a special order for Mrs. Llewelyn. I was holding it back for her, and she changed her mind."

"Well, it's just perfect for something I have in mind. You've just made yourself a sale."

"Fine." Adam moved the bolt to the counter. "And may I say that you'll look very pretty in this, whatever it turns out to be."

"Oh, it's not for me," she replied. "It's a present—a surprise."

She would have loved to explain that the gift was to be a maternity gift for Kate, who had just confided the thrilling news of her long-awaited pregnancy. But the announcement was for Kate and Jeff to make when they felt the time was right.

"A surprise? Then my lips are sealed," Adam declared as he commenced cutting the desired yardage from the hefty bolt.

As Anna watched him at work, she couldn't help but reflect on their two-and-a-half-year friendship. She regretted that she had never developed a closeness with the rest of his family, as she had so hoped. Sam had always made her feel comfortable. But Mrs. Burdick simply could not understand Anna's and

Adam's platonic relationship. And his sister, Helen, who had taken a liking to Matt Buchanan shortly after her arrival in Rosita, had looked upon her from the very beginning as competition. So Anna had never felt truly welcome in their home.

"So, how's business over at the Rosita Hotel?" Adam asked.

"Just fine." She then admitted with some reluctance, "Well, actually it's too slow."

"How many boarders do you have now?"

"Seven. The ones that didn't leave in the summer for Leadville headed over to Silver Cliff last month. When I first heard that the new strike was just seven miles from here, I was excited. But I didn't realize that people would desert Rosita to start a whole new town over there. Do you really think the Silver Cliff strike will be all that big?"

"I don't know. But I don't think there's cause for alarm, even if it is a major strike. A lot of people may go over there, but we've still got mines operating here. And until Silver Cliff grows into any kind of a town at all, Rosita will be the source of supplies."

"Just like Bassickville," Anna reasoned, referring to the small settlement that had sprung up around the Bassick Mine.

"Exactly. Bassickville has a few stores, but when anyone wants any real selection, he comes here. After all, Rosita is the county seat now."

Reassured by Adam's positive prediction, Anna smiled easily. "How's Lydia?"

Adam's pale green eyes flashed with pride at the mention of his new bride. "She's just fine. We're getting settled into our house now. It's small, but we don't really mind. We'll have you over sometime soon."

She nodded an acknowledgment to the invitation, comforted by her friend's sincere gesture but inwardly doubtful that the event would take place anywhere in the near future, if at all. She sensed an uneasiness in Lydia's behavior toward her, and she feared that Adam's new marital status would have a negative effect on their friendship. That Adam knew nothing of the awkwardness between herself and Lydia she was certain. Men seldom picked up on such undercurrents.

With her purchase tucked securely under her arm, Anna bade farewell to Adam, then stepped outside to brave the blustery wind once again. Upon reaching the boardinghouse, she had just deposited her parcel in her room when she heard the unmistakable sound of the front bell. She marched into the entry to greet the stranger who stood at the front desk.

She concluded at once that the rugged, middle-aged man was a cowboy. His skin glowed with a healthy tan not characteristic of miners. In addition to his western attire—brown hat, leather coat, and black trousers—the stranger wore a brace of pistols riding in carved leather holsters low over his hips.

"Good afternoon, sir. May I help you?"

The tall man stared at her blankly for a moment before answering. "Yes, ma'am. I . . . I'll be needin' a room."

Anna stepped behind the desk and pulled the hotel register from the top drawer, conscious all the while of the man's intense gaze. As his penetrating stare seemed to follow her every move, she grew increasingly uncomfortable.

"Do you want the room for just one night? Or will you be staying with us longer?" When he did not answer, her uneasiness heightened. "Sir, is something wrong?"

He shook his head as if to clear his thoughts. "I'm sorry, Miss. What did you say?"

She studied his changing expression as she repeated the question. "Will you be wanting the room just for tonight?"

"Yes, just for tonight." He removed his hat and ran his fingers through his shaggy brown hair. "I'm sorry. I didn't mean to stare at you. I was just confused for a minute."

"Oh, that's all right," Anna replied, her mind eased somewhat by his explanation. As she handed him a room key, she attempted a weak smile. "You'll have room number two. It's just up the stairs to your right. If you don't find everything you need, just let me know. The dining room doesn't open until six o'clock, but if you would like some hot coffee now, I'd be happy to get some for you."

"That would be nice, Miss. I've been ridin' since sunup, and I could use somethin' hot about now, if it's no trouble."

"It's no trouble at all. Why don't you take your things up to your room and then come back down to the parlor. I'll bring the coffee in there."

Nodding an acknowledgment, he stooped to gather his bedroll, saddlebags, and rifle, and plodded up the steep, narrow steps. Anna's heart went out to him in sympathy. He looked tired, and if he had been riding all day in the freezing wind, he was probably chilled to the bone. She hurried into the parlor to put more wood on the fire, then hastened to the kitchen to fetch the coffee. When she returned, she found the newcomer standing at the hearth enjoying the rousing blaze. She set her tray of coffee and cookies on the small table near the fireplace.

"Here you are, sir."

"Jake."

"All right then, Jake. Just help yourself. There's plenty more too."

His blue eyes sparkled with pleasure at the sight of the steaming brew and the large, rounded spice cookies. He reached for a cookie and took a hearty bite. "You make these?"

Anna nodded.

"Well, these are the best cookies I've tasted in a long time. You help with the meals here?" When she nodded again, he added, "Then I sure am lookin' forward to supper."

She beamed at the compliment, totally erasing from her thoughts any qualms that remained from their initial meeting. "Speaking of supper, I'd better be getting back to work. If you need anything else. . . ."

"Oh, Miss, there is one more thing. Some folks down the street said Billy Friedrich is still around these parts, and that he stays here off and on. Do you know if he's back down from the high country yet?"

Anna's interest in Jake's question surpassed her concern for supper. "Are you a friend of Billy's?"

"Yes—we go back quite a ways. I haven't seen him, though, since I came through here in '75. I just figured that since I was this close to Rosita, I might as well look him up."

"Billy did stay here, but he's not here now. He came back from the mountains in July when his gold diggings gave out. On his way, he hit a big silver vein over in Silver Cliff. It's about seven miles west of Rosita. His claim is on the southwest side of the camp. You shouldn't have any trouble finding him."

"His claim? You mean he actually filed a claim?"

"Yes. His strike was so close to town that he didn't have any choice. You'd think this strike is the worst thing that has ever happened to him, though. He's been moaning no end about hitting silver instead of gold."

"Sounds just like him," Jake laughed. "Gold is easier to reduce. Silver, well, that's somethin' else again. You need stamp mills, smelters, and all that. Silver spells people, and people spell trouble." He took a quick sip from his coffee cup. "Thanks for all the information. I'll be sure to head out that way when I leave in the mornin', though it's in the opposite direction of where I intended to go."

"And where is that?"

"Pueblo. I'd like to get there before the heavy snows set in. I'm not much for the higher elevations in cold weather. I'd just as soon winter it out down below."

"Well, it's been nice meeting you, Jake. If I don't see you again, have a safe trip. I'd best be getting back to work now." She started toward the door, then turned to speak to him once again. "Oh, if you wouldn't mind, would you say hello to Billy for me? I haven't seen much of him since he's been guarding his claim."

A serious expression crossed Jake's square-jawed face. "Well now, I just don't know if I can do that." Noting Anna's puzzled look, he loosed an easy laugh. "How can I tell him you said hello when I don't know who you are?"

She grinned along with him. "I'm sorry. My name is Anna. Anna Logan."

She turned and walked to the corridor, but as she did so, she experienced again the uneasy sensation that Jake's eyes were following her. The idea was strangely disquieting.

In the kitchen Anna found supper preparations already underway. Kate was stirring a boiling pot of beef stew, and the tantalizing aroma reminded Anna that she was late for her chores. She hastily donned an apron.

Jake was among the first to arrive at the dining room. As Anna chatted with him during the meal, she found herself enjoying his cheerful nature and quick wit. It wasn't difficult to see how he and Billy would have developed a close friendship.

Jake was among the first to arrive at the dining room. As Anna chatted with him during the meal, she found herself enjoying his cheerful nature and quick wit. It wasn't difficult to see how he and Billy would have developed a close friendship.

She hoped that she would see Jake later that night in the parlor. But when she peeked into the room after her work was done, he was nowhere in sight. Tom Hardy and Wes Bishop, the two boarders sitting on the couch, never seemed too willing to talk to her. How times had changed.

She thought back on the early days when Billy and Jason livened the evenings with their constant debates. Even when Billy was gone, Jason always added zest and a touch of controversy to the otherwise quiet evenings by the fire. Jason. She missed his informative, though arrogant presence. But who could blame him for moving to Denver to accept a position with the *Rocky Mountain News*?

She walked to her room, lit the oil lantern, and, on an impulse, pulled her family Bible from the bottom drawer. She carried the book over to her bed, but let it lie unopened on her lap for several minutes before leafing through the thin pages to the familiar middle section where her eyes rested upon one short entry.

Anna Kathleen Logan, born January 22, 1862

Anna Kathleen Logan. She had often wondered why her mother had chosen Kathleen as her middle name. Anna had been her grandmother Logan's name. But Kathleen? Grandfather had told her that her mother had simply liked the name.

She glanced at the tintype, studying anew each of the three faces pictured there. Grandfather looked so stern. But she credited much of his appearance to the photographer's practice of taking only serious poses. Yet despite the pious, mechanical poses, she fancied detecting a softness in her mother's eyes, a gentleness in her grandmother's expression. How she wished she had known them.

She carried the tintype to the mirror and compared her features to those of her mother. Her own hair was lighter, but aside from that she bore a striking resemblance to the lovely fifteen-year-old girl in the picture. Of course, she was older now—she would be seventeen before long. But the similarities definitely existed, and she took pleasure in them. For aside from the fact that she thought her mother to be a very attractive woman, she felt strangely honored by the resemblance, as if God had in this way allowed her a small knowledge of her mother.

Her heart ached again for information about her father. But she dismissed the nagging thoughts as quickly as they came. She had struggled with her questions over and over to no avail. Rehearsing them yet another time would bring her no closer to a solution.

Anna placed the picture inside the Bible, closed the book with finality, and returned it to its place. As she readied herself for bed, she reasoned that what was done was done. She could not revisit the past, so she would just have to let it rest in peace.

chapter

16

THE DAY BEGAN QUIETLY ENOUGH. While Kate worked in the kitchen, Anna served breakfast to the customers in the dining room.

But the peacefulness did not last long. After Anna had refilled Mr. Anders's coffee cup for the fourth time, she glanced up to see Billy and Jake standing at the entrance.

She rushed over to greet them. "Billy, it's so good to see you! And Jake, you certainly take a job seriously, don't you?"

"What do you mean?" Jake asked.

Anna grinned. "I just asked you to say hello to Billy for me, and here you are bringing him over so that I can say it myself."

"I've never been one to do things halfway," he joked.

She guided the men to a table, then brought them some hot coffee.

"Jake, how in the world did you ever persuade Billy to come over? I've been hoping he would, but nothing I ever do seems to work."

"Now Anna, that's not exactly true," Billy countered. "You see, when Jake said hello for you, he started in tellin' me what good meals you had fixed for him. It was more than I could stand." His eyes twinkled. "Anyway, I figger I have to come over every once in a while to check up on you. Are you stayin' out of trouble?"

Her voice was touched with mischief. "Yes, I am. But I doubt that I'd admit it if I wasn't."

When Billy released one of his low, familiar laughs, Anna's heart filled with warmth. It was so good to see him again.

"So, what do you have for us this mornin'?" Billy asked.

"Fried cornmeal mush and sausage."

Billy beamed. "I'd say we picked us a good time to come, then."

"I'll bring it right out."

Anna left their table and within minutes was back with their breakfast. As she set a plate in front of Jake, she could not resist making a comment.

"Jake, I'm surprised that you haven't started for Pueblo yet. The sky looks pretty dark. You could get snowed in here if you're not careful."

"I know. I'll be movin' on just as soon as I eat. I didn't plan on stayin' this long, but Billy and I got to swappin' tales yesterday and I ended up stayin' the night. Then Billy said he was comin' over here." He gave Anna a quick wink. "So, I figured that as long as I'd already wasted this much time, I'd make sure Billy here didn't get lost on the way over."

"Lost?" Billy exclaimed. "You're the one likely to get lost around here!"

"I'll tell you, Anna," Jake continued, purposely speaking as though Billy were not present. "You've really got to watch out for miners once they start gettin' old. They're so used to diggin' around in little holes that once they get out into the daylight, they can hardly find their way around." He grinned, casting a sidelong glance at Billy.

"Who you callin' old?" Billy demanded. "As far as minin' goes, at least I'm makin' some money at what I do. I've never known anybody to get rich by hammerin' railroad spikes all day."

"That so? Well, money or no money, I'd sure rather spend my days above the ground instead of tunnelin' around in the dirt like some mole."

Anna knew full well that they relished giving each other a hard time. Yes, indeed. They were quite a pair.

Two new customers entered the dining room, so Anna reluctantly left Billy's company to take care of them. When she returned to check on Billy's and Jake's progress, the two had almost finished breakfast. She fetched more sausage, mush, and coffee for them. Then, since the dining room was almost empty, she lingered by their table to visit.

"Mighty good eatin', Anna," Jake commented.

"Sure is," Billy agreed. "Like I always said, it takes a southerner to fix good cornmeal mush."

"Being a southerner myself, I'd say you hit the nail on the head," Jake maintained. "It takes a southerner to make good mush and decent fried chicken."

"Where in the South are you from?" Anna asked.

"Richmond."

"Then were you involved in the War at all?"

"Yep. I was in Kentucky when the fightin' first broke out. But I managed to get back to Virginia to help, for all the good it did."

Anna raised her eyebrows at the mention of her home state. "You lived in Kentucky?"

"For a while."

"Whereabouts?"

"Oh, I traveled all through the state. I worked where I could. Odd jobs, mostly."

"Did you ever go through Frankfort? That's my home."

Jake's eyes widened. "Frankfort? You're from Frankfort?"

She nodded. "I was born there. Well, not *in* Frankfort, exactly. Outside of town on my grandpa's farm."

"Your grandpa?" As he questioned her, his expression reminded her of their uncomfortable first meeting.

"Yes. Grandpa's name was Caleb Logan. He owned a tobacco farm about twenty miles south of town."

She eyed Jake curiously. What was going on inside his mind? He sat motionless, a distant look in his eyes, as if he were a thousand miles away. But she had little time to consider Jake's sudden silence, for at that moment another customer entered the dining room.

When at last she found time to stop by Jake's table, it was as if she had never been away. Jake immediately resumed the conversation.

"Did you live on the farm with your folks?" he asked, his voice noticeably strained.

"No. Just Grandpa and I lived there. He raised me after my parents died."

"When was that?"

"My mother died in February of '62, just a few weeks after I was born."

His eyes fastened on her. "And your pa?"

"I never knew my father. Grandpa said he was killed in the War."

Jake glanced away for a moment, then turned to face her again. "What's your grandpa doin' now? Is he still in Kentucky?"

"No. He died when I was nine, and since I didn't have any other relatives, I went to live at St. Matthew's in Frankfort. It's an orphanage."

Jake seemed unable to look at her any longer. He stared down at his plate and toyed nervously with his spoon.

Just then two customers waved Anna to their table. After

accepting their payment and clearing the dishes, she came back to Billy's table with her coffee pot.

"More coffee?" she asked. Billy nodded, but Jake shook his head. "Can I get you anything else?"

"Nothin' for me," Billy declared. "How about you, Jake?"

"No, nothing, thanks."

Anna removed Jake's plate, noting with surprise that he had left sizable portions of mush. Odd, she thought, since he had specifically requested more.

"Much as I hate to go, Anna, I really do need to get back to that blasted claim of mine," Billy confessed. "I'll probably have two or three jumpers fightin' over it when I get back there." He heaved a sigh. "I've half a mind to let 'em have it. It's more trouble than it's worth."

Anna's heart sank at the news of Billy's immediate departure. But she did her best to conceal her disappointment. She cared for Billy, and she knew that in his own way he returned the affection. But he had never truly understood the extent of her need. He would always be a loner who did not want anyone depending on him. And though she understood his need for freedom, the knowledge gave her little comfort.

She swallowed hard and cleared her throat. "Can you at least wait a few minutes before you go? You too, Jake. We've got some ham in the icebox, and I'd be more than happy to pack some sandwiches for you to take along."

Hearing no arguments, she carried her load of dishes to the kitchen, hurriedly packaged meals for them, and returned to the dining room to deliver them.

She handed the first parcel to Billy. "Here you are."

But as she handed the second to Jake, her eyes met his for a moment. She detected in them a subtle difference, as if this man of many moods had undergone yet another change. For their former sparkle had been replaced by a look of wistfulness.

Despite his sorrowful expression, Jake commenced another comical argument with Billy as they walked to the door. His action left Anna more puzzled than ever. She had met many unusual people during her three years in Colorado, but never had anyone left her so totally baffled.

chapter
17

"IT'S BEEN QUITE A DAY," Kate sighed late that evening as she stretched her long arms above her head to place the clean serving bowls on their proper shelf. She turned and leaned against the counter. "Is there much chili left from supper?"

"A few bowls," Anna replied. "Why?"

"I'm still hungry. I think I'll heat it up and have some more."

Anna watched the still slender blond pull the container of chili from the icebox. "Kate, I always thought that expectant mothers were supposed to avoid spicy foods."

"Not *this* expectant mother! I just can't seem to get enough of it. I'd do most anything to have a good enchilada about now." She poured the thick mixture into a pan and set it on the stove. "Would you hand me the chili powder? I think it could use a little more."

Anna winced as Kate sprinkled generous quantities of the seasoning into the already spicy soup.

"Why the sour face?" echoed Jeff's voice.

Anna looked up as Jeff entered the kitchen from the hallway. "It's your wife," she said with a smile.

"Anna doesn't approve of my diet," Kate explained. She stirred the chili vigorously and tasted a spoonful. "It still needs a bit more chili powder."

"Katie, Katie," Jeff laughed softly. He stepped behind his wife and circled her waist with his arms. "Before you add any more spices," he chuckled, "do you think you could dish out a bowl for our new boarder? That is, if you can spare some."

"Our new boarder?" the women chimed.

Jeff nodded, then motioned to the tall man standing in the doorway. "Mr. Tyler, come right on in. Kate, this is Mr. Tyler. Mr. Tyler, my wife, Kate Patterson. And this is Anna Logan."

Anna stared at the man who had just entered the room. "Jake! I thought you'd be halfway to Pueblo by now!"

"Do you two know each other?" Kate inquired.

Jake tossed a smile in Anna's direction. "We're both friends of Billy's."

"Just have a seat, Mr. Tyler," Kate requested. "I'll have your supper ready in just a minute."

When Jake took a place at the table, Anna crossed the room to join him.

"What brings you back to Rosita?"

"Oh, I just got to thinkin' that there wasn't really any good reason for travelin' on and risking gettin' snowbound out in the middle of nowhere. I might as well winter it out right here."

"But I thought you said you didn't like the high country."

"It shouldn't be all that bad. This way, I can see a bit more of Billy. Besides, I got a job, so it's too late to change my mind."

"A job?" Anna repeated in surprise. "Where in the world did you find a job on a Sunday?"

"At Carlin's Freight Company. I start haulin' ore first thing in the mornin'."

Anna stared at him, more puzzled than ever by this revelation. Just two days ago he had been anxious to move on to a warmer climate. Now he sat in the kitchen, announcing his intention of staying in Rosita to work. His decision didn't make any sense at all.

With Kate and Jeff to see to Jake's needs, Anna excused herself and retired to her room. She dressed for bed slowly, still deep in thought. She climbed into bed, smiling at the thought of Billy's unpredictable friend. For, though she didn't really know Jake, she was sure of one thing. With him at the boardinghouse, the winter would be anything but dull.

Anna's first opportunity to visit with Jake came three days later. After completing her supper chores, she carried a pile of mending into the empty parlor and, sitting down on the worn green sofa, began sewing two buttons onto a white dress shirt belonging to Tim Randall.

Jake entered the room shortly thereafter. He moved to a chair near the sofa and took a seat.

"I haven't seen much of you since Sunday," he remarked. "I guess they keep you pretty busy here."

"There's always plenty to do. I enjoy coming in by the fire in the evenings. But usually I'm just too tired on Mondays and Tuesdays. Those are the days we do the laundry and the ironing."

He nodded toward the shirt she was holding. "Don't you ever stop workin'?"

"Sometimes it doesn't seem so," she sighed. She snipped the thread on the last button, set the shirt aside, and reached for the next item on her mending pile.

"Girls as young as you don't usually know how to do half the things you do. Cookin', servin', sewin', and all. Did you learn all that from your grandpa?"

She looked up, suprised but pleased by his interest in her background.

"No. Grandpa took good care of me, but he didn't teach me much about working. I learned most everything I know at St. Matthew's."

Just then Tim called to her from the hallway. "Excuse me, Anna, but have you gotten to my shirt yet?"

"Just finished."

The lanky boarder grinned as he crossed the room to fetch his prized apparel. "Thanks a lot. I hated to bother you with it, but, with the dance coming up on Saturday . . ."

"I know. You want to look your best."

"That's right," Tim replied sheepishly. He thanked her again, then started back down the corridor. Anna couldn't help but chuckle as he disappeared around the corner.

"Is that your beau?" Jake asked.

"My beau? Oh, no. Tim has been seeing a lot of my best friend, Claire McMahon."

"You got a beau?"

His question embarrassed her, so she focused again on her mending. "No. I'm not seeing anyone regularly right now."

Their conversation lagged a bit. But after a few quiet moments, Jake broke the silence.

"What was that orphanage like, if you don't mind my askin'. I hear tell that some of them places . . ."

Anna's embarrassment faded as she jumped to the Home's defense. "St. Matthew's was a good home. Miss Sarah, the headmistress, made me feel like I belonged, and I made a lot of good friends while I was there. And, as you can see from my job here, their training has come in handy." Her voice dropped, losing its former intensity as she reflected further. "The only part that bothered me was being hired out to work for people. You never knew what to expect, or how they would treat you. But," she ventured with renewed enthusiasm, "that's how I wound up coming to Colorado, so I guess it worked out for the best."

"Are the folks who run this place the ones you worked for back there?"

"Well, I came out with Richard Patterson, Jeff's brother. Richard helped here a lot during the first year. He built all the beautiful furniture in the dining room and hotel rooms. But since he did such a nice job on them, people started asking him to build things for them. After a while he was so busy that he opened up a shop down on Euclid Avenue. I was only going to stay in Rosita for a year, but by the end of my stay I decided that I liked my job enough to make it permanent. Speaking of jobs, how is yours coming along?"

"Fair enough."

"Doesn't Carlin's Freight haul ore for the smaller mines?"

"Yep. And there's a lot of 'em."

"Have you had any trouble locating them all?"

"None to speak of. If things go like I expect, I figure I'll be makin' more runs over to Silver Cliff before long. Mines are poppin' up all over the place there, and they'll be needin' to use Rosita's stamp mills and smelters 'til they can build their own."

"I'd like to go over to Silver Cliff myself before too long to see Billy's mine. That is, when I get some free time and can get away."

Jake's eyes flashed. "Oh no, you don't, young lady!" he ordered. "You just stay away from there. Even by my standards, Silver Cliff is a rough camp. It sure isn't a place for a girl. The only women there. . . ." He stopped short, then proceeded in a calmer tone. "Well, you just take my word for it, and don't let me catch you headin' over that way."

Anna gazed at him uncertainly, wondering whether to be annoyed by his command or touched by his protectiveness. It then occurred to her that their conversation so far had been centered on herself. So she purposely changed the subject.

"What did you do before coming to Rosita?"

"Guess you could say I'm a jack-of-all-trades. You name the job, and I've probably done it. I left Virginia when I was twelve, after my folks died. I didn't get very far west, though, 'til after the War. I was workin' for the Denver & Rio Grande up until a week ago."

"That's the narrow gauge railroad?"

"Yep. The 'baby road,' they call it. Folks gave us a hard time at first for layin' the smaller track. But it's easier to put down, especially here in Colorado where you don't always have much clearance."

"Pardon me," interrupted a clear tenor voice from the entryway. Judging from the speaker's crisp English accent, Anna recognized the man as a hotel guest. As she turned her head, the willowy, middle-aged Englishman struck a rigid pose in the doorway.

"Do excuse me, Miss Logan, but Mildred has changed her mind and would like you to draw her a hot bath after all. Could you see to it at once?"

Anna set her sewing materials aside and rose to her feet. "Certainly, Mr. Whitfield. I'll take care of it right away."

"Also, my dear, could you bring up a fresh pot of tea when you come? Millie rather enjoys sipping a cup while she's soaking in the tub. And could we have a few of those fresh cakes to accompany the tea?"

"I'm sure I can find something for you, sir."

"Very well, then, I shall tell Millie that you will be up directly. Good evening."

As the English visitor disappeared around the corner, Anna breathed a sigh. "I'm sorry, Jake, but I've got to get back out to the kitchen. It's been nice talking to you."

Jake rose and followed Anna down the hallway. Instead of entering his room, he followed her to the kitchen where he insisted on helping. In short order, Jake hauled the heated water up the hotel steps while Anna led the way with her loaded tray of refreshments. When their task was accomplished, they walked back down the squeaky stairway.

"Those hotel folks," Jake grumbled. "It doesn't seem fair that they can expect you to do for them this late at night, especially after you've put in a full day."

Anna couldn't help but appreciate the fact that he was sticking up for her.

"How long have those two been here?" he asked.

"Three weeks."

"And they've probably made you wait on 'em hand and foot all that time."

"Well, Mr. Whitfield hasn't been too bad, but Mrs. Whitfield has been a little difficult."

"Isn't it kind of late in the year for them to be here?"

"Yes. Normally the sightseers have all left by mid-September. But the Whitfields are here on business. A lot of the mines in the area have eastern and foreign backing. Mr. Whitfield has been trying to buy some of the mines over in Silver Cliff. But they'll be leaving for Colorado Springs on Friday morning. Mrs. Whitfield would be more than a little upset if they got snowed in here."

"Well, I wouldn't like that any more than she would," Jake muttered as they reached the entryway. "So, for all of our sakes, I just hope the snow holds off long enough for the two of them to get out of town."

chapter
18

THE WHITFIELDS TIMED THEIR DEPARTURE PERFECTLY. Just one day after they left, winter descended in full force. By Saturday afternoon, the season's first storm had dumped several inches of snow onto the Wet Mountain Valley.

Since the storm showed no sign of relenting, few people attended the scheduled dance that evening. Despite the low attendance, however, the level of merriment remained high. The ratio of men to women stayed the same, leaving Anna with an abundance of willing partners who danced with her as often as her escort, Mike Ridgeway, allowed. Mike, an acquaintance from the Methodist church, seemed disgruntled by the numerous requests to share Anna's company. After sitting out three dances, he grew especially aggravated when at the start of the next number Jake stepped in to whirl Anna away with him.

After enjoying a lively Virginia reel with Mike, Anna accepted an invitation to a leisurely waltz with Tim Randall. Though Tim led her skillfully through the steps on the dance floor, she knew that he was miles away in thought. For his eyes remained fastened on Claire, who was moving gracefully in step with her current partner, Jim Lowry.

"Would you mind if we stopped to get something to drink?" he inquired halfway through the dance.

Anna could sense his inner frustration. "That would be fine. I could use a rest."

They made their way to the refreshment table where Tim filled two cups with the well-spiced apple cider. As they sipped their drinks, Adam Burdick approached the table.

"I see we all had the same idea," he commented. "Dancing is a thirsty business!"

Anna watched him closely as he ladled cider into two cups. His comment seemed typical of his normally jovial behavior, but she detected a forced gaity in his tone. He lifted the cups, ready to depart, then changed his mind and glanced awkwardly toward Anna.

"Anna, could I talk to you for a minute?"

"Of course," she answered, suspecting what the subject would be—Lydia. But before they could speak further, Adam's bride crossed the room to join them.

"Adam, I see you have our drinks," the petite, plain-looking brunette called. "Anna, how nice to see you again," she added, her voice even, but as biting as the cider. "Oh, Adam, there are the Burkes. We really do need to see them about that dinner invitation. If you'll excuse us, Anna. . . ." She nudged her husband forward.

As she did, Adam glanced back to Anna, as if to apologize for his young wife's unfounded jealousy. From the reassuring look in his eyes, Anna knew that they would still be friends. But his unspoken message had been clear. Their friendship would have to change.

The incident upset Anna greatly. She drew some consolation from the knowledge that Adam at least understood the situation now. But his commiseration did little to soothe her injured feelings.

She could not recall ever giving Lydia cause to consider herself a rival for Adam's affections. In fact, she had encouraged Adam to see Lydia, and had listened happily as he related his growing fondness for her. That Lydia had now cut her off so suddenly seemed a gross injustice. And that Adam would condone such behavior seemed even more cruel.

No longer in a partying mood, Anna was glad that the dance was almost over. When she finally arrived back at the boardinghouse, she said goodnight to Mike, then made her way to the dimly lit kitchen. There, to her surprise, she found Jake sitting at the long, empty table.

"Jake, what are you doing up so late?"

"Oh, hello there, Anna. I couldn't sleep, that's all." His voice took on a stern tone. "Aren't you up kind of late yourself?"

"I suppose it is late, but Mike and I had to stay afterward to help clean up."

"Oh. Did you have a nice time?"

Anna nodded, then glanced downward and began unbuttoning her heavy blue coat. By avoiding his eyes, she hoped to conceal from him her inner turmoil. But she was unsuccessful.

"Is something wrong?" She shook her head, but her troubled expression betrayed her true emotions. Jake's voice rose, his face tensing as an idea occurred to him. "Did that young fella get out of line when he brought you home?"

"Mike? Oh, no," she assured him, anxious to put that thought to rest. "It's nothing like that. Something is bothering me, but it's something altogether different."

Having acknowledged that she did indeed have a problem, Anna hesitated, unsure of whether or not to confide further in him. But she did need to talk to someone, and Jake seemed genuinely interested. So she moved over to the bench, sat down next to him, and related in detail the situation with Adam and Lydia.

Jake listened attentively. "So, you're kind of caught in the middle."

Anna nodded. "What should I do?"

"Appears to me there's not much you *can* do. You say Adam's a good friend?"

She nodded again, then murmured, "Well, I *thought* he was."

"First rule about friendship, Anna, is don't sell a friend short," Jake scolded. Anna looked up, confused by the reprimand. She had hoped for some sympathy.

"I know you feel let down, but if you think you're caught in the middle, think about him. He's tryin' to be fair to you on the one hand, but then he does have his wife to consider. He wouldn't be much of a husband if he didn't put her first, now, would he? He's havin' to decide whether to hurt his wife's feelings or his friend's. And that's a tough spot to be in. What would you do if you were in his place?"

"I hadn't thought of it like that before," she admitted. "Of course he'd have to go along with Lydia, even though he didn't agree with her, if it was something that really bothered her."

"Right. He's got to *live* with her. You just give 'em both a little time. They'll come around."

"I guess I've been pretty selfish, then. I'm sorry, Jake. You must think I'm awful."

"Awful? Why, not for a minute!"

"But you made it seem so clear."

"That's because I'm lookin' at it from a different angle. You just couldn't see the woods for all the trees, that's all. Now— don't you think it's time the both of us called it a day? You may be a spring chicken, but I'm sure not!"

As she giggled at his remark, she realized that her mood had changed entirely. She smiled fondly at the peculiar man who had just worked a minor miracle with her tangled emotions.

"Thank you, Jake."

"Any time, Anna," he replied, patting her smooth arm with his large, calloused hand. "Any time at all."

They rose to part company, but as they did, they heard a tapping sound at the back door.

"Who could that be at this hour?" Anna questioned. She moved toward the door, but Jake got there first.

"Better let me see."

As he opened the door, Anna peered around him. Her heart sank at the sight that awaited her. A frightened, battered Claire hovered in the darkness, her face blotched with bruises and tears. Her father had obviously been on the rampage again.

Anna immediately guided Claire into her bedroom. She then returned to the kitchen to fetch water and washcloths.

"Will she be all right?" Jake asked, his face clouded with concern.

Anna nodded and briefly explained Claire's dilemma.

Jake's expression grew grim. "Does this happen often?"

"I'm afraid so. But she only comes here when it gets really bad."

"You want me to go get Tim?"

"No, Claire's upset enough without having to worry about his reaction to all of this. Let's just wait until morning."

At that, she bade goodnight to Jake, entered her room, and tended to Claire's wounds. When her friend fell asleep at last, Anna pulled a chair up to the bed and sank into it, sleeping as best she could in the uncomfortable position. She felt almost relieved when dawn approached and Kate's clatter in the kitchen beckoned her to her morning duties.

After serving breakfast to the boarders, Anna told Tim what had happened. The young man was livid. Nothing she said could stop his plan for taking immediate physical action against Mr. McMahon. As he stomped angrily toward the back door, Jake called to him.

"Tim, you go right ahead. I'd say he's got it comin'. It's high time he learned a lesson. Just answer me one thing first."

"What is it?" Tim snapped.

"Why do you think he beat Claire up in the first place?"

"Because he's a miserable excuse for a father, that's why!"

"There's no denyin' that, that's for sure. But that's not what I meant. Why do you think he hit her?"

Tim calmed ever so slightly as he replied. "He usually beats on her when he's upset about something."

"All right. Let's just say you go find him and rough him up. When you're through with him, and that's assumin' that you come out the winner, do you think he's gonna be mad at you for layin' into him?"

"Yes, I'm sure he will be. But don't worry," he added, anticipating the direction in which Jake's question was leading. "He won't be taking it out on Claire again. I'll see to that."

"Fine. Then who's he gonna take it out on?"

Tim stood motionless as he considered Jake's question. His frustration grew as Jake elaborated. "If Claire's not there, and her old man feels like layin' into someone, who's it gonna be?"

"Her mother," Tim sighed, his towering frame suddenly limp from defeat as he realized the sickening truth. He leaned against a chair, gripping the back so tightly that his knuckles whitened.

Anna lay a gentle hand on his shoulder. "I know how you feel, Tim, and I'll tell you something. I'm glad Claire has somebody who cares about her as much as you do. Why don't you go in and check on her. She's in my room, and I know she'll want to see you."

The lanky Texan loosed his hold on the chair and stepped

toward the closed bedroom door. As he disappeared inside, Anna, Kate, Jake, and Jeff all breathed a sigh of relief. Though all four would have welcomed the chance to sit down and discuss the matter, the fast-filling dining room allowed them no time for reflection. Anna jumped headlong into her remaining duties, using all the energy she could muster to complete her chores.

Since Tim insisted on staying with Claire, Anna attended church. Afterward she saw to her responsibilities at the boardinghouse. But by early afternoon, the sleepless night with Claire began to wear heavily upon her. So after finishing the dinner cleanup, Anna slipped into her room to rest for a while.

At four o'clock Anna found herself in the kitchen again. She could have waited another hour before beginning supper preparations, but since Kate and Jeff had left her in charge of the light evening meal while they attended a Patterson family gathering, she wanted to be certain that she had everything under control. Although it was still too early to heat the vegetable soup, she set the table for the boarders, laid out the serving bowls, and sliced a heaping platterful of ham and cheese. As she stepped to the cupboard to pull glasses from the upper shelf, she heard the swishing sound of the swinging doors. Expecting to see Tim and Claire returning from their walk, she turned with a smile.

But her smile faded when she saw, not Claire and Tim, but Claire's father. She could tell by the look on his face that his visit meant trouble.

chapter

19

"WHERE'S CLAIRE?"

Mr. McMahon's narrow green eyes flashed angrily through the thick circle of red hair that framed his face. From the smell on his breath, Anna knew that he had been drinking again. His gruff manner frightened her, for she knew the violence he was capable of inflicting. But her outrage at his actions against his daughter surpassed her fears. She returned his glare with one of equal intensity.

"She's not here."

"Don't you lie to me. I know she comes here. Either you tell me where she is, or I'll tear this place apart looking for her."

As if to demonstrate his intention, he marched across the kitchen and opened Anna's bedroom door. Upon finding it empty, he slammed the door angrily.

"I'm not lying to you, Mr. McMahon," Anna insisted. Claire is staying here, but she's not here now. And you are trespassing. This is private property, and if you don't get out of here right now, I'll go get the sheriff."

"Why you little. . . ." He lunged across the room in quick, jerky strides, raised his hand, then struck her sharply across her left cheek. The force of the blow sent her reeling sideways until her shoulder and hip slammed against the stove. Dizzy from the blow, Anna leaned against the stove for support.

"You and your interference," he screamed, heading for her again with uplifted hand. "I'll teach you once and for all to mind your own business!"

Even as Anna's heart pounded with fear, a force within her swelled upward, giving her unexpected courage. Her pride would not permit her to cower. For no matter how frightened she felt, she refused to give Mr. McMahon the satisfaction of knowing that he had scared her to death.

"Go ahead and hit me, Mr. McMahon," she cried defiantly. "Just go ahead. Because I'm not Claire. Claire won't report you to the sheriff. But I will, believe me! There's nothing I'd like better than to see you behind bars, where you belong!"

He stopped short, seething with rage, his hand still positioned to strike her. But as he glared at her, another voice sounded from the hallway.

"You touch her, and you won't *live* long enough to go to jail!"

Anna's heart flooded with relief as Jake entered the room. His rugged, tall frame moved steadily, his eyes fastened firmly on the unwanted intruder.

"Now, you get out of here before I throw you out. And don't come back, or you'll be dealing with *me!*"

Judging from the look on Jake's face, Anna doubted that Russell McMahon would be fool enough to defy him. When Jake took another step toward him, Mr. McMahon hurried through the swinging doors and across the dining room.

Jake then headed straight for Anna. His stern expression was replaced in an instant by a look of compassion.

"Are you all right?"

Anna nodded, then touched her face gingerly. When Jake saw the red mark, he exploded.

"You mean he'd already hit you? Why, I'll. . . ."

Feeling dizzy again, Anna reached for his arm to steady herself. Realizing her plight, Jake pushed his anger aside.

"Here. Let me help you. Let's get you over to the bench where you can sit down."

He led her to the table where she sat until her lightheadedness subsided. After making sure that she had sustained no other injuries, Jake scolded her.

"You know, young lady, when I came walkin' down that hallway, I could hear you invitin' that old guy to hit you. Now that's askin' for trouble if I ever heard it!"

"Maybe so, but I meant it. You saw Claire last night."

"I sure did. And I don't want you to end up like that."

"Oh, Jake, I haven't even thanked you for coming to my rescue when you did. But, you know, if Mr. McMahon had beaten me up, I think some good might have come from it. Maybe a little time in jail would do Claire's father some good. At least Claire and her mother would be safe for a little while."

"Then again, a stay in the calaboose might make him mad enough to come after you again, just to get even," Jake reprimanded. "I don't want you takin' chances like that, Annie. You hear me?"

Though moved by Jake's concern, she was even more touched by the name he had called her. *Annie.* Not since the years with her grandfather had she heard that endearment.

"Oh, Jake, would you do me one more favor?" she begged. "Would you please not mention this to Claire?"

"But . . ."

"She'll feel terrible if she thinks her father did this to me. If she thinks I'll be in trouble for helping her, then she might not come here anymore. And she doesn't have anywhere else to go when things get bad. Please, Jake?" As she pleaded, she could see his reservations melting away.

"Well, all right. But how are you gonna explain that bruise on your face?"

"Oh, I don't know. I'll think of something."

But the issue never came up. For when Claire and Tim returned, they announced happily that they had just gotten married. The excited couple was too busy making plans to notice the injury. To Anna's delight, Tim decided that he and his wife would stay in the hotel until he could arrange for permanent housing.

That night, Anna lay awake for some time before falling asleep. So much had happened. She was so happy for Claire and Tim. Claire's life had been filled with such hardship. How inviting the idea of running away must have seemed to her at times. She had confided to Anna on one occasion that she had even been tempted to marry absolutely anyone just to escape her father's wrath. But her faith, her perseverance had paid off. Tim would take good care of her now.

Claire and Tim. Kate and Jeff. Adam and Lydia. Two by two, the couples surrounded her on all sides. Even Pamela had found the plain but wealthy Arthur Wolford. Yet here she was. Anna. Always—just Anna.

Perhaps she was too selective. She could marry if she really wanted to. There were plenty of available men. Lonely men. What was she looking for? Perfection?

No, not perfection. But she did know what she expected. After watching Kate and Jeff together for over three years, observing their closeness, their honesty, their love, she knew that she wanted a marriage like theirs—like the one Claire had found with Tim. Her mate would have to share both her desire to serve the Lord and her commitment to show His love to others. She would accept nothing at all before settling for less.

On Tuesday night Anna sat in the parlor, her body exhausted but her eyes and mind not quite ready to call it a day. She watched Wes Bishop carefully. As soon as he laid down the *Rosita Index,* she snatched it from the table before anyone else could lay claim to the popular journal.

As usual, the front page carried more information on the railroad struggle outside of Cañon City. She glanced through the articles halfheartedly, curious as to any new developments in the "Grand Canyon War" but disappointed by the same old news. Since April, reports on the fight between the Denver & Rio Grande and the Santa Fe Railroads had dominated the front page. Each issue outlined the legal and physical battles that had been raging since the moment both lines claimed possession to the same route to Leadville.

"Anything goin' on that I should know about?"

Anna glanced up at Jake as he sat down next to her on the sofa. She laid the paper aside.

"Not really. Just more talk about the railroads." As she mentioned the dispute, a thought occurred to her. "Jake, you said you worked for the Denver & Rio Grande, didn't you?"

"For a couple of years."

"Were you involved in the fight over at Cañon City?"

"Right from the start."

"Is the gorge really too narrow for two sets of tracks?"

"Annie, it's too narrow for *one* set of tracks. You ever see it?"

"No. I've only been to Cañon City once, and that was when I first came to Colorado."

"Well, I'll tell you," he began. "The Denver & Rio Grande started surveyin' that gorge long before the Santa Fe ever thought about it. The plan was to follow the Arkansas River up to Leadville to take advantage of all the silver shipments up there. That gorge, though, that's been quite a problem." He shook his head. "It's the steepest thing I've ever seen. It's a thousand feet to the bottom, and it runs for a full ten miles. The Arkansas cuts through hard and fast all the way."

"And they're actually trying to lay track along the bottom? Right along the river?"

"That's what they're doin'. There's hardly room to stand, let alone lay track. In some places we had to hang from ropes and drill holes in the rock to blast enough rock loose to make a roadbed."

The previously stale subject grew fascinating. "You mean you hung there? Right over the river?"

"I sure did! It was quite a time. I'd still be there workin' on it if it wasn't for all the fightin'. Not that I'm afraid of a showdown—not on your life. But the Santa Fe keeps layin' track too, sayin' that the route belongs to them. Both sides tear up what the other's got done, snipers shoot at you while you're tryin' to work—it's a real mess. I left because, the way I figured it, I hired on to lay track, not to stand guard and fight. I had my fill of that during the War."

His reference to the War brought to mind another question she had wanted to ask him. "Jake, you mentioned leaving Richmond after your parents died. I was just wondering. . . ." She hesitated, afraid that he might find her inquiry offensive. "Didn't you have any relatives? Or were you like me?"

"Oh, I had some kin livin' back there," he volunteered, his expression giving no indication that the question had bothered him. "As best I know, they're all still in Richmond—an uncle, aunt, and some cousins. I have a brother, too. His name is Vince. He's two years younger than me. We stayed with Uncle Ben for a while right after my folks died. But he and his family were all city folks, and I just couldn't take bein' hemmed in like that. Vince, now, he's different from me. He took to their ways right off. But after they sold my folks' farm, there just wasn't a reason for me to stay."

"What's your brother doing now?"

"I don't know. I went back after the War, but he was gone somewhere on business. Aunt Clara said he was happy workin' in town. That's the last I've heard of him. We never were real close. By now we wouldn't have much in common at all. After I talked to Aunt Clara for a while, I went on out to the farm, just to see the place again. Then I headed West."

"I've often wanted to do that—go back to Grandpa's farm in Frankfort to see if it's like I remembered it. Had your farm changed much?"

He cast his gaze to the fire. "It wasn't even there. The house, the barn—everything had been burned to the ground."

He turned to her, his eyes fixed upon her face, his voice calm but deadly serious. "Don't ever try to go back, Anna. Because nothin' is ever the same, and you can even end up losin' what good memories you had. Just remember things like they were. Because if you try to go back, you're liable to end up wishin' you hadn't."

chapter
20

TIM LOCATED AND REPAIRED A SUITABLE HOUSE less than a week after his marriage to Claire. With few possessions to their name, the couple required little help moving in on Saturday.

Anna spent every spare minute working with Claire on projects for the cozy, sparsely furnished three-room cabin. Located just a half-mile south of town on Grouse Street, the Randalls' home was within easy walking distance of the boardinghouse.

After a quick stop by their house on Thursday afternoon, Anna stepped carefully through the thick snow that blanketed Claire's front yard. Once on Grouse Street, she followed the deep imprints left by the heavy ore wagons as they plowed regularly from the mines to the smelters, their schedules slowed but not stopped by the moderate snowfall.

Hearing the familiar rumble of a wagon behind her, Anna instinctively waded into a high drift at the side of the road to wait for the cart to pass. As the heavily laden wagon rolled by, she waved a greeting to its driver, Mr. Anders, a regular customer at the dining room. She laughed inwardly as she recalled the countless cups of coffee that she poured for the ever-thirsty gentleman. How the small man found room for such volumes of the liquid she would never know. His insatiable desire for coffee brought to mind other acquaintances, with their assorted idiosyncrasies. Mr. Harmon's preference for pale griddlecakes. Mr. Whitaker's insistence on cold syrup. How many peculiar people she had met through the years. But how many special ones too.

As her heart filled with thankfulness for her friends, her mind flew back to the old sampler that doubtless still hung in the entryway at St. Matthew's, back to those two verses that she had thought so strange when she was younger. But now she understood their significance. Now, as she repeated the entire passage, she claimed it for her own.

And Jesus answered and said, Verily I say unto you, There is no man that hath left house, or brethren, or sisters, or father, or mother, or wife, or children, or lands, for my sake, and the gospel's, But he shall receive an hundredfold now in this time, houses, and brethren, and sisters, and mothers, and children, and lands, with persecutions; and in the world to come eternal life.

Mark 10:29, 30

She had not purposely left her family, but she had *been* abandoned by her parents and grandfather. That harsh fact had at times caused her much heartache. But she had tried to accept each trial, trusting God to work in it for her good. And God had rewarded her faith by giving her a family of sorts, in fact, several families—her St. Matthew's family and her ever-changing, ever-growing Colorado family. He had indeed blessed her a hundredfold. This knowledge did not lessen her curiosity about her father, but it did remove any traces of bitterness that lingered inside her heart.

Another low rumble echoed from the roadway, so she stepped to the side again to get out of the way. But instead of passing her, the wagon squeaked to a halt.

"Anna, I thought that was you!"

She recognized the driver even before turning to look at him. "Good afternoon, Jake."

"Want a ride? I'm headin' your way."

"I'd love one."

Anna walked to the side of the wagon and climbed up. With his passenger seated, Jake snapped the reins and the two black work horses plodded forward.

Anna glanced behind her. "I see your wagon's empty. Where are you going?"

"The Lucille. This'll be my last run for the day. What's for supper?"

"Chicken and dumplings."

"Sounds good. But then, most anything hot would sound good about now." He shivered as he spoke, his action reminding her of their first conversation when he had freely admitted his dislike for cold weather. She had never understood why he had changed his mind so suddenly and decided to stay in Rosita for the winter.

"I take it you were at Claire's."

As she nodded, a shiny object under his coat caught her eye. "Jake, why are you wearing your guns?"

He shrugged his shoulders. "I always wear them when I have to make a run over to The Cliff. That's where I was all mornin'."

"I know you told me that Silver Cliff isn't a safe place for me to go, but is it dangerous even for you?"

"Yes—it's nothing at all like Rosita."

"Have you ever had to use your guns?"

"Just last week."

The news troubled her. "What happened?"

"Oh, it was just a little scuffle, that's all. Don't worry. By the way, you told me that you were born in January. What day?"

"The twenty-second. Why?"

"Oh, I just wondered. You'll be seventeen then?"

She nodded.

Jake's face suddenly lighted. "You know how to ride?"

"You mean horses? No."

"Well, we'll have to take care of that come spring. Ever drive a wagon?"

"No."

"Then now's as good a time as any to learn." He slipped the reins into her hands. "Now don't be afraid. Just hold them loose like that . . . no, don't give them back to me. There. That's good. You're doin' just fine."

As they bounced slowly into town, Anna's heart surged with the thrill of her new accomplishment. Following Jake's directions, she brought the team to a stop just outside the boardinghouse. After thanking him for both the ride and the lesson, she jumped down from the wagon and headed for the hotel's front door.

"Don't you get any ideas about stealin' my job," Jake called.

"Don't worry. It's too cold out here for me. I'll stick to working in warm kitchens."

She waved goodbye, but stood watching until he disappeared around the curving road that would lead him to the Lucille. She was pleased that his last run for ore would take him to a local mine. A trip to Silver Cliff this late in the day would mean that he would stay overnight in the town, an action that would deprive her of his company in the parlor that evening. With Jake at the boardinghouse, she looked forward again to the nights by the fire, as she had when Jason and Billy roomed there.

Jake's interest in her still baffled her, for no one had ever given her such consistent, personal attention. His offer to teach her to ride in the spring indicated both that he enjoyed her company and that he intended to continue living in Rosita past winter. But although she appreciated his consideration, a part of her remained skeptical. For Billy had made promises too—to take her fishing, to show her how to spot gold traces in quartz—but he had never carried through on them. And Billy and Jake were alike in many ways.

They differed, too, she thought as she entered the hotel. Both made her laugh; both treated her as if she were special to them. But with Jake she sensed more than friendship. He demonstrated an almost parental concern. Then again, she reasoned with a touch of sadness, perhaps she only imagined the fatherly affection because she longed for it so desperately.

chapter
21

WITH JAKE AROUND the month of November was a lively one. The frequent, heavy snowstorms made his delivery schedule erratic, so he often had days at a time when blizzard conditions kept him off the road. When he was not working, he kept Anna company in the kitchen, helping the long, monotonous hours pass with stories of his extensive travels and adventures.

The snow stopped briefly during the first week of December, giving the braver area residents a chance to come into town. As usual, business picked up in the dining room. Anna and Kate worked steadily on Saturday, preparing extra food and quantities of hot coffee for their cold, hungry customers.

Late that night Anna dressed for bed, then crossed over to the chest of drawers to extinguish the oil lantern. As she reached for the lamp, she spotted an envelope perched atop the bureau. The letter from Jessie. She had forgotten all about it.

The note, penned six weeks ago, had arrived just that afternoon. With her full schedule, she had only been able to scan the letter when Jeff gave it to her at suppertime. She could not retire for the night without rereading it.

October 27, 1878

Dear Anna,

Please forgive me for being so late in answering your last letter. You know how terrible I am at correspondence. But thank you for your faithfulness in writing to me.

I have been very happy with my position here at the Commerce Bank. Knoxville is a nice town. Two weeks ago I was able to visit with the Forresters after church. I have the distinct feeling that Miss Sarah has asked them to keep an eye on me.

Well, I am finally an aunt. Danny and Karen had a little boy on August 31. They named him Daniel Robert Meyers. Daniel is after Danny, of course, and Robert is after my father. My parents would be so proud to know that they have a grandson.

I have not seen little Daniel yet, but I hope to this Christmas. I am looking forward to spending the holidays with Danny and his family.

My one regret at not spending Christmas in Knoxville is that I will miss someone very special. His name is Nicholas Powers, and he works at the bank with me. I didn't know if he liked me at first, but I decided that he did when I dropped a loaded cash box on his foot and he didn't get angry at me. Fortunately, he had on hard boots and only broke two toes.

It is quite late, so I had better close. Miss McNamara here at the boardinghouse makes all us girls keep strict hours. And since I am already in trouble with her for staying out late last week (I was having dinner with Nick's family), I had better obey her rules to the letter (at least for a while). Please write again soon.

Love as always,
Jessie

Anna chuckled at the note, realizing that her friend from St. Matthew's had not changed. The letter reflected both the buoyant spirit and the independent attitude that made Jessie unique.

Her eyes moved to the section referring to Danny's

newborn son. Daniel Robert Meyers. Anna Kathleen Logan. Anna after her Grandmother Logan, Kathleen after ... perhaps a relative on her father's side? She wondered.

The information about Jessie's young man grated ever so noticeably. Another pair. She blew out the lantern with a disgusted huff, the anger directed at herself, not Jessie. She was genuinely pleased that her friend had found someone. She would not give in to the jealousy that lurked within, to the envy that had reared its head earlier in the evening when Claire and Tim stopped by for supper. She would not go to bed in such a foul mood.

She would think of something positive. The approaching holidays. No, she still had too much work to do on her gifts. Billy. Yes, that was it. Billy had sent a message with Jake that very day informing her that he would be coming in for breakfast in the morning. She would set aside her negative thoughts and concentrate instead on how good it would be to see Billy again.

But the unpredictable prospector did not show up the next morning. As she cleared away the breakfast dishes, she tried not to be discouraged. Billy had let her down again, though, and she could not escape the depression that accompanied that fact.

That afternoon, as she finished drying the dinner dishes, Anna cringed inwardly when she saw Jake approaching. She felt certain that she could not tolerate either his cheery enthusiasm or his comments about Billy at this particular moment. Fortunately, he managed to avoid both.

"Annie, I know you're busy, but if you've got some time now, I was wondering if you would do me a favor."

"What is it?" she sighed, resenting his intrusion upon the time she had intended to spend alone.

"Well, I've got this friend. I've told him a lot about you, and he's been wantin' to meet you. I was goin' to bring him by, but he's hurt his leg. I'm on my way over to see him now, and it would sure mean a lot to me if you'd come along."

"Could you just bring him by when his leg gets better?"

"I'd rather not."

"But today's not a very good day. . . ."

"It'll only take a minute."

He had helped her so many times that she could not very well refuse his request. She agreed, donned her coat, and accompanied him out the front door and down the street. They strolled past F. L. Miller & Company, turned left onto Euclid Avenue, and stopped when they reached the Rosita Livery.

"Your friend works here?" she inquired. But Jake remained silent until they reached the fourth stall from the end.

"Well now, Amigo, how are you doing? I brought Annie here to see you, just like I promised. Annie, meet Amigo, the best horse this side of the Mississippi. And Amigo, this is Annie. Isn't she the prettiest thing you ever laid eyes on?" The brown and white pinto snorted, shaking his head in agreement.

"So, this is your friend," Anna chuckled. She patted Amigo's nose but stiffened when he nuzzled her.

"Don't be afraid." Jake reached into his pocket for a chunk of sugar and pressed it into her palm. "He just wants something to eat. Hold out your hand . . . there. You see? There's nothing to be afraid of."

"How did he hurt his leg?"

"He sprained it in a pothole. He'll be fine in a week or so. I wanted you two to meet, because the more you see of each other, the quicker you'll get used to each other. Then, come spring, teachin' you to ride him will be as easy as pie."

"Then you were serious about teaching me to ride?"

"Sure. That is—if you want to."

"I'd love it," Anna replied eagerly, her mood changed again by Jake's thoughtfulness.

They spent another few minutes with Amigo before heading back outside into the cold, clear daylight. Anna turned instinctively toward the boardinghouse.

"Where are you goin'?" Jake asked.

"Why, back to the hotel."

"Oh no, you don't. Not yet."

"But Kate will need me soon to. . . ."

"Kate won't be needin' you 'til four-thirty. I know that for a fact, because I asked her. So, since there's no rush, you just come along with me, because I've got somethin' in mind for us to do."

There was no arguing with Jake. He grasped Anna's arm firmly and pulled her alongside him as he crossed the street. Before she knew it, he had led her to a small building hidden in an alleyway away from the central business district.

"A Mexican restaurant?" she gasped as he opened the door and pushed her inside. "But Jake, we just ate. And I feel like a traitor! We do have our own restaurant, you know! What if someone sees me here?"

"Just tell them we're checkin' out the competition," he laughed as he followed a young Mexican waitress to a table. "Besides, we're not havin' a whole meal. You ever have a buñuelo?"

"A what?"

"A buñuelo. You'll like it."

And she did. Expecting the food to be spicy, Anna studied the platter suspiciously when the girl brought their order. But her eyes brightened with pleasure as she bit into the crunchy, round flour tortilla sprinkled with cinnamon and sugar. She

had difficulty deciding which she liked better—the warm
buñuelo or the steaming Mexican chocolate drink that Jake
had requested to accompany the crispy treat. He promptly
ordered second servings for them both.

As they walked back to the boardinghouse, Anna thought
she would burst.

"You were right, Jake! I loved the Mexican food—especially the buñeulo. And I know why you did this today. You
were trying to cheer me up."

"I just don't like to see you feelin' sad, that's all."

"I'm sorry that I let everything get to me like that."

"No need to apologize. We all get to feelin' pretty low
every now and then."

"Even you? In all the time you've been staying with us, I've
hardly ever seen you discouraged. You always seem so happy,
so cheerful."

"Well, I have my moments too." His deep voice grew
suddenly still. "There've been times when I thought the whole
world was crashin' down on me."

Noting the change in his tone, Anna could not help but
glance toward him. As she did, she observed again that
sorrowful, distant look in his eyes. She wanted to reach out to
him, to encourage him to confide in her as she had in him.
But before she could express herself, they had arrived back at
the boardinghouse.

Once inside, Anna busied herself at her tasks, reflecting
upon her afternoon excursion. But she was troubled by Jake's
reference to his difficult past. She chided herself for not
speaking up, for not letting Jake know that he could trust her
with whatever it was that was bothering him. But perhaps it
wasn't too late.

After her cleanup duty, she peered into the parlor. Jake was
not there. She returned to her room, but after working on

Kate's maternity blouse for a while, she decided to check the parlor again to see if by chance he had come in. She found him standing in front of the fire, his back to her as he rested his right foot on the low stone hearth.

She waited, almost afraid to disturb him. Then, mustering her courage, she approached him.

chapter
22

"Jake?"

He looked up.

"I was hoping I'd find you. I looked for you earlier, but I guess you must have gone out."

"I went to check on Amigo."

Anna took a seat on the sofa. "I'd like to apologize for what I said, Jake. I didn't mean to upset you."

"It wasn't your fault. Not at all. Sometimes I just get thinkin', that's all."

"About what?" she ventured, hoping to draw him out.

"About my wife."

He said the words so calmly, so lovingly, that her heart went out to him.

"Your wife? I didn't know you were ever married."

"It was a long time ago. We were only really together for two days."

"What happened?"

"She died." He stood silently for a moment, then turned to sit on the hearth. "It was during the War. We ran off and got married while her pa was away on business. We were plannin' to head for Texas to get a little place of our own. But when we got to the preacher's house in Lexington, we heard about the War breakin' out. I told her we'd best wait, since I'd have to go back to Virginia to fight. She had her heart set on gettin' married then and there, though. I guess I did too, or else I wouldn't have let her convince me that we should still go through with it."

"But why wouldn't you have wanted to go through with it?" Anna inquired innocently. "I'd have thought that the War would have made you both want to be together more than ever."

His eyes widened in exasperation. "I didn't have any way of takin' care of her, that's why! I couldn't send her to my uncle's in Richmond, not after I'd run off the way I did, and I didn't know how long I'd be gone!" His fervor lessened as he added, "She said she wanted us to get married before anything could happen to spoil it."

"Didn't she have a family of her own? Parents? Brothers and sisters?"

Jake breathed deeply. "Yes—she had her pa. She stayed with him, but it was hard for her. You see, her pa didn't think much of me. I was afraid of what he might do if he knew we were married."

"Why didn't he like you?"

"Oh, lots of reasons. For one, I was a southerner, and he was strong for the Union. Then too, I didn't have much schoolin'. He took a lot of pride in book learnin'. But I guess mostly he just thought I wasn't good enough for her. No matter how much work I did for him, he just figured I wasn't responsible enough. I was just a hired hand, you see, and I'd traveled all over, like I told you before." His voice grew intense. "But just because a man's a drifter, it doesn't mean he can't settle down and put down roots. I'd have made a good life for us, I swear it!"

"I know you would have, Jake," she agreed sympathetically.

"And your wife must have believed in you too, or she never would have gone against her father's wishes and married you. I'm sure the two of you would have had a wonderful life together. How did she die?"

He remained silent for so long that Anna wondered if she should have asked.

"How'd she die?" he reflected, his voice laced with bitterness. "Well, I always figured I knew that. I came back from the War during a short leave, and I found her grave there by her ma's. Her pa came out and told me to leave, told me she'd died from a fever. He said she'd been real weak from being sick, and that the fever was just too much for her. But he lied to me, Anna." His clear tone rang out angrily as the monstrous truth dawned on him afresh. "He stood there, and he knew the truth, and he lied to me!"

"You mean she wasn't dead?" Anna gasped.

"She was dead, all right—but she didn't die from a sickness. She was weak from having a child. *My* child." He stared at Anna, his voice pleading. "I didn't know, Anna! All those years, I didn't know! I swear it."

"Of course you didn't know," she assured him, attempting as best she could to console the guilt-stricken man. "If you had known that you had a child, I'm sure you would have done everything to make a good life for the two of you. But how did you find out about all of this? And do you know what happened to the baby? Is he living with your wife's family?"

"*She,*" he corrected quietly. "I have a daughter." He paused, then pulled a round, shiny object from his shirt pocket. After fingering it for a moment, he handed it to Anna. "It's a locket," he explained. "Abby gave it to me when I had to leave. Her picture's inside."

Anna held the medallion carefully, opening it slowly for

fear of breaking the delicate hinges on the beautifully engraved case. As she studied the small, round portrait, her eyes widened in disbelief. She stared at the painting, then at Jake, her face reflecting the shock that she felt. The woman in the locket was her mother!

"My wife's name was Abigail Logan," Jake announced as evenly as he could. "She lived on a tobacco farm twenty miles south of Frankfort, Kentucky, with her pa, Caleb Logan."

"But, then . . . then . . ."

"I'm your father, Anna."

Anna stared at him, her mind racing.

"I swear to you, Annie, I swear on Abby's grave that I didn't know. Not 'til that Sunday when we got to talkin'. Before that I just thought it was a coincidence, you lookin' so much like her and havin' her ma's name. But when you told me the rest, then I knew. And I knew what Caleb had done. I always knew he didn't like me, but I never figured he hated me so much as to keep me from knowin' about my own daughter."

Dumfounded by Jake's startling claim, Anna sat motionless while he continued talking.

"I know you might not believe me, Anna, but I can prove it to you. I've got somethin' else here, too." He produced a faded yellow paper which he promptly unfolded and placed in her hand. "It's Abby's and my marriage license. You see? We got married on April 15, 1861. I know it's a lot to take in all at once. But it's the truth."

She finally found her voice. "Why didn't you tell me sooner?"

"I wasn't sure you'd believe me, me bein' a stranger and all. Then too, I didn't figure it would hurt us to get to know each other first." He cast his gaze downward. "Anyway, you bein' almost seventeen, I wasn't sure you'd even want a pa now.

And besides, I didn't know what all Caleb might have told you about me."

"He didn't tell me anything! Nothing at all!" she cried, blinking at the tears that filled her eyes. "How could he do that when he knew you were alive?" Her wonder increased as the meaning of Jake's declaration sank in. "There were so many times I needed somebody! And I've imagined every possible explanation for Grandpa never saying anything about you. I thought you didn't want me, that my mother didn't want me, and, with my name being Logan like her maiden name, I was even afraid sometimes that. . . ."

Jake knelt in front of the sofa and grasped her shoulders firmly in his hands. "Annie, now you listen here. I showed you the wedding paper. Your ma was a fine woman, and I know she loved you more than anything. I would have too, if I'd have known. But I do know now. Your grandpa cheated us out of a lot of good years together. We can't go back, but we can start from right here, if you want to."

His words touched her deeply, increasing the flow of tears down her cheeks. She could hardly believe his story. Yet his account made sense. The locket and marriage certificate provided positive proof of his claim. He was her father. After all the long years of wondering, she knew.

"Then my name . . . my name is really . . ."

"Your name is Anna Tyler."

As the initial shock began to wear off, Anna was flooded with excitement.

"Annie, we both know all the facts now, but if you want to wait awhile to tell other folks, I'll understand. It might be kind of embarrassin' for you."

"Don't you ever say that," she insisted. "As far as other people are concerned, well, my friends will be delighted. And I don't really care what anyone else has to say about it. I can't

think of anyone I'd rather have for a father than you, Jake."
She hesitated, then ventured, "I mean . . . Pa."

Jake beamed with pride. "Well now, I'd say we've had quite
a night!" He rose to his feet. "I guess we both have a lot to
think about. What say we call it a day, and I'll walk you to
your room. We can talk more about all this in the mornin'."

Anna stood, nodding in agreement. They walked slowly to
the kitchen, but as they reached her bedroom door, Anna
could not resist the urge to ask him one final question.

"Jake, I mean, Pa, what were your parents' names?"

"William and Kathleen Tyler. Why?"

The glow on her face fairly illuminated the dark kitchen.
"Oh, I just wondered, that's all."

In bed, Anna could hardly sleep. She was overjoyed with
the revelation that Jake was her father. Yet her grandfather's
deception troubled her greatly. Despite his plan, however,
God's intervention had overruled Caleb's effort to keep Jake
and her apart. How different her past would have been had
Jake known the truth from the beginning. But God had
brought them together at last, and she would not question
His timing. She would simply treasure the second chance He
had given them.

The next morning Anna's friends were astounded by the
news. Since she did not wish to disclose all the personal
details of the complicated story, Anna presented Jake's case
discreetly by revealing only the very basic facts. The marriage
certificate and locket, in combination with her own tintype,
left no doubt in anyone's mind as to their relationship.

Beginning that very day, Anna and Jake spent as much time
together as possible. Whether they bundled up for a quick
walk, visited with Amigo, or merely sat by the fire, they
talked, filling in the gaps of history that each was curious to

know about the other. Through the cold, snowy weeks, they caught up as best they could on the years they had lost.

Although Anna valued all the personal information her father shared with her, the stories most precious to her were his memories of her mother. Through Jake's eyes, Anna saw her as the loving, loyal, beautiful woman he had loved.

But his bitter remembrances of Caleb cut her deeply. To her he had been a kind, loving grandparent, the only real parent she had ever known. Until now. The fact remained that he had perpetrated a cruel deception that had drastically altered their lives. Anna determined not to feel bitter, but to make the most of her time with her newfound father.

chapter
23

JAKE CELEBRATED BY LAUNCHING A CAMPAIGN to spoil his daughter. Through the Christmas season he surprised Anna with gifts and took her on short outings.

Four days before her birthday, on a Sunday after church, Anna joined Jeff and Kate as they walked back to the boardinghouse. As they neared the hotel, Anna noticed a handsomely decorated sleigh parked right in front.

"Somebody's going to have fun today," she commented. "It's a perfect day for a sleigh ride. I wonder who. . . ."

But there was no time for further musing. Just then Jake emerged from the hotel door. He deposited a stack of folded blankets into the sleigh before spotting the trio as they approached him.

"Well now, it's about time you got here!" he barked in mock anger. "Anna, you'd best get inside and get changed— and make it quick!"

"Pa, what . . ."

"Don't argue, now. We've only got this thing 'til nightfall, and that comes plenty early this time of year."

"You mean you *rented* this?" she exclaimed, slightly aggravated by the outlandish gesture. "Pa, you know I can't go for a sleigh ride. I still have work to do!"

"Not today you don't." He glanced toward Jeff and Kate. "Isn't that right?"

"Absolutely," Kate affirmed.

"But . . ."

"It's called having a day off," Jeff stated. "We think you're about due one."

"And don't worry about a thing," Kate assured her. "Jeff is going to help me."

"That's right," he boasted. "I'm going to do the serving in the dining room."

"Of course, Jeff isn't a permanent replacement by any means," Kate laughed. "Or we might lose what business we have."

"Well, what are you standin' there for? Get goin'!" Jake insisted.

"But we'll need some lunch. I'd better pack . . ."

"Lunch and dinner both are in the picnic basket on the kitchen table," Kate announced. "Just pick it up on your way out."

Although still somewhat dizzy from the unexpected turn of events, Anna hurried inside, changed into her warmest clothes, and fetched the heavy basket. Not until she and Jake were actually situated in the sleigh did the entire situation seem at all real.

Jake snapped the reins, and the horse picked up speed. They glided down Tyndal Street, leaving Rosita behind them as they wound their way around the low hills west of town.

"I hope you aren't too mad at me," Jake ventured quietly.

"Mad at you?"

"You sounded like you were, back there in town."

"Well, Pa, you just took me by surprise, that's all. I'm sorry if I gave you that impression. It's just that, with you. . . ." She paused, then laughed brightly. "I never know what you're going to do next!"

As Jake relaxed, his face assumed its natural, placid expression. "Well, somebody's got to keep you on your toes, and I figure that's my job."

They wandered through the snow-covered hills, and Anna's heart thrilled at the beauty all around her. After weeks of being confined indoors, with people everywhere she turned, she welcomed this taste of solitude. Today she felt as if she and her father were the only two people in the world.

Jake followed the curving road for some time. Turning off the main path, he proceeded north, heading into territory totally unfamiliar to Anna. When he made yet another deliberate turn to the left, Anna could not contain her curiosity.

"Pa, are we going somewhere in particular?"

Jake grinned. "It seems to me that I remember a young lady tellin' me once she'd like to see Billy's mine."

"We're going to Silver Cliff? Really?" she cried. "Does Billy know we're coming? Isn't it dangerous there anymore? I can hardly believe it!"

"Now just slow down there," he laughed, visibly delighted with her enthusiastic response. "One question at a time. Yes, we're goin' to Silver Cliff. We won't be ridin' through town, since this is a shortcut, but you're still to stay away from it unless I'm with you, understand? And yes, Billy knows we're comin'. I told him we'd be over this way with some lunch. So he should be there waitin' for us."

The knowledge of their intended destination added to her pleasure. But one more surprise lay in store for her. As the sleigh descended onto the open plain in which Silver Cliff was situated, Anna was able to see the entire range of the Sangre de Cristos, the full view unobstructed by the foothills that had previously concealed much of their beauty. The panorama before her literally took her breath away.

In the distance Anna could see clusters of brown buildings that she guessed to be the town of Silver Cliff. She also spied the steep white cliff from which the town drew its name.

At last Jake pointed to a tiny cabin just ahead. "There it is."

Billy's house reminded her of those first pathetic homes she had seen when she first arrived in Colorado—the houses built in haste, with the intention of being improved upon at a later date. Directly behind the cabin hovered the familiar wooden hoist, a simple tower constructed with more care than the house since, to the miner, it served a more practical purpose than did a comfortable dwelling.

Billy greeted them enthusiastically and offered immediately to show them around his claim. Anna would have preferred going directly inside to warm herself. But she did not want to hurt Billy's feelings, so she accompanied the men as they walked past the rickety cabin toward the mine shaft. When they reached the hoist, Anna peered through the sturdy timbering into a deep, black hole.

"There she is," Billy boasted. "The Sitting Duck Mine."

"How deep do you have her now?" Jake asked.

"Twenty-five feet."

Anna shuddered at the very thought of lowering oneself to such a depth in total darkness. Remembering the many deaths each year attributed to falls and other mining accidents, she thanked God that her father had chosen a less hazardous occupation.

"Why did you name it 'The Sitting Duck'?" Anna asked.

"Because that's what he feels like with all the claim jumpers around here!" Jake laughed.

"That's not far from the truth," Billy chuckled. "Actually, Anna, when I was on my way through here in July, I saw a duck just restin' on the ground, takin' his own sweet time. And I thought he'd make a real good supper. So I got my shotgun, got him in my sights, pulled the trigger, and darned if that little bugger didn't up and fly off. So instead of hittin' the duck, I blew a hole in the ground—a hole that showed a good vein of silver."

"So you see," Jake added with a grin, "sometimes it pays to be a lousy shot."

Once in the house, Jake and Anna stood by the potbellied stove, anxious to thaw out after their chilling trip. The drafty, one-room cabin seemed no warmer to Anna than the boardinghouse's back porch. She wondered how Billy expected to live there through the winter without catching pneumonia.

Since Billy seemed ready to eat, Anna sorted through the various packages of food to separate their lunch from their supper. Kate had packed enough for an army. Anna laid out the roast beef sandwiches, bread and butter pickles, applesauce, and chocolate layer cake. That left ham and cheese slices, biscuits, and ginger cookies for the evening meal.

Without a doubt, Billy enjoyed the lunch. Before Anna and Jake were half through with their sandwich, Billy had polished off his first and had bitten heartily into a second. Judging from his eagerness at the table, Anna guessed that it had been some time since he had eaten a well-rounded meal.

"Are there any good restaurants here in Silver Cliff?" she inquired.

"That depends on what you mean by a restaurant," Billy replied between mouthfuls. "Ed Austin—he runs that general store in Rosita—he opened up a place last week. The Horn Silver Saloon. And Lou Slavich has opened up a saloon too. But there's nothin' like your hotel, if that's what you mean. No sir, this lunch here is a real treat. How's your business, by the way?"

"Slow. But that's pretty typical for winter."

"That's true enough. Oh, Jake, that reminds me. I'll be needin' you to make a run for me by Wednesday. Can you schedule that in?"

"No problem. This isn't exactly the busiest time of year for Carlin's either."

"Speakin' of winter," Billy mentioned, "how are you farin' in the cold, Jake?" He grinned. "You know, when you decided to winter it out in Rosita, I knew somethin' was up. I just knew it! You've never liked the cold—never. So I knew you were up to somethin'."

"Oh, you did, did you?"

"I figured either you'd gone completely loco—which could well have been the case, now that I think about it—or else you had a mighty good reason for stayin' put." He glanced at Anna with fondness. "I'd say you had a pretty good reason at that."

The rest of the afternoon passed quickly. Anna listened with amusement as her father joked and reminisced with the gravel-voiced miner. But with the hour growing late, the visit ended.

Anna thanked Billy for his hospitality, then insisted that he keep the rest of the food. She and Jake climbed into the sleigh and departed, retracing their route in relative silence, neither wishing to break the quiet spell created by their glistening, serene surroundings.

Dusk had settled on Rosita when Jake halted the sleigh outside the hotel. Anna offered to go with him while he returned the rented sleigh, but he insisted that she had been out in the cold long enough.

"Besides, since you gave away my supper, I figure you owe me somethin' to eat," he teased. "Now you just get inside and see what you can rustle up."

Anna slid closer to him on the hard wooden seat and gave

him a warm hug. Climbing down from the sleigh, she gathered the empty picnic basket and the rumpled collection of blankets. While Jake pulled away, she stepped over to the front door, numb from the cold but tingling from a warmth inside. As she opened the door and entered the small, cozy room, assurance encompassed her as completely as did the warmth of the building. For her father was there, and he really loved her, as she loved him. Never had she felt more secure.

Anna's feelings of security did not last long. Throughout the next day, her pleasant memories of the outing with her father were disrupted by a sobering thought. St. Matthew's might not believe Jake's incredible story. If not, they might make her go back.

She had never really discussed the orphanage with her father. After his initial questioning about the care she had received, he seemed to have purposely avoided the topic. Anna could sense that he felt a tremendous guilt about her having to live there. So, to avoid hurting his feelings, she had put off explaining the fact that she was still very much under their care.

Through the years, Anna had needed and appreciated the Home's protection. Now she feared it.

From St. Matthew's point of view, Jake might easily appear to be a drifter who was taking advantage of a vulnerable young girl—a girl who happened to have a sizable inheritance waiting for her when she turned eighteen.

Her father knew nothing about Caleb's will, for she had never mentioned the trust to anyone. But St. Matthew's would be within their moral and legal rights to question Jake's claim. And knowing the integrity of the officials there, Anna was certain they would do just that.

She would have to write to Miss Sarah soon. The longer

she waited, the more suspicious the situation might look. And she would have to talk to her father about St. Matthew's too. As much as she dreaded doing both, she knew that she could not delay much longer.

chapter
24

THREE DAYS LATER Anna still had not taken any steps to clarify her position with either St. Matthew's or her father. But the fault was not entirely her own. For she was absorbed with another problem—the economy of the community.

She pondered the matter as she kneaded a ball of bread dough on Wednesday morning. She knew to expect a slump at this time during the year. But the situation this winter seemed worse than in the previous year. No one had stayed in the hotel for almost two weeks, and the boardinghouse was down to five roomers. Today she had been instructed to bake only half of her regular quantity of baked goods. Half! Financially, the business was getting by. But its present status simply would not do.

As she mulled over the problem, an idea occurred to her—a ridiculous, intriguing idea that grew more promising the more she considered it. She could hardly wait until Jeff and Kate returned from Kate's appointment with the doctor to confront them with her proposition. After making them sit down at the table, she began.

"You know how slow business has been here lately." She allowed them time to nod before continuing. "Well, I may have come up with a way to make more money."

Jeff looked at Kate, then back at Anna. "Well . . . go on."

Before outlining her actual plan, Anna confessed that something had been bothering her since her visit with Billy. When he mentioned Silver Cliff's lack of adequate eating places, an idea had taken root. The camp needed a good restaurant. But she had reasoned then that opening a new restaurant in the neighboring town would be impractical. It was the middle of winter, and no one knew how long Silver Cliff's diggings would hold out. Despite the negative factors, however, she could not forget Billy's voracious appetite or his sincere appreciation for the meal she and her father had shared with him. And if Billy had welcomed the food with such eagerness, other miners would probably do the same.

"So," she concluded, "what would be wrong with trying something for a day or two? Kate, you and I could make up simple meals like the one you packed for us on Sunday. And Jeff, you could ride over to The Cliff around lunchtime and see if there are any buyers. What do you think?"

Kate spoke first. "You know, Anna, that sounds like a pretty good idea!"

"It's certainly worth a try," Jeff speculated, his enthusiasm growing as he considered the prospect more carefully.

After a session of excited chatter, the three decided to prepare twenty sandwiches and two spice cakes for the following day's experiment.

That next afternoon, as Anna served the meager luncheon crowd, she wondered how Jeff was faring in Silver Cliff. She so hoped that her plan would prove successful. But when Jeff returned later in the day, his face bore a serious expression.

"Didn't . . . didn't the food sell?" she stammered.

"Let's just say we misjudged the market," he sighed. But his somber expression cracked a second later. "I could easily have sold *three* times as much food as I took there!"

"Then ... then ... they *wanted* it?"

"And did they! Anna, my dear, it looks like we're in business."

With her financial worries laid to rest, Anna set her mind on writing to St. Matthew's. Late one night she finally finished the long letter. She read it one last time, then folded it carefully and placed it on her dresser. Her part was finished now. Tomorrow the news would be on its way. She would try not to worry about the outcome.

Feeling suddenly hungry, Anna donned her robe and stepped into the kitchen. To her surprise, Kate, Jeff, and Jake were still gathered around the table. Aside from drinking coffee and eating leftover apple brown betty, the group seemed to be in the middle of a serious conversation. Not wishing to disturb them, she started back to her room. But Jeff called to her.

"Anna, don't go, please. You should be in on this too."

She joined the threesome, curious as to what subject could be so engrossing as to keep them up past eleven o'clock.

Jeff explained that they had been discussing the incredible success of their lunch wagon venture. Anna's perception and inventiveness had provided the hotel with a healthy supplemental income.

"Since the new business has no building to maintain and no expenses to speak of, we can't help but make money," Jeff pointed out. "But in mining towns, as you well know, fortunes can change in a very short time. Kate and I feel that, with a little foresight and some careful planning, we may be able to turn the extra revenue we're getting now into more permanent gain."

"What do you have in mind?"

The plan, Jeff admitted frankly, involved considerable risk.

Not until spring would they know with any degree of certainty whether Silver Cliff would still be in existence. If the ores died out, so would the town. In that event, "Anna's Lunch Wagon" would have served as an adequate means of profiting from the neighboring camp.

But if the silver did not give out and if more strikes were made, then Silver Cliff would become a boom town, drawing new prospectors like a giant magnet. If that happened, they could capitalize on the town's sudden prosperity. The incoming miners would need food and shelter—both of which could be provided by a new boardinghouse in Silver Cliff.

The investment would be purely speculative. For now would be the time to purchase a suitable property and the necessary lumber for the project. Waiting to buy either one after the boom would be putting money into someone else's pocket. The venture would also mean finding and training staff for the Silver Cliff boardinghouse, since Jeff preferred that Kate and Anna operate their present establishment. With Silver Cliff's reputation for violence, Jeff wanted the women to stay in Rosita. As supervisor, he would divide his time between the two towns.

"It's risky," he concluded. "But the more I think about it, the more I think we should go ahead with it. I'd like to start scouting out property right away. If we can get decent prices on the land and the lumber, we'll probably be able to pay for them from the profits on the lunch wagon. If Silver Cliff falls flat, then the worst that can happen is that we'll have lost our extra income. But if it booms, then we'll be in on the groundwork. And that's where the money is."

Anna could hardly believe her ears. Opening a second boardinghouse would be quite an undertaking. But Jeff's reasoning seemed sound. The more she thought about the venture, the more it fascinated her.

After discussing the matter for a while longer, Jeff and Kate retired for what was left of the night, leaving Anna and Jake alone in the cool, shadowy room.

"So, I take it you're all for the new place in Silver Cliff," her father remarked.

"It does sound like a good idea." She glanced toward him, detecting a look of uncertainty in his eyes. "You don't think it's going to work, do you. Why?"

"No, I didn't say that," he protested. "I just don't like the load that will fall on you. Do you have any idea what you'll be in for if they open up another place?"

"Me? Pa, Jeff said that other people will be running it. So it won't really affect me all that much."

"Yes it will," he corrected. "Maybe by the middle of summer things will get back to normal, but 'til then you'll be snowed under. First off, you'll have to help train the cooks and the other workers. And the new place will need blankets and sheets and curtains and who knows what else. They'll have you sewin' all that stuff, plus runnin' this place with Kate. And don't forget that the baby will be due. They'll probably want you to help with him, too. And, 'til the new place opens up, you'll be runnin' yourself ragged makin' food for that lunch wagon."

"Pa, I know it will be hectic for a while, but I'm used to working and I won't really mind."

"I know you won't. You're a fine girl, Annie. No matter what's come your way, you've met it head on. I'm proud of you. But, you know, things don't have to be like they are now, with you workin' from mornin' 'til night for other folks. I'm here now, and things can be different if you want them to be."

"What do you mean?"

"I've never come right out and said this before, because I

214

didn't know how to put it or even if you'd want me to. But I *am* your pa, and I can provide for you. You don't have to keep workin'. I have some money saved, and if you want to, we can leave and get us a little place somewhere. With the way things were when you were growin' up, I couldn't take care of you properly. But you can have a home with me—if you want it."

Deeply moved by his offer, Anna remained silent while she searched for the right words.

"Pa, the idea sounds wonderful, and I hope we can have a home someday. But I like my job here. And Jeff and Kate need me, especially with the baby coming. Besides, you and I are still getting to know each other. I think we should take our time before we do anything as major as moving away." She introduced the main reason behind her hesitancy, deciding that it was now or never. "Anyway, I've just finished writing to St. Matthew's. The Home is still my legal guardian. I couldn't go anywhere without their consent."

Her statement seemed to hit him like a ton of bricks.

"But you've been out here on your own for three years! And you're a thousand miles away!"

"I'm working here with the permission of the Home. I'm their ward until I'm eighteen. They keep a close watch on me in spite of the distance between us. The Pattersons report to them twice a year and I have to write several times a year to tell them how I'm doing."

"But I'm your father. You don't need them anymore."

"I know. That's why I wrote to them. I explained everything, and I'm sure they'll recognize your legal rights."

"They'll want proof that I'm your pa."

"We have proof."

His expression grew grim. "You're my daughter, Anna, and no orphanage is gonna have charge of you. Leastways not anymore. Not as long as I'm around. And if they try to give us trouble, they're in for a fight."

Judging from the look on Jake's face, Anna knew he meant every word he had said. He would fight if need be to claim her legally as his daughter. And though she loved him even more for the commitment he had just made to her, she hoped with all her heart that it would not come to that.

chapter
25

"It's just no use, Anna . No matter what you may have done to the dress, I'm still going to look like a cow."

Anna laid down the gown she was holding, struck a stiff pose, then placed both hands on her hips. "Claire Randall, enough of that kind of talk. You do not look like a cow, and you will not look like one in this dress. And how will you even know if you don't try it on?"

Claire's well-rounded form wobbled awkwardly as she trudged across the small front room of her home. But her eyes brightened when she reached the sofa and picked up the dress. "It does look pretty. You put lace on it and everything! It doesn't look like a blue gunnysack anymore!"

"I told you we could fix it up."

Anna helped her pregnant friend out of her housedress and into the transformed gown. Claire peered as best she could over her protruding stomach to examine the final product.

"Oh, Anna, thank you! It will be so nice to have something pretty to wear when I meet Tim's parents."

"You know, Claire, I'm a little surprised that Tim's parents are coming now, in the middle of July. If they would wait until the end of August, they'd be almost certain to see the baby."

"I know. But they're working their visit around a business trip." Claire patted her stomach and eyed Anna's slender waist with envy. "I think I'd make a better impression on them if I went in in the middle."

"Oh, Claire," Anna laughed. "You don't have a thing to worry about—except getting the house cleaned and supper fixed before the five o'clock stage gets here! So let's get busy. Where should we start?"

"Anywhere!" She grimaced as she began unbuttoning her dress. "Anna, I'm going to owe you so many favors. You fixed my dress, and now you're helping me with my work when I know you're swamped at the boardinghouse."

"Believe me, we're not swamped. The boardinghouse in Silver Cliff—now that's the hectic place. We have the workers all trained now, so my worries are over as far as the new place is concerned. I'm back to my regular routine. Kelly Patterson has been helping us since Kate had her baby. As a matter of fact, Kate told me that they could handle things just fine, so I'm to take my time and not worry about getting back to serve dinner. So you're going to have to feed me."

"I think I can manage that. Seriously, though, I do plan to come over to your house to help you out when you have a baby. So I will be paying you back eventually."

"Just don't be too anxious to pay me back," Anna warned. "Because you'll be in for a long wait. Now, let's get to work."

The two worked steadily, but made their tasks enjoyable by mixing plenty of chatter with their chores.

"Anna, I've been meaning to ask you if you've heard any more from St. Matthew's since they wrote asking all those questions."

"No," Anna sighed. "I just wish we'd hear something soon. At least I *think* I'd like to hear something soon."

"How does your father like working over in Silver Cliff?"

"Just fine. He doesn't say much, but I can tell that he likes construction work better than hauling ore. He did a beautiful job on the new boardinghouse. Jeff made a smart move when he asked Pa to help him build it."

After working all morning, the two women stopped to enjoy a relaxing lunch. They then tackled Claire's supper menu, preparing what they could ahead of time. By two-thirty they had completed their tasks, so Anna headed for home.

She strolled leisurely up Grouse Street. The hot sun beat upon her bare face and arms, its harshness countered by the cool breeze that whipped through the surrounding hills. Of all the seasons, Anna found summer the most enjoyable. Rosita's ideal location in the high valleys of the Wet Mountains provided its residents a cool, comfortable escape from the intense summer heat felt by those living on the prairies.

Before turning onto Tyndal Street, Anna glanced around her. Her heart was saddened by the distressing scene before her. How Rosita had changed. So many more people had left in the spring when they heard of more new strikes in Silver Cliff. And though their departures had not surprised her, she was dumfounded when she discovered that they were taking their houses with them. The high cost of new lumber induced many of the people to tear down their houses, haul the timber to their new location, and rebuild there. All around her, lots lay vacant—lots that just three months ago had contained sturdy homes, fences, and woodsheds. Today those same buildings stood in the ever-growing community of Silver Cliff.

Many hotels and businesses had moved too, though not as literally. But their departures proved beneficial to Anna and her co-workers. With less competition in town, the Rosita Hotel still drew a modest amount of business.

The hotel stood quiet as she entered. As was her habit, she peeked into the empty parlor to make sure the room appeared tidy. When it passed her inspection, she headed into the dining room. But the sight there filled her with chagrin—Kelly Patterson had once again done a haphazard cleaning job.

Anna sighed, then spun into action. She put the tables and chairs in order, then began sweeping the floor. But as she pushed the broom under the table near the window, she hit something. When she leaned over to retrieve the dark, rectangular object, she noticed with surprise that it was a carved leather wallet.

She stared uneasily at the bulky purse. She hated to open it, but she would never know who it belonged to if she didn't look inside. So she unfolded it. To her relief, its bulkiness was not due to a store of cash. Its principal contents were papers—contracts of some sort. She thumbed through the documents until she spotted a business card.

William Randolph Sinclair
Attorney-At-Law
Silver Cliff, Colorado

She folded the wallet slowly as she considered what to do. She did not know Mr. Sinclair, and since he lived in The Cliff, she could not return his lost property personally. Her father could deliver it, but he would not be returning from Silver Cliff until tomorrow night. She would take it to the sheriff. Perhaps Mr. Sinclair had already contacted him about the loss.

But when she arrived at his office, the sheriff was nowhere to be found. Disappointed, she turned to retrace her steps. But as she did, another idea occurred to her. What would bring an attorney from Silver Cliff into Rosita? The courthouse. Mr. Sinclair just might be there.

Pleased at her ingenuity, Anna marched purposefully to the City Hall, her slim figure erect with confidence as she entered the building. Once inside, she approached the middle-aged clerk who was seated at a desk in the foyer.

She cleared her throat. "Excuse me."

The heavyset, balding man looked up from his papers with some reluctance. "Yes?"

"Excuse me, sir. I'm looking for an attorney by the name of Mr. Sinclair."

"Sinclair?" His resonant voice reverberated through the tiny, silent room.

"Yes. William Sinclair from Silver Cliff. I was wondering if you knew whether or not he was still here."

He leafed through a thick black book on his desk. "Let me see. Yes, here it is. William Sinclair. A two-thirty session with Judge—"

"Are you looking for me?"

Startled by the man's remark, Anna turned abruptly. Her surprise increased when she saw the man himself. He did not look at all as she had expected an attorney to look. Well over six feet tall, the attractive young man seemed to be in his mid-to-late twenties. Curly black hair framed an oval face, drawing attention to the dark lashes fringing his clear blue eyes.

He moved toward her easily, crossing the room in but a few strides. His powerful form seemed unencumbered by the stylish dark gray vested suit he wore, with starched white shirt and black tie.

"If you're looking for William Sinclair, then you've found him. What can I do for you, Miss . . ."

"Tyler. Anna Tyler."

"All right, Miss Tyler. How may I help you?"

Anna suddenly felt self-conscious. "I—I don't need any legal advice," she stammered.

His full mouth formed a winsome smile. "That's too bad. I thought I might be getting my first pretty client. If this isn't a business call, then to what do I owe the pleasure?"

Embarrassed but flattered by his comment, Anna tightened her grip on the wallet. "I work at the Rosita Hotel. When I was sweeping the dining room just a while ago, I found this." She lifted her hands to display the leather purse.

The young lawyer's face flooded with relief. "My wallet!" He pulled it eagerly from her hands and made a hasty inventory of the contents. "Everything's here!" He then issued an immediate apology. "Not that I thought you would have taken anything. Please forgive me. But I've been working on these contracts all week, and I thought they had been stolen. What luck! Thank you so much, Miss Tyler." He pulled several bills from their resting place. "I'd be more than happy to compensate you for your trouble. These contracts are quite valuable."

Anna winced—the idea of accepting money for performing an honest deed was offensive to her. Her tone grew noticeably cooler. "No, Mr. Sinclair. That is not why I returned it."

Realizing his mistake at once, the young man replaced the cash and eyed her sheepishly. "Well, let me see. I've known you for two minutes, and I've already insulted you twice. I would say that I'm getting off to a pretty bad start, wouldn't you?" His expressive eyes locked onto her own. "I'm terribly sorry—again."

"That's all right."

"You said you work at the Rosita Hotel? I'm sure I didn't see you today when I was there. Believe me, I would have remembered."

She flushed again. "Today was one of the few days I wasn't working."

"Just my luck," he frowned.

"Speaking of work, Mr. Sinclair . . ."

"Will."

"All right, Will. I'm late as it is, so I must be going."

"Could I see you back to the hotel? I'm all finished here."

Seeing no reason to deny his request, Anna consented. The two left the courthouse and ambled up Tyndal Street.

As Anna studied her new acquaintance, she decided that in many ways he reminded her of Jason. Like the knowledgeable newspaperman, Will had doubtless received considerable formal education. His fashionable attire and polite manner suggested a well-to-do family background. And, like Jason, Will radiated a confidence that seemed to permeate the atmosphere around him. Yet, as she compared their likenesses, she noted with pleasure one marked contrast. Will lacked the arrogance that Jason had possessed.

"How long have you lived in Rosita?" the bright-eyed attorney inquired.

"Three years. Have you lived in Silver Cliff long?"

"I came here from Colorado Springs two months ago. I thought I'd try my luck up here, because, frankly," he chuckled, "the town needs all the legal help it can get. But I'm originally from St. Louis." He slowed his pace as they drew near to their destination. "How about you?"

"I came here from Frankfort, Kentucky."

"Does your family operate the hotel?"

"No. My father does construction work in Silver Cliff. I work here for Jeff and Kate Patterson."

"Jeff Patterson." Will's eyes narrowed as he considered the name. "Doesn't he have a hotel and boardinghouse in Silver Cliff too?"

"Yes. The Silver Cliff Inn." Anna stopped at the hotel's front door. "Well, here we are."

Will reached for the doorknob, but instead of turning it,

rested his hand on it. He gazed at her intently. "Thank you again, Anna Tyler. I hope to see you again very soon." He pulled open the door, and she stepped inside.

As the door closed behind her, Anna paused for a moment to allow her thoughts to settle. Her excursion to locate William Sinclair had turned into quite an adventure. The handsome young attorney was certainly charming. And he had seemed interested in her.

She shook her head as she moved through the dining room. Anyone as attractive and as interesting as William Sinclair could have his pick of women in Rosita, in Colorado Springs, and even in St. Louis. He was probably just being polite. Yet he had specifically said that he hoped to see her again. And, she decided, she rather hoped he had meant it.

chapter
26

TRUE TO HIS WORD, Will did reappear—and much sooner than Anna had anticipated. That very evening, he patronized the dining room before traveling back to Silver Cliff. While being most careful not to interrupt her serving duties, the young man did not miss any opportunity to talk with her again.

Will's attention greatly elevated Anna's mood. But she felt certain that his interest would wane when he discovered how little they had in common. So during the next two days, she pushed their two encounters from her mind, concentrating instead on her work. By Sunday evening she had all but dismissed any notion of seeing him again.

That night, as she was caring for the needs of the last four customers in the dining room, she heard the clang of the bell at the front desk. She paused just long enough to retrieve the "Dining Room Closed" sign before marching into the entryway to post the sign and to help the new arrival.

She stopped short when she saw Will leaning against the front desk, his back to her. Dressed casually in dark blue trousers and a blue plaid shirt, he stood staring into the parlor as if anticipating an answer to his summons.

Her quiet voice broke the silence. "Good evening."

He turned immediately, his handsome face bright with a pleasant smile. "Good evening, Anna."

She moved behind the desk. "Do you want a room?"

"Yes. I have an early court date tomorrow morning, so I'd like to stay in Rosita tonight. I just thought I'd give your place a try." His blue eyes fastened on her as she handed him the register. "I was hoping to see you tonight, but I didn't think it would be this soon."

His directness caught her off guard. She was relieved when he turned his attention to the hotel register, penned his name in a flourishing script, and pocketed his room key. Looking up, he spotted the small sign she was holding.

"Am I too late for supper?"

Anna ventured a mischievous grin. "Not if you can beat me to the door. I haven't hung the sign yet."

The two entered the dining room, where Anna guided the young man to a corner table and poured him a cup of coffee.

She took his order and promptly delivered his beef enchilada supper. After collecting payment from the departing patrons, she cleared their tables then approached Will's table to refill his coffee cup.

"Could I bring you some dessert? We have flan or apple pie."

"Flan? What is that?"

"It's a Mexican dish. A type of baked custard."

"Well, I've gone Mexican this far, so I might as well finish up the way I started. Flan it will be. And, Anna," he coaxed gently, "would I be presumptuous if I asked you to join me for dessert?"

Encouraged by his invitation, she responded positively. "Not at all. I'd be happy to join you."

She removed his plate, left the room, and returned quickly with two dishes of the pale caramel flan and a cup of hot coffee. While she placed the items on the small table, Will rose to help her with her chair.

"So, you're a teetotaler," he noted. "What other important facts should I know about you?"

Anna smiled at the charming young man, wondering how he could make her feel so comfortable yet so awkward at the same time. "There's not much to know."

"Oh, I don't believe that for a minute." He paused long enough to take a bite of creamy custard. "This is good!" When he scooped up another spoonful, Anna took advantage of his temporary silence to change the subject.

"Is your family back in St. Louis?"

He hesitated ever so slightly before answering. "Yes— parents, brother, and sister. My father has a law firm there."

"Living here would be quite a change from living in St. Louis. What brought you to Colorado?"

"The lure of the West, I guess. My uncle has a ranch just outside Colorado Springs. I used to spend summers there when I was growing up. It's not hard to fall in love with this country. I moved to Colorado Springs a year ago, and then decided to open a practice up here. How about you? What brought you all the way from Kentucky?"

Wishing to avoid discussing her complicated history, Anna answered as simply as she could. "Work."

"What about your family? Do you have any brothers and sisters?"

"No, I'm the only child. My mother died when I was a baby, so there's just my father and me."

The flan disappeared too quickly. Finally Anna announced that she needed to get back to her work. When she stood, Will rose as well. His impressive frame towered above her.

"If the parlor isn't off limits to hotel guests, I think I'll catch up on some reading."

"The parlor is for everyone, so feel free to go in. Will, thank you for the dessert."

"Thank you for joining me. And Anna, if you'll let me know when you're finished, I'd be happy to see you home."

She was unaccountably pleased with his offer. "Thank you, Will, but I *am* home. Pa and I live here."

As they spoke, Anna heard the swish of the swinging doors and a familiar call.

"Annie? Annie, are you . . ."

She and Will turned to see Jake entering the room. He stopped abruptly when he saw his daughter with a customer.

"Excuse me," he muttered. "I thought everybody was gone." He started to leave the room, but after scrutinizing his daughter's companion, crossed the room to join them.

"Here, Annie," he volunteered warily. "Let me help you carry the dishes." He stood next to Will, where his own lofty height allowed him steady eye contact with the stranger.

"Pa, this is Will Sinclair," Anna announced. "He works over in Silver Cliff. And Will, this is my father, Jake Tyler."

Will extended his long arm to offer a firm handshake. "I'm pleased to meet you, sir."

When Jake put forth his hand, Anna felt a sense of relief. Her father's reaction, though guarded, could have been worse. She was grateful that Will had worn casual clothing. For had Jake met him in his courtroom attire, he most certainly would have branded the young man a "city slicker," a breed for which he had little tolerance.

With the introductions out of the way, Will courteously excused himself. Anna said little as she and her father cleared the table and retreated into the empty kitchen to tackle the clean-up task.

Jake reached for a dry towel and wiped the dishes as she washed them. "That fella out there. You know him from somewhere?"

"We met a few days ago. I found his wallet on Friday." She tried to appear nonchalant, but by the time she finished relaying the incident, she was no longer able to disguise the sparkle in her voice.

Kate entered the kitchen to resume the tasks that had been interrupted by her hungry young son. "Here, Jake, let me do that," she insisted, pulling at the dish towel.

Jake gave up the wet rag willingly. "I guess I'll call it a day. I may go on out to the parlor for a bit. See you in the mornin', Annie."

Anna's heart plummeted. She could just picture him cornering Will in the parlor to grill him as to his intentions.

"Pa," she called out.

"Yeh, Annie, what is it?"

She stammered, unsure of what to say. For if by some miracle the idea of pumping Will had not yet occurred to him, she did not want to be the one to suggest it.

"Oh, I . . . I just wanted to check with you about your dinner tomorrow. Do you want me to pack roast beef sandwiches, or would you rather have some of the chicken left over from this afternoon?"

"The chicken would be fine."

She watched him leave, then continued washing dishes, trying not to think about the conversation he and Will might be having. After all, her father would never purposely embarrass her, nor would he embarrass Will. And if he did bring up the delicate subject of their friendship, she would just hope that the young attorney would not take offense.

The following morning Will's behavior appeared unchanged. His friendly attitude increased Anna's confidence, filling her busy day with anticipation. She mentally reviewed his complimentary remarks as she bent over her washtub to scrub the piles of soiled laundry. As she carried two dripping bedsheets to the clotheslines, she wondered if the proper young man from St. Louis would find her so interesting once he realized that she was little more than a maid. But her thoughts were interrupted by a sudden cry.

"Anna! Anna!"

Anna peered around the wet sheets to see Kate hurrying toward her, waving a piece of paper. Puzzled at first, Anna's heart jumped within her as her friend drew closer with what she could clearly identify as an envelope. She had finally heard from St. Matthew's.

After delivering the letter, Kate returned to the kitchen to give Anna some privacy. Anna clutched the envelope tightly, afraid to open it. Perhaps Miss Sarah would instruct her to return to St. Matthew's until they could reach a decision. Jake had assured her that he would accompany her if they requested that she come back, but she so prayed she could stay. Her hands trembled as she opened the letter.

June 2, 1879

Dear Anna,

I trust this letter finds you well. Thank you for your prompt reply to our last inquiries. The additional information you supplied has proven most helpful.

I hope you were not unduly upset by our last communication when we informed you that the Frankfort Courthouse had no record of your mother's marriage to Jacob Tyler. However, after learning from you that the wedding was performed in Lexington, we inquired there and have been able to trace those records. In light of this fact, we are quite willing to conclude that your legal name is indeed Anna Kathleen Tyler.

However, we must still verify beyond the shadow of a doubt that the Jacob Tyler currently living in Rosita is the same Jacob Tyler who married Abigail Logan, and that he is neither a misguided soul nor an imposter. It is our sincerest wish that you will bear with us in this endeavor and trust that we are interested solely in your welfare.

Using the information you sent us regarding Mr. Tyler's tour of duty with the Confederate army, we have begun an investigation into his service records. However, since his regiment records were stored in Richmond, we may not be able to secure them. As of yet, we have had no reply to our inquiries there.

In order for us to have a better understanding of Mr. Tyler's character, we feel that we must ask for local references from your friends and associates in Rosita. Please explain our dilemma to both Richard and Jeff Patterson and to your minister. We would very much appreciate hearing their evaluations of Mr. Tyler's claim.

After locating your parents' marriage certificate, we felt it necessary to inform the First National Bank of Frankfort of your current situation. They were most interested in Mr. Tyler's claim and have offered to assist with our investigation. They feel, as we do, that a personal interview with you and Mr. Tyler would help to speed up the process of reaching a correct decision. However, due to the time and expense involved in making such a trip, the bank has engaged a lawyer in your area to look into this matter for them. If you have not already heard from either the bank or their attorney, you will be receiving word from them directly.

Again, Anna, I thank you for your cooperation and your understanding. During this difficult time, please remember that we at St. Matthew's want only the best for you. We hope to have this entire matter resolved to everyone's satisfaction in short order.

Sincerely,
Sarah Johnson
St. Matthew's Home for Children

Confused by the multitude of details Miss Sarah had covered, Anna read the lengthy letter several times. She had hoped for either a "yes" or a "no" so that she and her father would at least know where they stood. But the letter only confirmed one thing—that the decision was still up in the air.

She scanned again the one encouraging paragraph. At least the Home now recognized her parents' marriage. They knew that she was really Anna Tyler.

But the rest of the letter filled her with anxiety. She cringed at their investigative techniques—tracing her father's service records and requiring local references on his character—as if he were a criminal. How humiliated her father would feel if they continued their relentless personal probing. And now the bank would be in on the digging too, with their inquisitive attorney. She dreaded the thought of sharing this new information with her father. She wouldn't blame him if he decided that claiming her legally just wasn't worth the embarrassment.

But her father did not share her feelings. When she discussed the new developments with him that evening, he assured her repeatedly that their personal inquiries would not upset him. So they settled back to do the only thing they could do—wait.

chapter
27

As Anna awaited further word from St. Matthew's, one factor made the frustrating period more tolerable. Will made a habit of stopping by whenever he came to town. Anna looked forward to his frequent visits, which, due to his unpredictable schedule, were generally unannounced. He did, however, make a firm date for the official statehood celebration on Friday, August first.

Since the party was one of the town's more formal occasions, Anna decided to wear the yellow silk gown that her father had bought her for Christmas. She thought the fitted dress looked especially becoming, since its pale color struck a contrast to her dark eyes and brown hair.

Her escort thought so too. As she entered the parlor where he was seated, Will eyed her approvingly while rising to his feet.

After exchanging quick greetings, the two stepped out the front door and moved slowly toward the City Hall. Anna glanced at Will, noting how at home he appeared in his stiff but stylish clothing.

"I'm sorry I was late. I hope I haven't made us miss anything."

Will seemed in no hurry. "That's quite all right. I know

how difficult it is for you to get away. And to be perfectly honest, I was almost late myself. A client needed some last-minute counseling."

"Then your business is thriving?"

"As a matter of fact, I won an important case today. I'm glad that Uncle Charles convinced me to come here."

"Congratulations! Then tonight's party was timed perfectly. We can celebrate statehood and your victory at the same time."

The celebration could not have gone better. Anna and Will spent a great deal of time visiting with Claire and Tim. The two men seemed to take a liking to each other. And to Anna's delight, Adam and Lydia Burdick were amazingly cordial.

But the most surprising event of the night occurred just as they were leaving. As they started out the doorway, they were accosted by Mr. Whitfield, the English businessman who was stationed once again at the Rosita Hotel with his demanding spouse. The stylishly dressed gentleman did not approach Anna, but Will.

"Good evening, Mr. Sinclair."

"Mr. Whitfield," Will acknowledged, extending his hand.

"I must say, sir, that in spite of our . . . what shall I call it . . . in spite of our ordeal this afternoon, I do believe that congratulations are in order. I was most impressed with your showing in the courtroom." He turned to Anna. "Young lady, this young man is quite an attorney."

"Excuse me, Anna," Will began. "This is Mr. Whitfield. And Mr. Whitfield, this is—"

"Why, Miss Logan! No need for an introduction, Mr. Sinclair. This young lady and I are already acquainted." He smiled pleasantly. "My dear, I didn't recognize you. You look positively smashing. Don't you agree, Millie?"

The dark-haired matron did not exude the same charm.

"Miss Logan? Not the same one from . . . my goodness! You're right, Edward. I wouldn't have recognized her either."

"Oh, do pardon me, Millie," her husband declared. "You have not yet met this gentleman. William Sinclair, may I present my wife, Mildred Whitfield."

"Were you representing Edward in that dreadful case this afternoon, Mr. Sinclair? Honestly, when you consider that the judge chose in favor of that shabby Mexican instead of Edward's company . . ."

"Millie, dearest," Mr. Whitfield interrupted, "if you will allow me to finish, I believe you should know that Mr. Sinclair was not furnishing my legal counsel. He was representing my opponent, Mr. . . ."

As he fumbled for the name, Will completed it for him. "Gutierrez. Carlos Gutierrez."

"Yes, that's it. You'd think that I could remember that name. It cost my company quite a bit of money. Or shall I say *you* did, sir. But that's all water under the bridge, as they say." He discussed the matter with remarkably good humor. "Yes, indeed, that was some defense you presented. You made me feel like a masked bandit robbing the poor man of his only income. But I have learned one thing. The next time I'm faced with a dispute over ownership of a mine, I know what lawyer to engage. If you ever need a good lawyer, Miss Logan, this is the man."

At that, the Whitfields excused themselves, leaving Anna and Will free to leave the party. Once outside the City Hall, Anna could not resist bringing up the topic of the courtroom battle.

"I didn't realize that your case today involved Mr. Whitfield. I knew that he was working on some kind of a legal problem, but I didn't know you were his opponent."

Will ventured a sly smile. "If I had known that you knew him, I might have asked you to spy on him for me."

"It doesn't sound like you needed any help from me. What was the case about?"

"Mr. Whitfield's corporation is investing in mining interests in Silver Cliff. Mr. Gutierrez had signed a contract selling his mine, but he changed his mind when he hit a really big vein of silver."

"But was that fair? If he had already agreed to sign . . ."

"He was railroaded into signing, Anna," Will exclaimed. "Mr. Whitfield seems like a nice enough man, but he's a shrewd businessman and he can be very devious. I know his type very well. And I know Mr. Gutierrez's type too. He was an easy target for someone like Mr. Whitfield."

"But how did you ever win? I've always thought that it was almost impossible to break a written contract."

"There was a small technicality," Will admitted unashamedly. "You see, Mr. Gutierrez basically owned the mine, but when he filed the original claim, it was on his wife's birthday. As a present to her, he put the deed in her name. So, technically, the property belonged to her, and she hadn't signed the contract." His voice grew strangely quiet. "For once I found a loophole that helped the victim, not the villain."

Anna gave him a quizzical glance. "Will, earlier tonight you said your uncle had talked you into coming up here. What did you mean?"

"You have a good memory." He stopped and leaned against a hitching post. "You said something to me once about the change it must have been for me coming here from St. Louis. Do you remember that? Well, Anna, changes can be good. This one certainly was."

He watched her closely, as if to determine whether she would be interested in his story. Satisfied that she was, he continued. "When I moved to Colorado Springs last year, it

236

was out of sheer disgust. I had gone through law school and was working with my father. His firm is very well known in St. Louis and in the eastern United States. Most of his clients are people like the Whitfields.

"Anna, when I went into law, it was to help people—not to supply greedy executives with legal ammunition." He paused. "When I left St. Louis, it was after having a real battle with my father. I was supposed to issue a foreclosure to an Italian businessman. The whole thing was just a scheme designed for stealing his business. Mr. Pasculari was successfully diverting the market from the business of one of Father's major accounts. And they wanted the man stopped.

"But I wouldn't do it. In fact, I switched sides and offered my services to Mr. Pasculari. With my knowledge of the case and of the tactics my father was going to use, we managed to win. Needless to say, my father was furious. But then, so was I."

"I don't understand the man, Anna! He's a genius! He could help people. He could fight corruption instead of encouraging it!"

He paused again, this time to calm down. "When I moved to Colorado Springs, it was simply to work for my uncle. I didn't practice law, and I wouldn't even consider handling any legal matters. I didn't do anything but ride horses and rope cows. But Uncle Charles—and the Lord—kept working on me. I finally decided to give the system one more try before throwing it all out. And so here I am."

Wishing to comfort him, Anna instinctively reached out, resting her hand on his arm. As she did, he covered her small hand with his large one.

Once outside the hotel, Will stopped Anna just short of the door. "Anna, I know this is short notice, but Mr. Gutierrez came by today to invite me to a celebration tomorrow night.

His house is just outside Rosita—not far from here at all. Would you come with me? I'll warn you, though, that Carlos may be the only one who speaks any English. And the place will be swarming with all his relatives. It starts at six o'clock, but I could come by for you at eight. I'm sure they wouldn't mind. Would you come with me?"

"Yes, I'd like to."

"Good. And Anna, before we go in, thank you for the lovely evening."

"Are you staying here at the hotel tonight?"

"Yes. And I told your father that I'd have you home at a decent hour. So, Anna, until tomorrow then." His eyes locked with hers as he pulled her hand to his lips and kissed it softly.

"Until tomorrow," she repeated. They stepped inside.

The next day could not pass quickly enough. Anna spent much of the day recalling the previous night's experience. But her excitement turned to anxiety when Jeff delivered a letter to her late that afternoon.

July 23, 1879

Dear Miss Tyler,

The First National Bank of Frankfort has informed me of your current situation and has asked that I act in their behalf in evaluating Mr. Jacob Tyler's legal claim. I would therefore like to meet with both of you to discuss this matter in its entirety.

For this purpose, I will be arriving in Rosita on Tuesday, August 12. If this date is not acceptable to you or Mr. Tyler, please wire me at once. Otherwise, I will look forward to meeting with the two of you then.

Sincerely,
Justin T. Cosgrove
Attorney-At-Law
112 Front Street
Pueblo, Colorado

After reading the letter, Anna waited restlessly for her father to return from Silver Cliff. But to her dismay, he did not arrive home that evening before Will stopped by to escort her to the Gutierrez party. So she joined him with mixed emotions, and said very little.

Mr. Gutierrez's party temporarily distracted Anna from her worries. The host and hostess welcomed them as the honored guests and happily introduced them to every member of their boisterous family. Anna was surprised to discover that they had prepared an elaborate supper, and that they had delayed serving it until her arrival. Never had she tasted such a variety of delicious Mexican dishes.

Few of the family members spoke much English, but they managed to communicate quite clearly both their joy in being able to keep their property and their heartfelt affection for Will, who had made their victory possible. Anna felt proud to be in his company.

With the hour fast approaching midnight, Will finally convinced his grateful client that they had to be on their way. He and Anna stepped out into the clear night where a full, round moon illuminated the darkness. When Will reached for her hand, his action filled Anna with a comfortable boldness.

"What did you think of that meal?" he asked.

"Delicious! The food was all so good."

"And spicy!" he chuckled. "I tried to warn you about that green vegetable dish, but you had already taken a big bite."

She laughed brightly as she remembered the episode. "I thought I knew what it would taste like, because I've had it before. I just hadn't had Grandma Gutierrez's version of it!"

"What was it, anyway?"

"Nopallitos. It's a cactus. And I think Grandma Gutierrez forgot to take the needles out!"

Will joined in with her laughter and squeezed her hand. But when he spoke again, his tone was serious.

"Anna, before I forget, I'd like to apologize to you."

"Apologize? For what?"

"For earlier this evening when I came to get you. Don't you remember? When we passed Mr. Whitfield in the entryway, he called you by the wrong name again. He keeps addressing you as Anna Logan. I should have corrected him."

"Will, I . . . well, Mr. Whitfield wasn't exactly wrong. Up until last December, that was the name I was using."

He stopped in his tracks. "The name you were using? I don't understand."

She briefly outlined her background, beginning with her early years at St. Matthew's and ending with the afternoon's unsettling notice from Pueblo. To her relief, Will reacted calmly. Far from being repelled by her story, as she had feared, he seemed to admire her even more for her courage and resolute faith.

Before resuming their walk, Anna timidly ventured a question. "Will, if this thing with Pa . . . if it ends up that I need a lawyer, would you consider . . ."

He reached to clasp both of her hands in his. "Anna, do you even have to ask me that?" He pulled her closer, leaning down to plant a light kiss on her lips.

As he pulled away, he moved his hands up her arms to gently grip her shoulders. "On second thought, maybe I shouldn't agree to represent you."

"Why not?"

"A good lawyer never becomes too involved with his clients, or he won't have the proper perspective." He slid his arms upward again, cupping her face in his hands. "And Anna, where you're concerned, I couldn't possibly be objective."

He leaned down again, finding her lips once more. This time, as his warm mouth lingered upon hers, the tender kiss built to such an intensity that it startled her. She gently but firmly pushed him away.

They walked the rest of the way back to the boardinghouse in silence, for neither wished to disrupt their newfound happiness by speaking. Before seeing her inside, Will embraced Anna once again, his kiss binding them firmly. As they parted company in the dark, chilly entryway, each knew that the small spark flowing between them had been fully ignited. They would never be the same.

chapter
28

AFTER WHAT SEEMED LIKE AN ETERNITY, the dreaded date of August 12 arrived. Though Anna did not look forward to meeting the four o'clock stage, she and Jake waited at the depot to greet the middle-aged attorney from Pueblo.

As the three of them walked to the hotel, Anna wished with all her heart that Will could be with her. But she understood and agreed with the reason for his absence. His presence could be misconstrued as a premature legal confrontation. Will did not want to start their interview off on the wrong foot by putting Mr. Cosgrove on the defensive.

Mr. Cosgrove himself showed little emotion. His stony face and expressionless eyes gave Anna no hint as to his reaction to their case.

Will stopped by briefly that evening to meet his traveling colleague and to offer what support he could to a weary Anna and a fidgety Jake.

"How are things progressing?"

"Who knows?" Jake muttered. "That man's a born poker player if I ever saw one."

"Will, when you talked to him, did he give you any idea at all as to what he's thinking?" Anna asked.

"No, I'm sorry, Anna. I haven't a clue. I didn't dare ask too many questions for fear of putting him on his guard. But if it's any consolation, I've made a few inquiries about him. He has a reputation for being very fair. But he's also very thorough. You may be in for a long siege."

The attorney stayed at the hotel, taking advantage of Anna's and Jake's residence there to continue his probing well into the night. Anticipating more questions the next day, Anna was surprised to learn that, after conducting interviews with Jeff and Kate, Richard Patterson, and the Reverend Scott, Mr. Cosgrove had departed for Cañon City on the noon stage.

Throughout the day she mulled over the wide range of questions he had asked her. She wondered what personal topics he may have discussed with her father during their private meeting. In her own session with him, she had been shocked to learn that, through the bank's wise investments of her trust fund, her inheritance had grown to the sum of eighty-eight hundred dollars.

While a part of her felt relieved to know that the meeting was finally over, the confrontation with Mr. Cosgrove in many ways increased her anxieties. For so much depended upon his evaluation. His reaction would influence both the bank's and St. Matthew's decisions. If he doubted Jake's credibility, then so would they.

She wished that the attorney had given her some indication of his feelings. Then she might at least know something. As it stood now, she was only certain of one fact—that she could not tolerate any more waiting. The more she considered her predicament, the more depressed she became. She could not bear to stand by helplessly while others dictated her future.

Both Will and her father sensed her despondency that evening. Though they attempted to be cheerful, neither of them could buoy her drooping spirits. When her depression continued through Friday, Jake resorted to extreme measures.

He waited until she had finished her supper cleanup duties before cornering her in the kitchen. "Annie, come here a second. I want to talk to you."

"Pa, I'm tired, and I'd just like to go to bed."

"I know. But this is real important."

Too exhausted to protest, Anna allowed him to pull her to the table. She sat on the bench and cast her gaze downward.

"I've got a plan, and I want you to hear me out. Are you listenin'?" She gave him a feeble nod. "Now here we are, just sittin' here hopin' to hear news that isn't likely to arrive soon. Will tells me that even if that poker-faced lawyer decides to believe our story, he's got to write all the details down and send them back to Kentucky. Then they have to think about it before they make their decision. Even after that, if everybody agrees, Will says that the Home will have to get a court date to go over all the evidence with a judge. It's the judge who'll have the final say. The court appointed St. Matthew's to look after you, so they'll have to be the ones to un-appoint them."

"Oh, no!" Anna sighed, discouraged even more by the new information.

"Now, just settle down. I can't believe that the good Lord put us together only to pull us apart again. And like I told you before, if they make you go back to Kentucky, then I'll go right along with you. And if the two of us end up going back, it looks to me like we just might have us some extra company on the trip."

"Extra company?"

Her father gave her a sly glance. "Don't you try to tell me that Will wouldn't be all bent out of shape if you were to head for Kentucky. He'd probably have all his fancy law books down off the shelves and into packin' crates in less than five minutes."

Her spirits perked at her father's conjecture. "You've seen Will's office?"

"A couple of times. I stopped in once or twice to chat, that's all. Anyway, to get back to what I was sayin', you and I aren't just goin' to sit here mopin' around. I happen to think that we'll come out of this fine. We should just feel glad that our part is all finished. We've done our best, and I think that calls for celebratin'."

She eyed him skeptically. "Celebrating?"

"That's right! I checked it all out with Jeff and Kate, and it's just fine with them. You and I are takin' a little trip."

"A trip? Pa—"

"Come Monday mornin', we're gettin' on that stage to Cañon City. We'll stay there Monday night. Tuesday mornin', we're headin' for the railroad station. We'll ride the Denver & Rio Grande straight through the Grand Canyon of the Arkansas, just like all the tourists. After that, I'm takin' you shoppin'. And we're gonna try every restaurant in town. You're not goin' to do any work at all. Then we'll head back on Wednesday."

Anna's mind flew in all directions at the same time. "But how can you get off work?"

"Don't fret about that. All you have to worry about now is gettin' your things packed and ready to go by Monday."

Jake's plan worked, for Anna's mood changed instantly. Through the weekend, she laundered the clothing they would need and made the necessary preparations for their upcoming adventure. The only problem she faced was putting aside her excitement long enough to get to sleep on Sunday night.

Their trip, the first real vacation Anna could ever remember, worked wonders for her lagging spirits. The ride itself followed the same route that Jeff had used to transport Anna and the Pattersons to Rosita upon their arrival in Colorado. She had forgotten what extremes in scenery could be found along the trail—sprawling meadows, winding mountain passes, and the spectacular view of Pike's Peak.

Jake had meant what he said about not working. After settling into their hotel, the two vacationers strolled through the city to do some sightseeing. The delicious french pastry Jake treated her to in no way spoiled her appetite for the tasty supper they purchased later at the hotel dining room. Before retiring for the night, as Anna sipped a cup of tea while soaking in a hot, sudsy tub, she felt positively sinful. But not nearly as sinful as she felt the next morning when she devoured a huge breakfast that had been delivered to her in her room. In spite of her occasional pangs of guilt, however, she enjoyed every luxurious moment.

As he had promised, Jake secured two tickets for the Tuesday morning train trip into the Grand Canyon of the Arkansas. As the excursion began, Anna sat calmly in her seat by the left window. For the first few miles, she gazed quietly at the Arkansas River, meandering alongside the narrow railroad tracks. But gradually the scene before her changed.

Though the train did not descend into the gorge, steep cliffs began to rise on each side, their height increasing with each bend in the roadway. Before she knew it, she was staring upward, craning her neck to take in the incredible sight. The solid granite walls rose one thousand feet on either side of her. The right side of the train ran so close to the mountain of rock that the passengers could touch the cold granite as they passed by.

But Anna could not reach the stone wall on her side of the train. For directly between her and the far cliff rushed the river, its swift current whipping forcefully through the ten-mile gorge. She shuddered at the thought of her father dangling by ropes above the white-capped water. The spectacle left her breathless.

When they returned to Cañon City, Anna had difficulty making the transition from the serene grandeur of nature to the noisy routine of the busy city. But after a late dinner, she and her father geared for an afternoon of shopping. Anna enjoyed browsing through the various shops. She made several purchases with the money she had brought with her. She found a new shaving mug and brush for her father, a tiny silver baby spoon for Claire's expected arrival, and some fabric and notions for a new dress.

The next morning, Anna and Jake boarded the stage for Rosita. Though reluctant to have her vacation end, Anna was ready to go home. The trip had been a wonderful, relaxing change of pace, but she had missed Will. She hoped that he would be coming into Rosita soon.

Late that afternoon, the stage rolled to a stop at the Rosita depot. After collecting their baggage, Anna and Jake made their way to the hotel. Anna hurried to the kitchen, where she found Jeff and Kate working side by side at the counter. After exchanging greetings, she jumped headlong into an excited recollection of the highlights of her trip.

"I've never felt so lazy in all my life," she concluded merrily. "If you'll give me a minute to change my clothes, I'll get to work. That is, if I can remember how!"

But Kate stopped her. "Anna, before you do anything, there's something you should know. Something . . . something happened while you were away."

chapter
29

"WHAT IS IT?" Anna asked. "It isn't Andy, is it? Nothing has happened to the baby, has it?"

"No, no," Jeff assured her. "Andy is fine. But there was an accident on Monday afternoon."

"An accident?"

"Yes. At Miller's. Adam Burdick was pulling a heavy box from one of the top shelves when the rung on his ladder broke. He fell."

"Adam's been hurt?"

Jeff glanced reluctantly toward Jake before fixing his gaze again upon Anna. "I'm sorry, Anna. He broke his neck. He's dead."

"Adam . . . Adam's dead? But he can't be. He just got married, and Lydia. . . . He just can't be." She thought she felt her father's arm around her shoulder, but she was still too shocked by the news to know that he was indeed standing next to her.

"Like I said, it happened on Monday," Jeff disclosed. "If it's any consolation at all, he never knew what hit him. He died instantly. We would have wired you, but since they planned the funeral for Tuesday, we knew that there was little chance of you getting back in time."

"The funeral was on Tuesday?" she whispered. "Then he's already buried?" The sound of her voice echoed strangely in her head, as if someone other than herself were speaking. "I've got to go over there—to the cemetery. And I've got to go see his family. Will you handle things here for me while I'm gone?"

"Of course we will, Anna," Kate assured her.

Anna moved to the back door as if in a trance. As she stepped outside, she grew aware of something heavy and warm resting on her shoulder. Her father still had his arm around her.

They trudged up the street to the cemetery where Jake quickly located the recently upturned plot. Even as she read the painted words on the wooden cross, she found them hard to believe.

Adam Burdick
April 13, 1858—August 18, 1879

How long she stood there she did not know. But at length her father guided her away from the grave, insisting that they be on their way. She would not go home, however, before stopping by to express her condolences to Adam's family. Although Lydia still did not wish to see any visitors, Sam seemed most grateful for her visit.

Only as she was leaving the Burdick home did the cold reality of Adam's death begin to dawn. Both the grave and Sam's reaction had confirmed what Jeff had told her. Adam was dead. By the time she reached the boardinghouse, the numbness had worn off completely. And in the privacy of her room, she allowed her tears to flow unhindered.

She slept little that night, but she rose early the following morning to assume her duties. Since she seemed determined to work, Kate and Jeff did not argue with her. She performed all her accustomed tasks save one, for Kate would not allow her to serve in the dining room. Adam's accident was still news, and since he was well known and well-liked in the town, his death was a principal topic of conversation among the patrons. Kate did not wish to expose Anna to the painful comments when her wound was still so fresh.

Everyone at the boardinghouse seemed to understand Anna's need for solitude. Even her father managed to give her a wide berth that evening, while at the same time making it clear that he was available if she needed him. He did, however, approach her before she retired to deliver a note from Will. Once in her room, Anna read the short message.

Dear Anna,

I stopped by to see you last night, but when Jeff relayed to me the tragic news of your friend's death, I thought it best to give you some time alone.

I met Adam only briefly, but he seemed to be a kind, likable person, as I'm sure he must have been since you valued his friendship so highly. Please know that I share your grief, and that my thoughts are very much with you.

With sincerest regards,
Will

Will waited until Saturday night before stopping by again. Knowing that Anna would not feel up to attending the town's scheduled square dance, he suggested instead that they take a walk. Anna readily consented to the change in plans.

As they stepped out the hotel's front door, Anna fell silently into step beside her lanky companion. Their limited conversation dwindled as they exhausted topics of discussion. Will questioned her about her trip to Cañon City, but she was not in the mood to detail her adventures. Silence hung heavily between them.

Finally Anna spoke. "You know, it's so ironic. Sam Burdick made Adam leave the mines because they were too dangerous."

Having voiced her thoughts, she felt more settled somehow, as if she had at least honestly shared her grief with Will. He said nothing, but reached for her hand. Though neither mentioned it, both could feel the tension lessening.

The slender moon barely illuminated the bumpy dirt road as they left the quiet streets of Rosita and moved north toward the tiny town of Bassickville. Will started to say something, but he hesitated, as if he expected this attempt at conversation to die away too. But at last he spoke.

"Did you hear that the Bassick Mine has been sold?"

"Sold?"

"That's right. One of my colleagues handled the transaction. The new owners will be taking over operations next month."

Her steady voice reflected a subtle change in her spirits. "Do you have any idea what the selling price was?"

"Five hundred thousand dollars, and a one-fifth interest in the company."

"Who are the new owners?" A thought occurred to her, so she did not allow him time to answer. "The Bassick Mine isn't one of the mines that Mr. Whitfield bought, is it?"

"No. I haven't met the new owners, but I do know they're from New York."

"I wonder what changes they'll make," Anna pondered aloud. "Most new owners tend to do that, you know. I hope they don't bring in their own crew. That would put a lot of men out of work."

"I haven't heard of any major reorganization plans so I would assume they'll keep most of the current employees. I do know of one change that's being made right now, but not by the new owners. By David Livingstone."

"Billy has mentioned him before. He lived in Rosita for a while just before I came, didn't he?"

"Yes. He's a nephew of the famous Dr. Livingstone in Africa. He left Rosita in '75, but he's back now with his wife."

"You said that he's changing something. What?"

"The name of the town."

Anna stopped in her tracks. "What? He's renaming Bassickville? Whatever for?"

Will shrugged his wide shoulders. "From what I understand, his wife doesn't care for the current name. They've picked out a Spanish one. I can't remember it at the moment. Anyway, with the new owners coming, Ed Bassick won't be living there anymore. So it won't really matter."

"But Ed Bassick discovered the mine and founded the town!" Anna cried, her voice rising in indignation. "You'd think that they would leave the name, if only out of respect for him!" She paused, then added decisively, "Well, they can call the town whatever they want to, but *I'm* still going to call it Bassickville!"

Will began to chuckle.

"What's so funny?"

"You are. I didn't realize that you have such a stubborn streak."

Anna found herself smiling. "Why not? You know my father."

Will squeezed her hand, and they continued their stroll. Anna sensed again the powerful current flowing freely between them.

"I've really missed you, Anna. I know you were only in

Cañon City for a few days, and I know that I often go that long without seeing you. But at least when you're in Rosita, I know you're within reach. Does that make any sense?"

"Yes. I missed you too."

Her words gave him all the encouragement he needed to wrap his arm snugly around her shoulder. She slid her arm around his waist.

"If Cañon City seemed like a hundred miles away, then Colorado Springs will seem like a thousand!" Will moaned. He turned to face her. "I don't want to go, but I must be there on Monday to handle a case."

She tried unsuccessfully to mask her disappointment. "How long will you be gone?"

He winced. "I don't see how I can get things worked out in less than three weeks. Anna, I'm going to miss you more than I can say." He leaned down and kissed her warmly.

She snuggled securely against him. "Just hurry back."

"Promise me one thing, though."

"What?"

"That you won't run off with some good-looking rancher while I'm gone."

"I suppose I can promise not to." She pushed him away just far enough to gaze into his eyes. "That is, if you'll promise me something too."

"Oh, no. I can see that I'm in trouble," he grimaced. "You're probably going to demand that I not look at any pretty girls."

She was about to confirm his suspicion when her mind unexpectedly flooded with thoughts of Adam. The smile on her face faded as her large brown eyes grew intense.

"No." She embraced Will suddenly and clung to him almost desperately. "Just promise . . . just promise me you'll come back."

Will returned her embrace with one of equal strength, assuring her all the while that he would come home soon and safely. When at last he managed to calm her fears, he held her at arm's length to study her face.

"I've just thought of something," he announced. "You know that expression 'Absence makes the heart grow fonder'? Well, I used to think it was true. But now I can see that it only works in some cases. It certainly can't apply to us."

"Why not?"

"Why not? Because if you can grow fonder of a person, then that means your relationship can stand some improvement. So, you see, that saying can't hold true for us. Because, my dearest Anna, how can anyone possibly improve on love?"

chapter
30

ORDINARILY, WILL'S LEAVING SO SOON after Adam's death would have increased Anna's anxiety. But his declaration had made their separation more bearable by erasing any insecurities she had concerning their relationship. Her heart thrilled at Will's expression of love. His acknowledgment had given her the courage to admit openly that the feeling was mutual.

At times, Anna's happiness would darken when she thought of the bereaved Lydia. She now understood more fully just how much the young woman had lost. But aside from these sorrowful moments, Anna felt a deep contentment.

The first week of Will's absence dragged by as visions of the handsome attorney dominated her thoughts. But an event in the second week pulled Anna suddenly from her remembrances of Will. For on Wednesday, September third, Claire gave birth to twin girls.

In the following days, Anna spent as much time with the new family as possible. She helped wherever she could with diaper changes, laundry, and meal preparations. Between her daily boardinghouse duties and her nightly visits with the infants, Sarah and Elizabeth, the remaining weeks of Will's trip passed almost before she knew it.

On September seventeenth, just two days later than he had anticipated, Will returned. The bright-eyed lawyer entered the dining room shortly before closing time. Anna wanted to drop everything to see him, but she still had three customers to serve. So she had no choice but to ask her visibly impatient beau to wait.

When at last she joined him in the parlor, she found to her dismay that he was not alone. Seated with him on the sofa were her father and Mr. Carlisle, their notoriously talkative boarder. Will looked up as soon as she entered the room. She crossed the parlor and, as casually as she could, chose the chair next to his.

"Welcome back," she ventured with a shy smile.

His deep blue eyes locked with her own. "It's good to be home."

"How was your trip? Did you win your case?"

He nodded but did not elaborate. "Your father tells me that you've been busy since I left. So, Claire and Tim are actually parents now. I'll bet they're delighted with twins!" He glanced toward Anna's father. "Jake, I know it's late, but would you mind if Anna and I went over to Tim's? Not for long, I promise. I'd just like to see Tim's new family and give him my congratulations." He turned to Anna. "That is, if you wouldn't mind."

In answer, Anna turned a radiant face to Jake. "All right with you, Pa?"

Unable to resist his daughter's plea, Jake gave in easily enough. Anna ran to fetch her coat, then met Will in the kitchen where they headed out the back door.

But before they had even left the porch, Will caught Anna in the shadows, pulled her against him, and embraced her longingly. "Anna, I've missed you so."

"And I missed you!"

"I hope I didn't seem too obvious in the parlor," Will apologized. "But I could hardly stand waiting one more minute to be alone with you."

The two moved hand in hand out the door into the cold September night.

"How were your relatives?" Anna asked when she had caught her breath.

"Fine. Uncle Charles is quite a character. I always enjoy seeing him."

"Did you hear any news of your family?"

"Yes. Aunt Clara got a letter from my mother while I was there. Father usually adds a note too. But since he didn't, I can only assume that he's still upset with Uncle Charles for taking me in. They've had their disagreements through the years, but in time they've always ironed things out. This rift has gone on for so long, though. I just hope I haven't involved Uncle Charles in the family feud."

Anna was about to offer consolation when Will changed the subject.

"Did you get my letter?"

"Yes. I was so glad to hear from you."

"I just had to talk to you, even if it was only on paper. Speaking of letters, have you heard anything from St. Matthew's yet?"

"No."

"Well, you will, believe me. And I'm sure it will be good news."

When they reached Tim's and Claire's house on Grouse Street, the new parents seemed more than eager to show off their newborn daughters. Sarah was sleeping soundly, but Elizabeth showed no inclination of joining her. So the couple had braced themselves for a long night.

With the hour already late, Anna and Will stayed only a

short time before bidding their friends goodnight and stepping back out into the chilly night. Despite the penetrating bite in the rising wind, neither Anna nor Will seemed in any hurry to reach the boardinghouse. They strolled at a leisurely pace until they neared a vacant building that shielded them from the wind.

Will stopped. "Anna, I wasn't going to ask you this yet, but will you marry me?" She had wanted to hear that particular question, but his timing caught her unprepared. Her heart raced as she opened her mouth to answer him.

But before hearing her reply, Will rushed into explanations. "I'd like to marry you tomorrow! But I'm not earning enough money to support a wife, so it can't be until I have more saved. And I want to ask your father for permission, not St. Matthew's. And he can't give his consent until this whole guardianship situation is cleared up. So, if you say yes, we can't really even tell anyone about it until heaven knows when. But Anna, I just need to know—will you marry me?"

"Yes, I will."

He gazed at her lovingly, his eyes mirroring his inner joy. "Then you won't mind the delay? Financially speaking, I need more time to build up my practice. I realize that you have a sizable inheritance coming to you when we marry, but I don't want to use that. That money is capital and should be saved for emergencies or for investments—not used for daily living. Day-to-day finances will be my responsibility. So I need to be sure I can handle them. And I'm serious about wanting Jake's permission to marry you. I know that technically we don't need anyone's consent. But I think a lot of your father, and it would mean a great deal to me to have his blessing. I want to have his approval before I take you away."

"I want that too."

"Then we're in agreement?"

"We agree. But Will, what if St. Matthew's says no? What if they want me to come back?"

"In that case, we will simply get married anyway. If the Home or the bank causes trouble for you after that, legally they won't have a leg to stand on."

"You're sure?"

"I'm sure. Just think about it for a minute, and you'll see that I'm right. The inheritance becomes yours when you turn eighteen or get married. Am I right so far?"

"Yes."

"Well, that little statement says quite a bit. Your grand-father's will gives you an option. It assumes that you may very well marry before you're eighteen. So the bank has no right to complain if you do, since the trust allows for that condition."

With her fears eased by Will's sound reasoning, Anna moved reluctantly from the protection of the building to resume their walk. But as they neared the hotel, Will let out a sudden cry. "Oh, no! I've just thought of something. I was planning on making a fortune out of your case," he teased. "But now that we're getting married, I suppose I'll have to give you free legal counsel."

Anna picked up on his playful remark. "Now, Will, don't take it so hard. After all, it's only money."

"Only money! Would you listen to that? It's only money!" He grew more serious. "Well, you're right. It is only money." His mouth formed a mischievous grin. "Besides, I'm very flexible on payments. I'll accept property, stock, or anything within reason as a substitute for cash."

"I see. But you only have one problem with that policy. Right now, I don't have any property or stock."

"Oh, don't worry," he assured her, giving her shoulder a gentle squeeze. "As I said, I'm very flexible. When the time comes, I'm sure we can work something out."

chapter
31

THE Home made ANNA WAIT one more month before announcing their decision. To everyone's relief, both the bank and St. Matthew's backed Jake's claim as legitimate and promised their support in seeking a transfer of guardianship from the court.

But not until November 12, 1879, did the official decision reach them naming Jake as Anna's legal father. Anna, Jake, and Will were elated with the news. Though Anna and Will wanted to ask Jake immediately for his consent to their marriage, both agreed that her father be allowed several days to enjoy his long-sought authority before being asked to relinquish it.

When at last Will brought up the question, Jake seemed in no way surprised. After consulting privately with his daughter, he gave the couple his wholehearted blessing.

With the personal and legal obstacles out of the way, Anna and Will forged ahead with their wedding plans. After deciding on an August date, the couple worked and saved diligently toward that end. They saw less of each other than they would have liked to, due both to the heavy snows and Will's determination to handle as many cases as he possibly could. But with the county seat in Rosita, they were at least assured some time together when Will's legal duties brought him to the land office, county recorder's office, or the courthouse.

When business at the Rosita Hotel hit its annual winter slump, Anna used her time wisely by concentrating her energies on sewing projects—two new dresses for her trousseau, bed linens, and a colorful patchwork quilt. Her sewing helped to pass the time, but it also increased her longing for August to arrive.

Her anticipation heightened in May when her father took her to Cañon City again, this time to select the material and laces for her wedding gown. Yet, in spite of her bouts with impatience, Anna did not really mind the months of waiting to marry Will. For during that time she spent many precious hours with her father—hours in which he confided more treasured memories of his secret courtship and short marriage to her mother. She would not have traded those moments for anything in the world.

Just five days before their wedding, Anna cleared the breakfast dishes away from Mr. Anders's table, breathing a sigh as she carried the heavy tray to the kitchen. She glanced at the clock. Almost a quarter past eight. Will had mentioned that he planned to stop by before his eight o'clock court appointment. It now appeared that she would have to wait until after the hearing to see him. He had probably gotten a late start from Silver Cliff again.

She fetched the coffee pot from the stove and moved back out to the dining room to refill the remaining two customers' cups. Business had certainly been slow. In fact, the hotel and boardinghouse had never pulled out of their winter slump. Each month fewer people patronized their establishment.

The Rosita Hotel was not alone in that respect. Through the summer, the entire town—or what was left of it—had felt the devastating financial impact of Silver Cliff's prosperity. The burgeoning town continued to draw more and more residents and businesses from Rosita. Anna understood the reasoning behind the ongoing exodus, but she could not help but resent Silver Cliff for sapping the lifeblood of her beloved town. She took pride in the fact that the house she and Will were buying was situated in Rosita, not Silver Cliff. The tremendous difference in housing costs between the neighboring towns had made Rosita a more practical place for the young couple to locate.

Focusing her attention back to the business at hand, Anna looked up to see a tall, solidly built gentleman of some fifty years passing through the dining room doorway. He smiled as she caught his eye, and though she felt certain that she had never met the gray-haired man before, she was equally sure that he looked strangely familiar.

"Good morning," she announced pleasantly as she crossed the room and guided the casually dressed man to a corner table. She poured him a cup of coffee, took his order, then returned shortly thereafter balancing a platter of hotcakes, scrambled eggs, ham, and a pitcher of warm syrup.

"Here you are, sir."

But apparently the stranger did not hear her. For just as she was placing the plate of food onto the table, he extended his arm to reach for his coffee cup. His hand hit the platter, tipped it sideways, and sent it crashing to the floor.

Realizing his error, he rose to assist Anna. But instead of helping her, he bumped her arm. His action caused her to dump the pitcher of syrup down the front of her apron.

"I'm terribly sorry," he apologized repeatedly. He stooped to retrieve the broken pieces of glass.

"That's all right," Anna replied graciously. "Please, sir, there's no need for you to clean that up. Let me get a broom."

She hurried to the kitchen, returning with the necessary equipment to clear away the scattered mixture of food and glass. In no time the dining room was back to its normal state.

"If you'll have a seat, sir, I'd be happy to fix you another breakfast. It will only take a few minutes." She moved back to the kitchen, donned a fresh apron, then brought an identical meal out to the gentleman's table.

The stranger saw her coming this time, so he called out to her. "Don't worry. I promise not to move until you set the dish down."

She smiled as she placed the plate in front of him. "Here you are. All in one piece this time. Would you like more coffee?"

"Yes, please."

She retrieved the coffee pot and returned to the man's table.

"This is very good," he remarked. "Are you the cook here?"

"Yes, along with Kate Patterson. She and her husband own the hotel."

She left him again, this time to clear the dirty dishes from the two tables near the kitchen. With the tables in order, she checked back with the lone customer.

"Can I get you anything else?"

"No, I've had plenty." He rose to his feet. "Now, what do I owe you for the meals and the broken dishes?"

"Forty cents." He started to correct her, but she interrupted. "I will not accept any money for the first meal. It was as much my fault as yours."

His lips formed a sly grin. "I can see that it would be useless to argue with you." He reached into his pocket to pull out the change, mumbling as he handed her the money, "I still say it was my fault."

"Don't be so sure of that. I'm usually careful, but my mind hasn't exactly been on work this week. I'm getting married on Saturday."

As she was speaking, another figure entered the dining room. When she glanced in that direction, her eyes lighted with pleasure. Noting her reaction, the stranger looked up too.

"I take it that's your fiancé?"

"Yes, it is."

Will walked toward them, his expression unusually stern. To Anna's surprise, he did not greet her but directed his remarks to the man next to her.

"Well, I should have known not to leave you alone. I had a sneaky suspicion I'd find you here."

"Now, William," the bright-eyed customer argued. "You can't blame me for being curious, can you? After all, I just couldn't wait any longer to meet the young lady who has managed to capture the heart of my favorite nephew."

"Your nephew!" Anna exclaimed, taken aback as she realized that the man had looked familiar to her because he bore a definite resemblance to Will. "Will, is this—"

"This is my Uncle Charles," he announced. "My infamous, sneaky, impatient Uncle Charles who was supposed to wait for me to finish in the courthouse and then come over with me to meet you." He moved closer to his intended bride and wrapped his arm around her shoulder. "So, Uncle Charles, what do you think? Does she pass your inspection?"

The spirited gentleman eyed her skeptically before speaking. "Well, she's pretty, just like you said. And she's a good cook." He winked at her. "She's a little on the stubborn side, but I'd say that's in her favor. Yes, she definitely passes my inspection." He reached for her hand and gripped it solidly. "Anna, welcome to the family."

The wedding took place as planned on Saturday, August 21, 1880. The Reverend Scott performed the simple ceremony at the Methodist church, then the newlyweds and their friends returned to the hotel for a rousing reception in the parlor.

Anna's heart felt as if it would burst with joy and thankfulness to God. Claire and Tim were on hand to offer their best wishes, as were the Pattersons, the current boarders, and an assortment of faithful patrons from the dining room. Mr. and Mrs. Gutierrez and several of Will's business acquaintances attended the gathering as well.

As was the custom at such functions, the newly married couple spent most of the time apart, separated by groups of well-meaning friends imparting last-minute advice and congratulations. Though the bride and groom often found themselves across the room from each other, their eyes locked repeatedly during the reception, their glances assuring each other that the party would not go on forever, that they would soon have time alone.

As Anna stood by the fireplace surrounded by Claire, Kate, and a crowd of others, her heart could barely contain its happiness as she viewed Will and her father receiving hearty handshakes. Her father had not lost her to Will, but had truly gained a son. He knew that, as did she. That she had been so blessed, that God had allowed her to find both Will and her father, was a joy that on this day brought her to tears.

She surveyed the people around her, finding among them Sam Burdick and Billy. Sam's friendship had not changed, despite his family's continued show of indifference. And Billy's appearance at the wedding represented a true sacrifice on his part. He seldom took time away from his precious, profitable diggings, and he held a general dislike for any semblance of formality. Their presence today meant more to her than she could express.

As she watched her smiling groom, only she could have

guessed his hidden thoughts and understood his unspoken disappointment at the purposeful absence of his parents. Though Will had not expected them, Anna knew how much he had hoped at least to hear from them. But she was thankful that his uncle and aunt had come. Their presence made up in part for his parents' silence.

She caught Will's attention again, translating the quiet signals in his bright blue eyes. Yes, she knew. They would be together soon, starting their new life as husband and wife in their beautiful little house. They had waited this long. A few more minutes wouldn't hurt.

She glanced around the room again, her eyes settling once again on her husband. Yes, it had been a long wait. But it had been worth it.

chapter

32

September 21, 1880

Dear Jessie,

Greetings from Colorado. I just finished reading your last letter dated May 17. Please forgive me for not writing any sooner. Summers are so hectic with all the extra gardening and canning (as you remember from St. Matthew's), so when you add wedding preparations to it too, there is little time left for corresponding.

It is a miserable night tonight—cold and dark with rain coming down in buckets. I am sitting by the fire waiting for Will to come home, but I doubt that he will attempt the ride in such a downpour. Twice last week he stayed overnight in his office because of the heavy rains. A major storm hit us last Monday and has caused a lot of damage in Silver Cliff.

I was so sorry to hear about the problems little Daniel Robert is having. I pray his lung condition will improve.

Will and I love our new home. The property includes a three-room cabin, woodshed, and a small stable. It is situated just outside of Rosita, so Will has to ride four miles to his office. But he doesn't seem to mind.

I am still working at the boardinghouse (for breakfast and dinner only). Our house is two-and-a-half miles from the hotel, which is an easy enough trip for me since Pa gave me a horse for a wedding present. She is a beautiful coal-black mare named Midnight.

Thank you for your good wishes concerning our marriage. I hope someday to see you again and to introduce you to both Will and my father.

Give my best wishes to Danny and Karen. My prayers are with your little nephew.

Love,
Anna

Anna perused the letter one final time, sealed the envelope, then carried the note to the kitchen table. Having completed her writing project, she wondered what to do next.

The house stood quiet save for the ticking of the small clock on the mantel. Long accustomed to the noise and traffic at the hotel, Anna felt uncomfortable in the overpowering silence. She all but welcomed the low sound of the recurring thunder as it rumbled through the surrounding water-soaked hills.

After fidgeting for a moment, Anna opened the icebox and reached for a platter of cold chicken. As she carried the plate to the table, a noise at the kitchen door startled her. Before she knew it, the door pushed open and a wet, windblown figure staggered into the house.

"Will!" She rushed over to him. "Oh, Will, you're soaked to the bone!"

She pulled off his soggy coat, then guided him to the fire, insisting all the while that he change into some dry clothes. She hurriedly fetched towels and clothing, then warmed each item in front of the fire until he was ready for them. As he finished dressing, Anna headed back to the kitchen to rekindle the hot coals in the cookstove.

"Have you had supper yet?"

"No."

"I have some chicken, so I'll heat it in some gravy and put it over biscuits."

He finished buttoning his blue sweater as he joined her in the kitchen. "Cold chicken will be fine, sweetheart. Don't go to all the trouble of heating everything up at this late hour."

"It's no trouble. You need something hot after that ride. Will, I'm happy to have you home, but you really shouldn't have risked going out on such a horrible night. I would have understood."

"I know." He stood directly behind her and slipped his arms around her waist. "But I missed you." His lips wandered from the top of her head to the base of her neck. "Besides, the ride in tonight was nowhere near as bad as those two nights in the office last week."

Though affected by his romantic overtures, Anna proceeded resolutely with her primary objective—getting a hot meal into her chilled husband. She slid from his grasp and crossed over to the icebox.

"How did it go in court today?"

When he did not answer, she looked up. One glimpse of his downcast expression told her that the session with Judge Morley had been as difficult as he had feared.

"I lost the appeal."

Anna's eyes widened in disbelief. "What? How could that have happened? You worked so hard on that case!"

"Well, it's like they say: You can't win them all. This isn't the first case I've lost, and I'm sure it won't be my last."

But his stoic acceptance did not pacify his wife. "I don't see how Judge Morley could have decided against you. He should know by now that you're an honest lawyer and that you wouldn't represent any client who didn't deserve it. Your reasoning on the new evidence was so logical. I'd just like to have a word or two with him right now!"

Her show of loyalty brought a smile to his face. "You, my dear, are what Judge Morley would call a partial witness," he chuckled. "Anyway, there's nothing more we can do, so let's just forget about it for now. And what is the news from the hotel?"

"The same as always." She stirred the bubbling gravy mixture. "Oh, Claire and the twins came by to invite us to supper on Friday."

"I don't have any commitments. You can tell her that we'll be there."

With the chicken and gravy prepared, Anna carried a steaming plateful to the table where Will ate heartily. When he finished, he banked the fire and helped Anna with the cleanup. Together they made short work of the job. With the kitchen neat and sparkling clean, they moved hand in hand toward the bedroom.

"Will, I'm glad you came home. And I'm sorry about your afternoon in court. Is it possible for Judge Morley to change his mind?"

"You mean reverse his decision? It's possible, but not at all probable."

"You're sure?"

"I'm sure. I lost my appeal, and that's that. Don't let it bother you."

But as they reached the bedroom door, Anna smothered a giggle.

"What's so funny?" Will asked.

"Oh, nothing," she laughed. But as her husband eyed her suspiciously, she confessed. "Well, actually, I was thinking about your case."

"What's so amusing about that?"

"Just one thing. You see, you and Judge Morley may believe you've lost your appeal, but I don't."

By Thursday morning the rain had turned to snow. Bundled in her woolen coat, knitted hat, and gloves, Anna sprang lightly atop Midnight and guided her carefully along the slushy road into Rosita.

After leaving the animal at the livery, she made her way to the hotel. She served breakfast to the four boarders and the few dining room patrons, then stepped into the parlor to begin the weekly cleaning.

As she swept the dusty floor, her thoughts drifted to Will. How she appreciated his willingness to let her continue working. She realized that the time would come when she would need to quit—either when they had children, or when Will's law practice grew to involve more entertaining, as he suspected it might. But for now, especially during the winter months, she had little to occupy her time at home. She needed the activity that her job offered.

But her desire to work stemmed from another reason as well, one that she had never voiced to her husband. Her life up to that point had consisted of a series of abrupt changes— of being forced to cut her ties to the past with little or no warning. By working even briefly during the early months of their marriage, Anna felt a deeper sense of security. She experienced the joy of beginning a new life without having to sacrifice the old one completely.

She straightened the chairs and dusted the furniture, then tidied the stack of newspapers that lay atop the table. While organizing the assorted issues, she glanced at the impressive array of titles. The *Daily Prospect,* the *Silver Cliff Republican,* the *Mining Gazette*—all printed in Silver Cliff. She spied a smaller paper at the bottom of the pile. The *Sierra Journal.* The name and the owner of the publication had changed, but she knew that the little newspaper would in her mind always be the *Rosita Index,* just as Querida would always remain

Bassickville. Change. In her life as well as the life of the town, there seemed no way to avoid it.

Her work accomplished, Anna moved back to the kitchen to prepare the dinner menu. As she worked, she felt a sudden blast of cold air when Kate entered from outside. She held the door open, calling out to her young son.

"Come on, Andy. Come inside, sweetheart. It's cold out there!"

At last the seventeen-month-old wandered into the room. Kate removed his bulky outer garments, turning him loose to run down the hallway. She breathed a weary sigh and sat down at the table.

"I'd take my own coat off, but I'm too tired," she groaned.

Anna stepped to the table with a steaming cup of tea. "Here, I just brewed this."

Anna poured a cup for herself. But as she approached the table, Andy ran back into the room, almost stumbling into her. She balanced her full cup to keep the liquid from spilling.

"Andy, you certainly are a busy little boy!" Anna laughed. "He's quite a character, isn't he."

"Just like his father," Kate nodded. "I don't know what we'd do without him. Or without you, either. As you well know, I can't keep up with business and Andy at the same time. I can't tell you how happy we were to find both you and Will agreeable to your staying on here."

As Anna studied Kate's face, she could not help but notice how tired the young mother looked. Since her fair-haired friend usually abounded with energy, Anna grew concerned by her appearance.

"Kate, do you feel all right? You look so pale."

"Frankly, no, I don't feel well. But it's nothing to worry about. Please don't tell anyone, except for Will, of course, but we've just found out that we're going to have another baby in late May."

"I'm so happy for you! I know how pleased you must be."

"Pleased, yes. But sick too," Kate moaned. "I'm feeling pretty miserable this time. Our only regret is. . . ." She stopped, her unnatural pause indicating that she had disclosed more information than she had intended. Anna picked up immediately on the unfinished statement.

"You only regret what?"

Kate remained silent for several moments. "Well, I suppose it's something we might as well discuss now. Since we found out about the baby, we've been forced to make some decisions about the hotel. You know how badly things have been going. The hotel is still holding its own, but just barely. Financially, the situation is fast becoming break-even. And a business cannot long survive on those terms."

Anna stiffened as the seriousness of Kate's inference sank in. "If my salary is a problem, I'm sure we could work something out."

"It's not that simple. Rosita is just not attracting business anymore." She hesitated before adding quietly, "The town is dying, Anna. You must know that."

Anna did know it, but the words still cut her to the quick.

"What are you going to do?" she asked feebly.

"We want to stay here through the winter. Silver Cliff has calmed down now that so many families are living there, but it's still crowded and noisy. We want Andy to live in this quieter atmosphere for as long as possible. This April, Jeff plans to build a house on some property we bought outside of Silver Cliff. Hopefully, we can be settled in before the baby's born.

"Since we're making a small profit here, we plan to keep the hotel and boardinghouse running until spring, with you handling breakfast and dinner, and Jeff and I managing the supper crowd. But we feel that by next summer Rosita's economy will be much worse. And we just can't afford to operate a business at a loss, no matter how much we like the town. We just have to be practical. I hope you understand, and that you can see our position. And I hope that this hasn't come as too much of a shock."

The news had indeed been a surprise. Anna knew that business had dwindled, but it had never once occurred to her that Kate and Jeff might close the hotel permanently. Now she was forced to face the issue realistically. Rosita was dying. The hotel was drawing little business and had no hope of attracting more in the future. Silver Cliff had claimed another victim.

The news greatly distressed her. But as Anna thought about it through the day, she appreciated one fact. She would not have to give up her job for a number of months. The hotel would not be closing immediately. The transition for her would be gradual.

Besides, spring was still a long way off. By then, anything could happen. She and Will might even be expecting a child themselves. In that case, she would have to quit working at the hotel anyway.

But, somehow, her rationalizations did little to affect her drooping spirits. And as she and Midnight plodded home late that afternoon, she felt as if she had just lost her best friend.

chapter
33

ANNA SAID NOTHING about the Pattersons' plans to anyone except her husband. But keeping the secret from Claire proved a difficult task.

On Friday evening, the inquisitive redhead sensed something peculiar in Anna's unusually quiet behavior. But try as she would, Claire could not break down Anna's resolve not to discuss the confidential topic.

Later that night, Will lauded Anna on her quick verbal maneuvering. "Claire doesn't give up easily, does she?" He stirred the fire and sat down next to Anna on their comfortable brown sofa.

"No, she doesn't."

Anna stared at the bright, crackling flames. She had such a busy day ahead of her tomorrow, and she had hoped to go straight to bed. But Will seemed in a talkative mood, so she snuggled next to him as he settled down to watch the roaring blaze.

"I'd hate to be in Tim's shoes if he ever had to keep a secret," Will chuckled. "I doubt that Claire would give him much peace until he came out with it. You did quite a job evading her questions. Remind me never to cross-examine you in a courtroom." He shifted his position slightly. "Oh, sweetheart, I forgot to tell you that Mr. Warner paid me today. The full amount—and in cash, nonetheless. Isn't that good news!"

"Yes, it is," she murmured, fighting to keep her eyes open.

"I've been thinking. With our finances in reasonably good shape, now might be a good time to take a little trip. I'm not handling any urgent cases, so it would be an ideal time to visit with Uncle Charles and Aunt Clara. Do you think Kate would mind getting a substitute for you for about two weeks? I know that we may be taking a bit of a risk as far as the weather is concerned, but if we leave early next week, I think it would be safe enough. What do you think?"

"I'd like that, Will—if Kate can get along without me."

"Good. Then let's plan to leave on Tuesday. But I'll need to wire Uncle Charles just to be sure. And you'd better let Kate know first thing tomorrow. All right?"

But she did not answer.

"Anna?" He turned his head, puzzled by her silence. "Sweetheart, would you rather we didn't make the trip? If so, then just tell me and we can do it some other time."

But she didn't hear a word he was saying. She was sound asleep.

Anna enjoyed the trip immensely. The stage and train rides went smoothly and offered the couple hours of relaxation as they viewed the splendid scenery en route to Colorado Springs.

Once at the ranch, Anna and Will received a warm welcome from Uncle Charles, Aunt Clara, and an assortment of cousins. Though moderately well-to-do, Will's relatives seemed down-to-earth and did not put on airs. Anna found that she fit right in.

The training in horsemanship provided by her father stood

her in good stead during their stay. In spite of the cold weather and light snowfall, the Sinclairs spent a great deal of time riding. When not in the saddle exploring the ranch, Anna traveled to town with Clara for shopping excursions or visits with friends.

Uncle Charles frequently invited people over for supper, a practice that kept Anna and Clara busy in the kitchen. On one such evening halfway through their stay, Anna met a short, balding man named Silas Carrington, a local attorney. He spoke to Will at great length while she, Clara, and Mrs. Carrington saw to their supper.

During the meal, the men dominated the conversation and continued to do so into the evening, even after the women joined them in the parlor. Anna sat silently beside her husband, her mind wandering as the men talked on and on. But her mind snapped back to reality when Mr. Carrington asked Will a question.

"Will, I know you're happy in Rosita, but have you ever considered moving?"

Though surprised by the question, Anna was even more startled by Will's response.

"Oh, I don't know. It would depend upon the job, I suppose. Why?"

Anna listened attentively as Mr. Carrington continued. "My firm has a branch office in Leadville. One of our top attorneys there is retiring next summer, so we're looking for a replacement for him."

"That wouldn't be John Gregory, would it?"

"Why yes, it would be. Do you know him?"

Will nodded. "I admire him a great deal. But I can't quite picture him retiring."

"Neither can we. We were hoping to convince him to stay with us longer. But he's made up his mind. He has a tremendous reputation, which is why finding someone to take his place is going to be difficult. Or at least my associates think so. Personally, I think you would be an excellent choice for the position."

"Me?"

"Yes. I've been watching you for some time now, and I've been most impressed. We want someone young, talented, and honest. You certainly qualify in those categories. The salary isn't enormous, but it's steady. Mind you, this is not an official inquiry. John won't be leaving us until July, so we're in no immediate need of a replacement. But if you're at all interested, I'd be more than happy to contact you for an interview sometime in the future."

Much to Anna's relief, Will replied skeptically, "Well, as you said yourself, Silas, we are happy in Silver Cliff." But her hopes were dashed when he added, "But the prospect does sound intriguing. I won't commit to anything right at the moment, of course, but I certainly wouldn't object to talking more about it at a later date."

"Splendid!"

At that, the conversation turned to other subjects. But in Anna's mind, the topic remained very much alive.

Had her husband been serious when he implied an interest in the position in Leadville? Certainly he knew by now how much she loved living in Rosita. And what about her father? She didn't want to leave him. Will had never mentioned moving before. Then, of course, she had never really discussed the possibility with him either. But she intended to tonight—and in great detail.

As Anna waited impatiently for the visitors to leave, she reconsidered her plan. Perhaps it would be better if she said nothing about it. Will had mentioned himself that he was happy in Silver Cliff. If he ever became serious about moving, he would certainly talk it over with her.

She thought the matter through some more and decided against debating it. For if she did not bring up the topic again, perhaps Will might just forget about it.

Fortunately for the traveling couple, the heavy snowfall did not begin until after their return to Rosita. Will soon became buried again in his growing law practice and never once brought up the subject of moving. Greatly relieved by his silence on the subject, Anna settled back into her regular routine.

As Will had anticipated, he began to feel more social obligations toward his clients and colleagues. So, beginning with the holiday season, he invited numerous guests into their home. The hostessing tasks required little effort on Anna's part since she had grown so used to preparing and serving quantities of food at the boardinghouse. Her new responsibilities blended nicely with her talent for cooking. Between the extra company and her job at the Rosita Hotel, January and February passed quickly.

The windy month remained true to its name, bringing with it more snow. Late on Wednesday, the ninth of March, Anna listened to the wind whistling through the cracks in the cabin wall. How she appreciated being in her cozy house on such a night.

She stacked two more logs onto the already robust fire, then spread her blankets and pillow on the sofa. With Will in Silver Cliff for the night, she was determined to sleep by a warm fire instead of freezing in the bedroom as she had the last time he was gone.

After dressing for bed, Anna bundled into the blankets and lay down on the couch. As she did, her thoughts traveled to her husband. Perhaps he was in his office by now, sleeping on that hard little cot. She hoped he would be warm enough. She wondered if his evening meeting with the town council had gone well. If it had, then he might still be at the meeting, for those sessions often ran into the night. At length she pushed the guesswork from her mind, and while listening to the crackling fire and the sound of the strong wind outside, she fell asleep.

After several hours, Anna wakened suddenly, startled by a strange noise. Her heart pounded in her chest as she listened, her body stiffening as she heard the sound again. Voices. Voices calling in the wind. And horses running swiftly along the snow-covered road in front of her house.

She jumped from the sofa and rushed to the window where she spied three men riding toward Rosita. They were shouting as they traveled up the road. She thought at first that they might be drunk. But as she gazed farther down the road, she froze in her tracks. In the distance, in the direction of Rosita, an eerie, reddish glow illuminated the night sky. Fire!

In no time, Anna donned her clothing and ran out the door, saddling Midnight faster than she ever thought possible. She mounted the horse, and allowed her to gallop as quickly as she dared on the slippery, uneven pathway. As she neared the town, her mind flooded with fear for Jeff, Kate, and Andy. She prayed with all her heart that they would be safe, and that the fire might be contained before it caused too much damage.

But when she reached the edge of town, her worst fears were realized. Two entire blocks along Tyndal Street were aflame, including the Rosita Hotel. Men and women were rushing everywhere, filling buckets at the spring, throwing the icy water onto the burning buildings.

Anna jumped from her horse to join them in the fight. Her eyes and throat stung from the dense smoke that filled the air. Having no container in which to carry water, she gathered chunks of snow and ice to hurl at the billowing flames.

Not far from her, she spotted Jeff calling orders to the bucket brigade. Kate was passing the buckets along the long line, Andy at her side. Anna thanked God that her friends had gotten out of the burning hotel alive.

Together, Anna and the townspeople rallied to battle the enormous blaze. But despite their frantic efforts, the fire spread. Even as she and the other residents worked, the fire ripped through more of the seasoned wood buildings, igniting them like dry matchsticks. At length, the people stopped struggling, Anna along with them. It was useless to fight anymore. Nothing could be done to save the town. Anna stared helplessly at the hotel, its upper story now engulfed in flames. Though she did not want to see her former home burning, she could not turn her eyes away.

Once again she heard the pounding of hoofs. Anna looked behind her to see men on horseback—riders from Silver Cliff coming to assist. But though she saw them approaching, their presence did not really register on her mind. For she could see only one thing—Rosita burning.

She heard voices too. Familiar, excited voices. Her father's and Will's. They kept talking to her, but she could not focus on what they were saying. She simply allowed them to lead her away from the fire. And though she could not understand why they insisted she ride with Will on his horse instead of her own, she bent to their wishes and mounted with her husband, clutching his waist tightly as they moved slowly back down the road.

She looked back, her eyes filling with tears, her heart sickened by the haunting, incandescent haze of gray and orange that lighted the surrounding hills. For Rosita, her home for so many years, was gone. And there was nothing that anyone could do about it.

Anna did not want to see Rosita again. She wanted to remember the happy little town as it had been in its early years—at the height of its glory. But she could not stay away. Late the following morning, she slipped away from the cabin to walk the winding road into the dark, desolate town.

She moved quietly toward the hotel, her eyes scanning the blackened ruins of the once sturdy building. For four blocks, charred buildings lined the street, their dark skeletons still smoldering from the previous night's fire. She did not understand how such a blaze could have started in the icehouse in the back of Miller's store. But start it had, its sweeping fury claiming Rosita's entire business district. Only those businesses situated away from the center of town had managed to survive. They might linger for a while. But with Silver Cliff so close, Anna knew that Rosita would never recover from the fire.

As she stood in front of her former home, she could not help reflecting upon her past. The hotel held so many memories for her. There she had met new friends, had found her father, had grown to love Will. She realized now just how much the little building had meant to her.

Yet despite her sorrow over the devastation, there was much for which to be thankful. The buildings had been destroyed, but not the people, not the memories. She still had Kate, Jeff, and Andy. She knew that Tim, Claire, and the children were safe. She had lost another home, but she still had Will and her father. She realized afresh that, though a place could be special, the people were what really mattered.

She gazed westward toward the Sangre de Cristos, still towering, still ruling the landscape, unchanged by the events of the past twenty-four hours. How she would miss their comforting presence if Will ever decided to move to Leadville, or anywhere else.

But as she viewed their snowy peaks, her heart filled with peace. For she knew that whatever lay ahead, God would be with her. He had led her in the past, and she had no doubts that she could trust Him with her future, whatever it held.

ABOUT THE AUTHOR

Dearest Anna is DEBORAH RAU's first novel. A native of Dayton, Ohio, she currently resides in Escondido, California, where she combines free-lance writing with homemaking. Although she has written numerous articles for Christian periodicals, her first love is historical fiction. Her husband and two children share her interest in history and, during family vacations, take an active part in her research.

A Letter to Our Readers

Dear Reader:

Welcome to the world of Serenade Books—a series designed to bring you the most beautiful love stories in the world of inspirational romance. They will uplift you, encourage you, and provide hours of wholesome entertainment, as thousands of readers have testified. In order that we might better contribute to your reading enjoyment, we would appreciate your taking a few minutes to respond to the following questions and return to:

> Editor, Serenade Books
> The Zondervan Publishing House
> 1415 Lake Drive, S.E.
> Grand Rapids, Michigan 49506

1. Did you enjoy reading DEAREST ANNA?

   ☐ Very much. I would like to see more books by this author!
   ☐ Moderately
   ☐ I would have enjoyed it more if _____

2. Where did you purchase this book? _____

3. What influenced your decision to purchase this book?

   ☐ Cover   ☐ Back cover copy
   ☐ Title   ☐ Friends
   ☐ Publicity   ☐ Other _____

4. Please rate the following elements from 1 (poor) to 10 (superior).

☐ Heroine   ☐ Plot
☐ Hero   ☐ Inspirational theme
☐ Setting   ☐ Secondary characters

5. What are some inspirational themes you would like to see treated in future books?

_____

_____

6. Please indicate your age range:

☐ Under 18   ☐ 25–34   ☐ 46–55
☐ 18–24   ☐ 35–45   ☐ Over 55